From Joseph J. Christiano,
Author of *Old Ghosts* and *Dark Annie*, comes
THE SHADOW MAN

…The Shadow Man turned in their direction.

Sarah did not pause. She all but dragged him in the direction of Rebecca's car. She threw open the passenger's door and tossed Nick inside.

"We have to go back for Rebecca," Nick said weakly. "Sarah, we have to go back."

Sarah got in behind the wheel. "It doesn't want her, it wants us." She slammed the door closed and threw a glance over her shoulder. The mass of darkness had changed course and was closing on the Hyundai. Sarah jammed the key into the ignition and turned it. The engine roared to life. She slapped the shifter into D and mashed the gas pedal. The car surged down the driveway and she did not look back…

The Shadow Man

Joseph J. Christiano

The Shadow Man

By Joseph J. Christiano

© 2015 Joseph J. Christiano

5174 Peri St. Swartz Creek, MI 48473

Cover design by Taria A Reed

Printed in United States of America

Nightshade Imprint

For Chris, Vinny,

Scozz and George

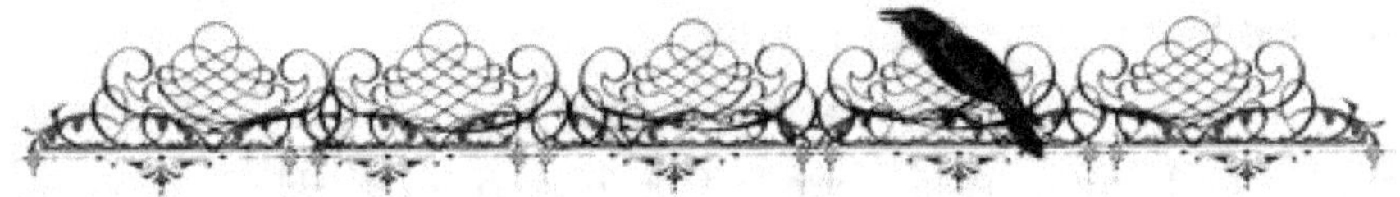

Chapter 1

Caught the Dragon

The first sensation of which Nicholas Wade became aware was something warm and wet on the back of his head. His hand moved seemingly of its own volition to the area and he felt the dampness on his fingertips. He had no idea from where the dampness had originated or its reason for being. He knew simply that the back of his head was wet. He tried to draw his hand back and have a look at the liquid on his fingers, but his arm resisted the commands from his brain. The appendage moved slowly, clumsily, and something, he knew not what, seemed to be in the way.

The second thing of which he became aware was the strobe lights that flashed somewhere on the other side of his eyelids. Why were his eyes closed? He tried to open them, but something wet and sticky frustrated his attempt. In the brief moment when he managed to get his left eye one-quarter open he could see nothing but a red haze.

Sounds began to intrude upon him. He had much difficulty sorting through them. Voices. The sound of many footsteps. A strange crunching sound he could best describe as Rice Krispies after milk has been added to the bowl. Softer, distant voices that sounded like walkie-talkie chatter.

He also became aware of the pressure on his right shoulder and his abdomen. A seatbelt? That had to be it. He had been in the passenger seat of Angie's Mustang, that much he remembered. Was he still there? The evidence of the seatbelt seemed to suggest just that. But why could he not remember? And why did his eyes and arm defy his commands?

Several of the voices closest to him faded in and out. He caught a word here ("bad"), a partial phrase there ("jaws of life"), but he seemed unable to string them together into a coherent sentence. He wished he could open his eyes. The multi-colored strobes that flashed around him were all that prevented him from existing in complete darkness.

He heard another voice, very close. He felt warm breath on his right ear. Nick could not understand what the voice told him, but part of him recognized the reassuring tone. There was unexpected pressure on his right hand. He tried to recoil from it, but it seemed his hand had not yet ended its rebellion. He could not pull away.

A moment after the man took Nick's hand in his own there was a loud thud that seemed to come from all around him. The whine of machinery, a small motor suddenly pressed into service. The sound of thin metal crumpling and finally tearing.

The cacophony did not so much fade out as it ended abruptly. More of the cereal noise, more voices. And then more hands, grasping his arms and legs, one cradling his head. The sensation of being weightless. He felt cool air on his arms, his face. And, of course, the warm wetness on the back of his head that now reached his neck.

Male voices, frantic; he wished he could understand them. A female voice that spoke only two words: "Call it." Nick felt himself come back to earth as the people holding him placed him on the ground. No, not the ground. Something soft. Soft and with a pillow. A bed? The sensation of being moved, rolled. The squeak of a bad wheel, like on a shopping cart.

The last thing of which he would be aware for some time was another voice. It was deep and tinged with a Hispanic accent. *You just remember Santos. Santos got whachoo need.* Nick would not realize until he awoke in the hospital that this last voice did not belong to anyone around him. It was a memory. And not a particularly pleasant one.

****

The first thing he did when he came to was open his eyes. They obeyed him now although he did not know why that should be noteworthy. When had they ever given him trouble before? He saw a young woman's face looming over him and he recognized the owner of that face immediately.

"Rebecca," he whispered. His throat felt raw, dry.

His cousin smiled at him and clasped his right hand in hers. "Hey, Nicky," she said. Her smile widened. "How are you feeling?"

He swallowed and it hurt to do so. He tried to see around her, but sudden pain lanced through his neck.

"Don't try to move, don't try to move," Rebecca told him. "You're wearing a neck brace." She looked him up and down. "Among other things."

His eyes moved down and he took in his prone body. He lay in a hospital bed. His right leg was sheathed in a cast from ankle to thigh. His left hand was wrapped in a bandage. Poking out of the top of his right hand and between Rebecca's fingers was an IV. His eyes followed the tube up to the plastic bag half-filled with a clear solution, hanging from a metal pole. After a moment he returned his gaze to Rebecca. "Hospital." It was not a question.

She nodded and squeezed his hand. "You're lucky to be breathing, Nicky. It was pretty bad from what I hear."

Nick closed his eyes and tried to figure out just how the hell he had wound up in the hospital. He tried for what felt like several moments, but he came up empty. Finally he looked at Rebecca again. "What happened?"

"You were in a car accident. A bad one. How much do you remember?"

Her smile remained in place, but even in his current state he could see it was forced. He swallowed again, winced at the pain. "How did it happen?"

Rebecca's smile faltered; it was her turn to swallow. She looked away, out the window to his right. He followed her gaze. His room was apparently high up; he could see the cityscape far below. Cars zipped back and forth along the stretch of highway perhaps a half mile distant. The sun was beginning its downslide behind the foothills on the horizon. Rebecca continued to stare out the window. Her grip on his right hand loosened.

"Becks," Nick whispered. When her eyes met his again he saw they were wet. There were no tears, but it looked as if some might be on the way. He nodded as much as the neck brace would allow. "Tell me what happened."

Rebecca bit her lip. "I don't know everything. The cops are still investigating, I think." She stood and began a slow orbit around the room. "It was bad, Nicky, very bad. Two days ago you were involved in a single-vehicle collision. I heard from a cop when I got here that they had a priest ready to give you Last Rites." Her smile returned, but it was weak, a shadow of its former self. "But you pulled through. That's all that matters."

Nick's brow furrowed. "I remember…" His voice trailed off. The truth was he could not remember a thing. Not really. He closed his eyes and concentrated. The fog that usually obscured his memory after he successfully caught the dragon seemed thicker than usual. Most of the time he could catch glimpses of scattered images. This time he could see nothing but the fog.

He squeezed his eyes tighter and felt his free hand curl into a fist. The IV tube pulled a little against the tape securing it to the back of his hand. The uncomfortable and unfamiliar sensation might serve to blow away some of the fog.

Success. He caught a glimpse of himself ascending the stairs to Santos's apartment. The staircase was dark and dirty. An ancient strip of carpet ran along the center of the steps; it was threadbare and its original color was anybody's guess. Paint peeled freely from the walls. Nick had been in plenty of other houses similar to this, but he had never been in this one. He was uneasy, he remembered that clearly. He had never met Santos and was only here because his usual dealer was taking a sabbatical in Danbury courtesy of the Feds. He remembered knocking on the door on the second floor, being invited in. He remembered the overall shabbiness and shittiness of Santos's apartment. He remembered the gap-toothed grin on Santos's weathered face as Nick forked over the cash. And he remembered Santos's parting shot as Nick closed the door behind him and descended the stairs. "You just remember Santos. Santos got whachoo need."

The fog threatened to cover everything else but Nick clenched his fist tighter. His fingernails dug deeply into his palm. He heard Rebecca say, "Nicky?" He ignored her and concentrated on the pain in his hand. It could not burn through all the fog, but it found him a small opening where it was not quite so thick.

He sat in the front seat of the Mustang. Something from Avenged Sevenfold played over the speakers. He held the empty toilet paper roll to his mouth and inhaled as deeply as he could. He tasted the sweet smoke and felt it work its way down his throat. It was always his second-favorite part of the whole ritual; the first was afterwards, when it kicked in. He remembered sitting all the way back in the seat and holding his breath. He eventually released that breath as a steady stream of smoke out the window. Then it was his turn to hold the tinfoil and light its contents for Angie.

"Angie," he whispered. Nick opened his eyes and looked at Rebecca. His look of concern was quickly replaced by one of dread. "Where's Angie?"

Rebecca swallowed. "Nicky…" She swallowed again.

Nick sat up in the bed. Pain lanced through his leg, his arm and his neck. Nick whimpered and lay back down as gently as he was able. When the pain was once again manageable he returned his attention to Rebecca. "Becks, where's Angie? Is she okay?" He did not like the look in his cousin's eyes.

She let go of his hand and took a few slow steps away from the bed. She faced the door and folded her arms across her chest. She started and stopped a few times before she was able to speak. "She's gone, Nicky. She didn't make it." A pause. "I'm so sorry, honey."

Nick blinked at her. He released a breath he was unaware he held. "Jesus, that can't be right," he said after a long moment. His head remained on the pillow, but he looked at Rebecca. "She was only twenty-eight, for Christ's sake." His voice became louder and took on an edge. "Tell me this is all a joke, Rebecca. Because if it's true—"

"It's true." Rebecca turned and faced him again. "Jesus, do you think I'd make that up?" She advanced a few steps and stopped at the foot of the bed. "You were in a bad car accident, Nicky. And from what I overheard the cops say, you should feel pretty goddamned lucky you weren't the driver. As it is you're in deep enough shit without that, too." She paused long enough to swallow again. "They found all this paraphernalia in the car. I'm sure they ran blood work on you and I'm just as sure they found something. Didn't they?" Now it was her voice that took on an edge. "Didn't they?"

Nick looked away.

Rebecca turned in anger, but it seemed to last only a moment. When she spoke again her voice was calm, measured. "I figured as much when the nurse told me they were giving you methadone instead of oxy-whatever. Because I'm pretty sure they only give you methadone when the patient is a heroin addict. Even I know that." She shook her head. "Your parents died from that shit, Nicky. Why are you in such a fucking hurry to follow in their footsteps?" She walked around the bed and took her original spot. She clasped his hand. "You're blood and I love you. But you can't keep this up. No one can." She leaned over him and looked into his eyes. "Your girlfriend is dead, Nick. This is your wakeup call. Because the next time my phone rings it'll be the cops asking me to ID your body."

Nick looked into her eyes for only a moment before he turned away as much as the neck brace would allow. "Can I be alone for a few?"

She let go of his hand. "Only for a few. There's a detective outside and I'm sure he's gonna want to talk to you. You'd better be straight with him, Nicky. You'd better be straight."

He heard her soft footsteps retreat from the room.

As Rebecca predicted it was no more than a few moments later when a man in jeans and a sport jacket entered the room. He knocked on the door as he walked past it. "Nicholas?" He did not await a reply as he made his way to the foot of the bed. "I'm Detective Connolly, Philadelphia PD. I need to speak with you."

Nick turned his eyes to the foot of the bed. Connolly was an older man with receding brown hair. He wore a white polo shirt beneath the sport coat. The coat looked to be a size too small; the man's tree trunk arms strained against the fabric and Nick could clearly see the bulge in the man's side where his weapon rested in its holster. His gold badge was clipped to the waistline of his jeans.

The two men stared at each other for a moment before Nick said, "What do you want?"

Connolly produced a small notepad from his back pocket and a pen from behind his ear. "I want you to tell me what happened two nights ago. As much as you can remember." He smiled.

Nick did not buy into the smile for a moment. He was a veteran of too many arrests and interrogations to believe Connolly wanted anything other than enough evidence to put him away. If he could get the evidence without having to resort to an investigation, actually *doing his job*, then so much the better. Nick disliked him immediately. "I don't remember shit."

Connolly's smile remained in place. "I don't believe that." He lowered the pad and pen. "Can I speak frankly with you? Man to man?"

Nick remained silent.

"I already know what happened, the broad strokes, anyway. All I need from you is the details." He looked away, at the walls and floor and finally out the window. "A young woman is dead, Nicholas. I assume you've heard?"

Nick nodded. His mouth felt as dry as his throat.

"We already know she was high on heroin. And so were you. Your blood work tells all sorts of tales. I want to know where you got it. Give me the fucker's name and I'll make sure he pays for this."

Nick continued to stare at the ceiling.

Connolly walked slowly about the room. He kept his eyes on the floor. "Don't think you're being noble, Nicholas. We know Angela Grey withdrew two hundred dollars from her checking account ninety minutes before the collision. The two of you bought it, you smoked it up and now here we are. But that's after Ms. Grey effectively demonstrated that law of physics known as fusion. You should have seen her car. It was not recognizable as an automobile." He stopped his walk around the room and placed both hands on the bed's safety rail to Nick's right. "Why would you protect the bastard who sold you that shit? He's partially responsible for her death. Help me do my job and put the prick away for a long time." His tone changed, became warmer. "That's a promise."

Nick ignored him. He stared at the ceiling, but what he saw was Angie leaning over in the driver's seat and taking a big hit from the powder burning atop the foil in his hand.

Connolly readied his pad and pen. "Give me a name and I'll tell the judge you were cooperative. I'll ask the D.A. to do me a favor and recommend substance abuse counseling for you instead of prison. Now that's a way out, man. And if you're smart you'll take it and say 'thank you.'"

Nick had somehow managed to avoid prison until now. He had been arrested plenty of times, but he had always lucked out when it came to the actual sentence. Although in those prior arrests there had been no deaths. Never once had there even been the possibility of it except his own from an overdose. This was different. This was Angie.

"I don't remember everything," he told Connolly. "Just flashes of memory here and there."

"Tell me everything you do remember." Connolly's pen hovered above the small pad like a lion about to pounce on a snoozing gazelle.

Nick swallowed, felt the pain in this throat. "Get me a glass of water first."

Connolly did as he asked.

They spoke at length. They were interrupted only once when the nurse, a pretty little thing with short blonde hair whose ID badge sported the name "Elizabeth," entered to swap out his IV bag. By the end of the interview (*interrogation*) Nick had given Connolly everything he had.

Chapter 2

Welcome to Springbrook

Nick eased himself out of the car. He closed the door and waited for Rebecca to extricate herself from behind the wheel. When she had done so he limped around to the back of the car and stood next to her. She pulled his duffel bag from the back seat and placed it on the sidewalk. The sun was just starting to hit the street, finally overcoming the crest of the foothills in the distance. It felt warm on his face and he welcomed the sensation.

Eight weeks after he awoke in the hospital and Angela Grey was lowered into the ground he found himself standing in front of what would be his home for the next ninety days. In theory, anyway. He was already looking for the cameras that undoubtedly kept watch on the front entrance. It was probably too much to hope there was a blind spot, but if there was he would find it.

He had spent the previous two weeks, since his appearance in court, in a smoky haze of near-oblivion in Staci's shadowed apartment. Staci had been good to him, he had to admit. Considering how their relationship had ended he was fortunate she even spoke to him. To say nothing of giving him a place to crash and providing him with enough H to keep him nearly comatose during his stay with her. That the price of his room and board had been sex whenever he was physically able to perform was beside the point. He was fairly certain she had fucked him once or twice while he drifted in and out of consciousness. It made little difference to him. If he could be out of it and still satisfy her then so much the better. It was a memory he could live without.

Something else he could live without was Rebecca's reaction when he answered the door thirty minutes earlier. He was high, having just smoked what would be his last hit of heroin for the next ninety days. (Again, in theory.) She recognized the signs and walked back to her car, disgusted. That was fine with him, too; she seemed angry enough to forego any lectures or character assassination, but not so angry she refused to drive him to the rehab facility. He had thrown his duffel into the backseat and all but collapsed into the front. They drove in silence.

Now they stood next to each other and looked at the façade of the Springbrook Healing and Recovery Center. It looked like the rehab facility began life as a school or perhaps an office building. There were three floors and numerous large windows facing the street. A set of short, wide stairs led to the double entry doors. Panes of glass stood on either side of the doors and colored sheets of paper with messages printed on them were taped to the inside. A flagpole stood to the left of the stairs and the Stars and Stripes fluttered in the light breeze. The top floor stood in direct sunlight and made the tan brick exterior seem white.

"Are you gonna be okay?"

Nick grunted. "Why wouldn't I be?"

"This is a pretty big deal, Nicky. And you won't be getting off on the right foot with these people. Not once they realize you're arriving already stoned out of your mind."

"I'm not stoned out of my mind. I'm high, yes, but I've been a lot worse than this. I'm pretty well practiced at hiding it, believe me."

"Oh, I believe you."

They stood in silence for several more moments, Nick with his eyes closed and enjoying the feel of the sun on his skin, Rebecca holding his hand. In truth Nick could have remained that way for hours.

"I looked up this place online. They have several family events planned in the next month. That's when the patients can invite family members to come visit for the day. They have cookouts, volleyball, shit like that. They also have a gym, which, frankly, you could use. You're getting a little thin there, cuz."

"Comes with the job," he said. His eyes remained closed. "Have you ever seen a fat heroin addict?"

"Nicky."

Something in her tone made him open his eyes and look at her. Her anger was gone. She looked both nervous and hopeful. There were tears in her eyes, but they had not yet spilled down her cheeks. He hoped she would retain control at least until she made it back inside the car. He already felt like shit without having to see Rebecca cry.

She said, "Do good in there. Listen to them and do what they tell you and beat this thing. I don't want to go to your funeral. Please."

He squeezed her hand and that turned into a hug. The moment his arms closed around her he heard her lose the battle with her tears. Her breath hitched in her throat. She was not sobbing, not yet, but he felt she would be before long.

"It's okay, Becks. It'll be okay, I swear. Don't cry."

"Just get better, Nicky." She was clearly on the verge of losing it. She hugged him tighter and made it difficult for him to breathe. "Just get better. Promise me."

He hesitated. Until that moment it had been his intention to go over the wall at the first available opportunity. He could shack up with Staci again until he found someone more stable. And on the plus side she would keep him high and guilt-free. The cops did not know about Staci and he trusted Rebecca to keep that information to herself so they would not be a factor. And if no better opportunity came around, well, there were worse fates than living with someone who would keep the white flowing and ask only for sex in return.

But now, for the first time since his mid-teens, he felt a pang of guilt regarding his addiction. He waded through the fog in his head and realized that time the guilt had been about Rebecca, as well. He could not remember the exact circumstances, but he thought perhaps she had caught him about to smoke up and he had invited her to join him. If the guilt had been enough perhaps he would have sought help and beaten the dragon at the age of fifteen. But it had not. He felt a pang when he realized this time would likely end with the same result.

He pulled away just enough so he could look into her red, wet eyes. "I promise, Becks. I'll do everything I can. I promise."

She hugged him again and forced all the air from his lungs. He enjoyed the knowledge that she cared for him and loved him as only family could. At the same time a part of him resented her for bringing on the heavy emotions and preventing him from truly enjoying the remnants of the white smoke in his system. He pushed that feeling as far down as it would go. He was not altogether successful but he managed to hide it from Rebecca.

"I think I have to go, Becks. The last thing I want is to be late for my first day. Know what I mean?"

She squeezed him more tightly before releasing her grip. Nick gulped air but did not make it obvious. Rebecca was not a big girl, but she had been for most of her life. It would not do to give her any reminder of that.

"Love you, Nicky."

"Love you, too, Becks. I'll call ya."

She hugged him one more time and turned and walked back to her car. She did not look at him again. He remained on the sidewalk and watched her start the Hyundai and pull away from the curb. The car stopped perhaps fifty feet away. It was too far for Nick to see her eyes watching him from the rearview but he knew that was precisely what she was doing. *Making sure I go inside and not take off down the street the second she's out of sight. Smart girl.* Nick picked up the duffel and slung it over his shoulder. He walked slowly up the steps to the Springbrook Healing and Recovery Center. Rebecca's car remained parked.

Nick paused when he reached the doors. His hand rested on the handle, but he stopped and turned. Rebecca's car inched slowly away. His eyes surveyed the street. Nearly every house within his field of vision was multi-family. Trees of various sort decorated the yards and the strip of grass between the sidewalk and the blacktop. Some of the houses had seen better days but this was by no means a slum. It looked to him like a street you could find in just about any town in any state. It was quiet except for a lone dog barking somewhere a block away.

"Could be worse."

Nick turned his attention to the fliers taped to the glass beside the doors. One promoted a family get-together that occurred two days before. Another showed a cartoon image of a disheveled man surrounded by darkness and huddled in a corner, clutching his knees to his chest. The caption stated: *YOU DON'T HAVE TO GO IT ALONE. WE'RE HERE TO HELP!* A third sheet of paper was an advertisement for a bail bonds company. Nick smiled and shook his head and opened the door.

The reception area was small. Two uncomfortable-looking chairs accounted for the only furniture. The receptionist, a miniscule young woman with a deep tan and wearing a white coat sat behind a glass partition. She looked up when the door opened and greeted Nick with a smile.

"Hi. How can I help you?" Her smile was warm but somehow disingenuous. Her name tag read *Amanda.*

"Nick Wade. I'm here to check in."

Amanda slid open the glass partition. "Do you have your admittance paperwork?"

"I do." Nick pulled a folded envelope from his back pocket. He handed it to her.

After Amanda read through it and typed the information into her computer she smiled again and said, "Have a seat. The nurse will be with you in a moment."

"Thanks." Nick took one of the seats and leaned all the way back. The heroin was still there, still made him feel good, but he could feel it starting to slip. He was unable to sneak any from Staci before he left the house. That meant he would have to rely on someone within rehab to hook him up. He knew people snuck that shit inside all the time; it was simply a matter of identifying his most likely source as soon as possible. In the best of all worlds that would be whoever was his roommate. Nick said a silent prayer he would ID the source before the shakes got too bad.

"Mr. Wade? I'm Karen Gaudiosi. I'm one of the nurses here at Springbrook."

Nick opened his eyes and looked at the source of the voice. "God, you're short." In point of fact, she was. Karen could not be more than 4'10", and that was probably being generous. She was of medium build and sported long, black hair. Her scrubs were pink and white and there was a clipboard in her left hand. She stood in the doorway to his right, holding the door open with her free hand. "Is this place populated entirely by hobbits?"

"Not entirely." She seemed to take a dim view of his attempt at humor. "Come with me, please." She opened the door wider and allowed him to pass into the facility.

The corridor was wide and brightly lit. The floor was white tile and the walls were an off-white that Nick thought he had never before seen. Several closed doors lined the walls. They were labeled *Maintenance* and *Staff Only* and the like. He squashed his nervousness when he failed to see anything labeled *Dispensary*. There had to be one. But it seemed he would have to wait until Karen decided he needed to know where it was located.

She stopped at a door and pulled a ring of keys from her pocket. She unlocked the door and motioned him inside. He read the label on the door as he entered. *Interview and Testing*. Nick grimaced.

Karen closed the door behind them and said, "Place your bag on the table, please. We have to have a urine sample. It's standard procedure in admitting new patients. The bathroom is over there behind that curtain."

"I'll save you the trouble. I smoked up this morning. In fact, no more than two hours ago."

"I see." She wrote something on her clipboard. "I'll still need a sample." She took a small plastic cup from the table where he had placed his duffel bag. "Fill it as much as you can, please."

"Waste of time, but all right." He took the cup and walked behind the curtain. "It's gonna come up positive. I can tell you that right now."

"I understand."

Her voice was neutral, almost pleasant. *Like you're the first asshole to show up here high,* she said without speaking. Nick had to concede the point. In fact, he was probably in a better position than some simply because he was not trying to sneak anything into the building. That, perhaps, might win him some points and get Karen to drop her guard. Not that he thought that was remotely likely. But it did not hurt to hope.

He filled the cup roughly halfway and came out from behind the curtain. Karen had put on latex gloves and took it from him. She capped it and affixed a label to it. "Okay, we'll just see what that says. We'll have the results in about five minutes. We do our own testing onsite."

"That's convenient."

"And necessary. I have to go through your bag, make sure there's nothing in there that shouldn't be. Is that okay with you?"

"Do I have a choice?"

"Not if you want to stay here, no."

Nick smirked at her honesty. "Knock yourself out." He sat in one of the chairs and watched Karen investigate the contents of his duffel. He had packed shirts, jeans, bathing trunks and toiletries. That accounted for most of his earthly possessions. A few pairs of socks and a couple of well-worn paperbacks he had managed to sneak out of Staci's (including one on Jack the Ripper that he had somehow never come across) filled out the rest of his belongings.

"Okay, you're clean."

Nick snorted. "Not by a long shot. Like I said, wait'll you get the results of the piss test."

"Be that as it may, I can show you to your room now. Normally, that would be a no-no. It's a major violation of the rules to expose the patients to someone under the influence. But your roommate is out with the others on a field trip so I can at least show it to you and let you get situated. Then I'll take you to see Dr. Buckley."

"Sounds like a plan." Nick picked up his duffel and followed Karen out of the room.

They walked down the corridor in silence. The stairs at the end of the hallway proved to be a pain in the ass and Nick was forced to hop up each step one at a time. His leg brace, far from comfortable, anyway, bit into his skin. Karen slowed her pace accordingly.

"Your limp. How bad is the pain?"

"I can manage. It's the goddamned brace they gave me that sucks. The metal clasps wear through the fabric pretty fast and they start digging into my skin." He tapped the side of his right knee. "I can't wait to get rid of the thing."

"Well, we're almost there. You'll be on the second floor. All male patients are on two, the females are on three. And there is never, never any fraternization between the two after lights out. Just so you know. Socializing is fine during the day in the common areas."

"You guys really know how to take the fun out of everything," he remarked.

"Oh, we're quite good at that," Karen agreed.

They reached the second floor and Karen led him down a hallway that looked precisely the same as the one below. Numerous doors lined the walls. All were open. He peeked in the first few and saw them identical in their size and appointments. Two twin beds, a couple of nightstands and lamps, two small dressers and a television mounted to the wall in the corner. At least two small cameras were affixed on the walls as well, and these made Nick uneasy. He expected them to be there and would have been suspicious by their absence, but he disliked them nonetheless.

Karen stopped next to an open door and indicated the room on the other side with a nod of her head. Nick ambled up to the door and read the placard on the wall. There were two names there: *John Curran* and, beneath that, *Nicholas Wade*. "This is your room."

Nick peeked inside and saw the exact same layout he had seen in the other rooms. The only exceptions were the personal belongings of John Curran. Nick made his way inside and looked about. There was a small bathroom to the immediate right of the doorway that had been obscured by his viewing angle. He looked inside and then moved farther in.

It seemed Curran had claimed the bed nearest the door. Nick dropped his duffle on the bed next to the windows. It would have been his choice, anyway. Easier to get to the window without waking his roommate. He looked back at Karen. "Cozy."

"It can be," Karen replied. "We want to make you as comfortable as possible while you're here."

"And what about my roommate? What's his deal?"

"John is a decent guy. I think you'll like him. I'm afraid I can't say beyond that, patient confidentiality and all. If he wants you to know something he'll tell you himself."

Nick nodded. "Fair enough."

He hobbled to the window and looked through. His room faced the street and would have been to the right of the front entrance when he viewed the building with Rebecca. A large tree partially blocked his view of the street. He noted with some irritation the tree was too far away to use to get down to street level. *Well, you can always jump,* he thought. *And break your other leg and maybe your head while you're at it.* Nick smirked. His inner voice still had enough of its usual heroin-infused sarcasm. But that still did not change the fact that getting out that way was probably out of the question.

"If you're ready we'll go back downstairs. Dr. Buckley is expecting you."

"Sure." Nick exited the room.

The walk down the stairs was only slightly less of a pain in the ass than the walk up, but he managed without too much discomfort. Karen led him back up the main hallway. They stopped in front of the door with *Administration* etched onto the placard. She waved her ID badge in front of the small scanner next to the placard and Nick heard the lock disengage. Karen opened the door, stepped through and motioned him inside.

There was another corridor, this one narrower than the one outside. It was carpeted and the walls were adorned with cheap art prints most likely purchased at a discount dollar store. Karen led the way to a closed door. She knocked on it and Nick heard a deep female voice from the other side say, "Come in."

Karen opened the door and stepped aside for Nick. He ambled past her and entered Dr. Buckley's office.

The room could have been situated in an Ivy League university. Beautiful paintings that most certainly did not originate in a dollar store were hung with care and at strategic places on the walls. Behind the desk were Dr. Buckley's diplomas and certificates and a few plaques. The desk itself was enormous and looked and smelled like oak. Plants grew in pots in the corners; bookshelves took up the rest of the wall space. The chair in which Buckley sat was tall and made of dark leather. Two chairs, much more modest, were placed in front of her desk. The only thing the room lacked was a decent view out the window. The office faced out from the side of the building. He caught a glimpse of a narrow alley between the window and the stone wall that bordered the property.

Buckley herself was pretty much as Nick had pictured her. A well-fed, middle-aged white woman whose dark auburn hair was simply too auburn not to be artificially colored. She was most definitely not a hobbit; even while sitting she seemed to loom above him. She wore a smart pantsuit that cost more than his first car. Her fingers were adorned with rings except, ironically, her ring finger. Several thin, gold bracelets clanged together on her wrists. Her lips and her cheeks were far too red and he could almost picture her slathering on the makeup in the morning before she left the house, perhaps even hiding away in her office bathroom at some point during the day for touchups. He disliked her immediately.

Buckley indicated one of the chairs in front of the desk. "Please, have a seat. Thank you, Karen."

Nick took the seat and regarded the tall woman on the other side of the desk. Karen mumbled something and exited the room. She closed the door behind her.

"I'm Dr. Buckley, Mr. Wade. Welcome to Springbrook."

"Thank you."

She looked at the open folder in front of her. "Your urinalysis came back as positive for diacetylmorphine, more commonly known as heroin."

"Yeah, I told the nurse it would."

"That's not uncommon here. Most patients, in fact, arrive under the influence. It's a big deal, but it's not the end of the world. In fact, you can look at it as quite the opposite. See it as the last time you'll ever be high."

Nick kept his expression neutral. "I'll do that."

"You have quite an extensive history," Buckley said as she turned the page. Her eyes skimmed down the paper. "Fewer arrests than I would have expected, though. You were careful not to get caught too often."

"Not carful enough, I guess."

"Indeed. But let's not focus on that." She closed the file and took a sheet of pink paper. She readied her pen and asked, without looking at him, "How long have you been addicted to diacetylmorphine?"

Nick shifted his weight. "The first time I got high I was fifteen. Been doing it since."

"And that is how long?" Her eyes remained on the pink piece of paper.

"I'm thirty-one."

She scribbled his response. "Describe the manner in which you first tried the narcotic, please."

"My father had just died. He was a heroin addict for most of his life. He committed suicide at thirty-nine, OD'd, of course.. He wasn't in the ground a week before my mother asked me if I wanted to try it."

"So this first time was with your mother? She provided you with the drug?" Her tone was neutral, matter-of-fact.

Even among his fellow addicts the idea of a woman influencing her young son to take heroin elicited surprise. Buckley did not so much as arch an eyebrow. Nick's dislike of the woman deepened. "That's right."

Buckley continued to scribble. "Any idea why she would do that? Was she an addict as well?"

Nick shifted in the chair again. "Yes. She OD'd about two years ago. Or so I was told. We lost contact over the years."

"I see." More scribbling. "Can you describe that first time to me?"

"The first time I used heroin? Well, that was a long time ago. I can't remember every detail."

"Just tell me what you do remember."

"Okay. She loaded up a syringe and injected me with it. Then she took whatever was left in there for herself. I hated it. Not the being high part, that was actually okay. The needle part. I hate needles."

"That's a pretty common phobia."

"After that she offered to teach me how to smoke it. That's my preferred method, by the way. Smoking it. It's painless and you feel the effects instantly. Injections suck."

"And how much do you use in a day?"

Nick shrugged. "I don't know. I go through it pretty fast. If it's available to me I'll stay high until it's gone. Then I'll go out and find some more."

"And how do you do that? Your file says you're unemployed. How do you get the money for it?"

"Mostly hook up with someone who has money. Or shoplift. I got really good at that. Before it got too bad I used to pawn my belongings or my roommate's belongings. Where there's a will..." He was surprised at how easily he could relate his story. Even Angie had not known most of this.

Buckley stopped writing and placed her pen on the desk. She folded her hands in front of her. "Mr. Wade, what I see here is a young man who has been given a chance to escape from a downward spiral. Your addiction controls you completely. If left to your own devices you'll follow the path your parents took. I don't think you want that. I don't want that for you. We can help you avoid that fate and become a contributing member of society. But you have to determine that that's what you want. This won't work if your heart isn't in it. If you think you'll just humor us and then go right back to that life once you walk out the door then there's really nothing we can do for you."

Don't I know it, Nick thought. What he said was, "I'm here, right?"

"We'll speak more in group. I think you'll be better encouraged to talk about your experiences in a room full of your peers. We have some decent people here, Mr. Wade. They've made the same mistakes you've made and they're working hard to get back on the right path. I think it will be very healthy for you to listen to them and speak with them. And, of course, the staff and I are here for you twenty-four-seven. Whatever help you may need we'll provide. That's my promise to you." She unfolded her hands and placed them palms-down on her desktop. "But we absolutely will not tolerate narcotics usage here. If you somehow managed to sneak something in here and you get caught using, or you're showing signs of intoxication, the staff are instructed to call the police and that will end your time with us. Our policy is zero tolerance. I can't stress that enough. With all that in mind, does Springbrook sound like a positive environment to you?

"Pretty positive, yeah," Nick lied. "I'm looking forward to meeting everyone."

"You'll be in quarantine for the next six hours. That's the rule when a new patient shows up under the influence. You'll be under constant surveillance that whole time. Anything you need, the nurses or I will provide it to you."

Nick shrugged. "Okay."

She nodded and called out, "Karen."

The door at his back opened.

"Take Mr. Wade to quarantine, please."

"Yes, doctor."

Nick stood. Buckley did, as well, and Nick saw his impression of the woman's height was not incorrect. She was well over six feet tall, maybe 6'6". She extended her hand and Nick shook it. Her smile was pleasant, if forced. He had reached the door when Dr. Buckley called to him, "Again, welcome to Springbrook."

"Thanks," Nick replied without looking back. He followed Karen from the office.

Chapter 3

Hope in Her Eyes

He took both his lunch and his dinner in quarantine. He could have joined the others in the cafeteria, but he did not want their first impression of him to be at the table. He also did not want to meet the other patients all at once. His decision was based in no small part on the fact that he was starting to feel the early effects of withdrawal. He did not feel sick, not yet, but he would soon enough. He thought it best to remain in quarantine until he could get a grip on both the symptoms and his irritability. Karen brought his dinner to him along with a methadone tablet. He downed the tablet and picked at his dinner. It was a different nurse, an older woman named Carol, who picked up his plate and informed him Karen had gone home for the night.

She wanted to take him to his room, but Nick knew better. He was in that uncomfortable zone where the heroin had abandoned him and the methadone had yet to take hold. The last thing he wanted was to go to his room agitated and maybe piss off Curran; if the man turned out to have anything stashed away Nick would have to start on good terms with him. Nick instead elected to go outside. The backyard of the center was fenced in for privacy and contained a shallow pool and several picnic tables. He could go out there and wait for the methadone to kick in and then he could meet his new roommate.

Carol escorted him outside. There were two young women sitting at the edge of the pool, smoking cigarettes. Their legs dangled in the water. They chatted with their backs to him and took no notice of his presence. That suited him just fine. He selected the picnic table in the corner. Most of it was wreathed in shadow and it was there he sat.

He felt the cool night air on his skin. It made the sweat feel like ice and raised the gooseflesh on his arms. It was still better than full-on withdrawal. The methadone, it seemed, was starting to go to work. He would sit there until it did its job and he trusted his stomach to retain its contents. Then he would make his way upstairs and meet Curran. Nick had spent enough time around addicts to spot the signs of someone holding. It would take a resourceful person to sneak something inside Springbrook; Nick hoped his roommate proved to be the resourceful kind.

His stomach rumbled and Nick closed his eyes and concentrated on keeping his dinner where it belonged. He succeeded but it took most of his willpower. Fresh sweat broke out on his forehead and chilled him. He felt his heart racing and purposely slowed his breathing. It took several moments during which he thought he might pass out. When the brief episode had run its course and order was restored to his lower abdomen Nick opened his eyes.

The two women at the pool were now on their feet. They toweled off their legs while they chatted. One of them, the older of the two, sported short blonde hair and tattoos up and down her arms. *Coke addict*, Nick thought. *Cokeheads love their tattoos.* She giggled at something her companion said and turned toward the building. The other, with longer, brown hair and with tattoos of her own, joined her. The two women went inside without ever looking in Nick's direction. He did not get a good luck at the older woman but the younger one appeared to be no more than twenty or twenty-one. *What's so fucked up in her life that she's in here already?* Then he remembered himself at that age and answered his own question. They slid the glass doors closed and vanished from his sight.

Nick remained at the picnic table for another ten minutes before he followed them inside.

He made his way slowly and painfully up the stairs to the second floor. On the landing he paused for breath and to quiet the throbbing in his knee. He could hear female voices on the floor above him. There was laughter and the sound of softly running feet. It sounded to Nick like the slumber parties the girls next door to him threw seemingly every other weekend when he was a kid. He would sit at his window and look across the way. The silhouettes of teen girls would move across the curtains and Nick would imagine what was going on inside the room. But he never got to see anything, which was a shame. What preteen boy wouldn't have loved a peek inside those curtains? But the DeGroate girls had moved away when he was twelve and the house was bought by an old couple and Nick had never again felt the urge to try to peek through those curtains.

It took some effort but he pushed those memories down. Thinking of the DeGroate girls was just fine, but those thoughts inevitably led to his own home life at that time and that was something he did not need to think about, certainly not with the symptoms of withdrawal threatening to claw their way past the methadone. Not when he was about to meet his new roommate.

Nick lingered on the landing for only a moment longer before he continued on to his room. Several of the doors on the second floor were now closed. It was not yet lights out but it seemed the day's field trip had taken a lot out of the patients. He could see the telltale light of a television under one of the doors but the other rooms were dark and silent. He moved past them as quietly and as quickly as he was able.

The door to his room was likewise closed. Light from the television spilled a few inches onto the tiled floor. Nick took a deep breath and opened the door.

John Curran lay on his bed with the pillows propped up on the headboard and looking disinterested in whatever was on the TV. He sat up a little straighter when Nick walked in. "You must be my new roomie." He looked Nick up and down.

Curran looked to be around Nick's age. He had short, dark hair and looked like someone who worked out often. He wore no shirt and his pajama bottoms displayed the KISS logo at various angles. Curran stuck out a beefy hand. "John Curran."

Nick took the accepted hand. "Nick Wade. Nice to meet you."

Curran settled back on his bed. "What are you in for? Wait. Let me guess. It's either meth or heroin. Am I right?"

"No to the first, a definite yes to the second." Nick negotiated his way toward his small bed. His duffel bag remained where he left it but he knew Curran must have taken a peek inside at some point. It did not bother Nick at all; he would have done the same thing. He lowered himself onto the bed slowly, grimacing at the fresh pain in his leg.

"Broken wheel?" Curran asked.

"You should see the other guy."

"I bet. Listen, I wasn't really watching this. If there's something on you wanna watch, feel free." He offered the remote.

Nick held up a hand. "Whatever. I'm not really in the mood for TV." He glanced at the set, anyway. *"Hogan's Heroes*? I used to watch this all the time when I was a kid. Great show."

"Fuckin A." Curran's eyes went back to the television.

Nick removed his shirt and tossed it onto his dresser. He rummaged through his duffle until he found his toothbrush and tube of Crest. He eyed the cameras looking down at him from the corners and thought, *Fuck it.* "So, what's it like here? Anything around?"

Curran's eyes did not move from the TV screen. "Not that I'm aware of. I asked the same question the day I got here. I guess every once in a while someone gets something past our dungeon guards but you can't count on it. This place is pretty fucking dry."

"Shit." Nick pursed his lips. He felt Curran was telling the truth. Nick knew most of the tells an addict used when it came to lying about their stash. He saw none of them from his new roommate. It was possible he was lying but if he were then he was even more accomplished at it than Nick himself.

When it seemed Curran would volunteer no further information Nick got back to his feet and hobbled into the bathroom. After his teeth were brushed and his bladder emptied he returned to his bed.

"Wish I had better news for you," Curran said as Nick pulled his sweatpants off. They joined his shirt on the dresser and he slid beneath his sheets. "Buckley runs a pretty tight ship. The only way to get shit in here is to wait for family day and have someone bring it to you. But even that's dicey. If they even suspect someone's trying to bring something in, they search the shit out of them. If they don't wanna go along with the search then they're invited to leave the premises. And the nurses here have that shit down to a science. You'd need a nun to get something past Karen or Carol. And even then…"

The news made Nick sweat. "What about you? Why are you here?"

"Painkillers and alcohol," Curran replied right away. It was clear he had expected the question. "Blew out my knee in a pickup basketball game. Doc gave me oxycodone and I guess I took a little too much of it. When that got scarce I started drinking. That was four years ago, by the way. I say if you're gonna fuck up do it in a big way."

"Oh, I did," Nick informed him.

Curran laughed and after a moment, Nick joined him. *Hogan's Heroes* was followed by *F Troop* and then *The Brady Bunch*. Neither man paid much attention to the TV; they continued their conversation even after Carol came in and told them it was lights out.

Nick did not get much sleep that night. Even after the conversation with Curran trickled out he remained wide awake. With the methadone working its way out of his system and nothing to take its place his stomach began to protest. He got the shakes around 2:30. He barely made it to the bathroom the first time he vomited. The second time he made it with time to spare mostly because he was intimately familiar with the onset. The third and fourth times he did not need to dash to the bathroom because he was already there. He spent most of his first night at Springbrook Healing and Recovery Center on the bathroom floor with one arm slung across the toilet and wanting to die.

This was not going to work.

Karen found him there the following morning. He was half-asleep with drying vomit clinging to his lips. When she pulled his head away from the toilet a long string of half-solidified bile stretched and finally broke. Most of it landed in the toilet but Nick was past caring or even noticing.

She helped him to his feet and back into the room. Curran was starting to stir when they made it to Nick's bed. He felt himself drop onto the mattress, heard a sigh from both Karen and Curran. He opened one eye and regarded his roommate.

Curran propped himself up on one elbow and rubbed his eyes with his free hand. He squinted at the sunlight beaming through the curtains. "What time is it?"

"You ask me that every morning. Six forty-five AM. Time to get up."

He kicked off the sheets and sat on the edge of the bed. "He don't look too good."

"No, he doesn't. And neither did you after your first night."

"Don't remind me about that," Curran said. He disappeared into the bathroom.

"Just let me die," Nick mumbled. He was aware enough to know Karen probably had not heard or understood his plea. She surprised him.

"Can't. That would look pretty bad on my eval next month."

He tried to say, *Like I give a shit*, but it came out as incoherent babble. This time Karen made no reply. He heard her cross the room and a moment later he saw a clean shirt land on the bed inches from his face.

"You'll have to get dressed, Nick. Morning meeting is important. Dr. Buckley expects all the patients to be there." A pause. "Even you."

Nick mumbled his protest.

"And I suggest you brush your teeth before you go downstairs. You won't win any friends if you smell like vomit. John, give him a hand, will you?"

"Sure thing," Curran replied from the bathroom.

Nick heard Karen retreat from the room. A moment later he heard her knock on the door next to theirs.

Nick remained motionless. His stomach continued to threaten another eruption at any moment but he had gone through this enough times to know it was an empty threat. Whatever had been in his stomach before had long since made good its escape. He dry-heaved a couple times but that was all.

"Gotta get a move-on, man. Buckley starts the morning meeting at 7:05 on the dot. If you're late the only excuse she'll accept is you're dead."

"I *am* dead," Nick mumbled.

His new roommate laughed. "Nah, you only think you're dead. C'mon, I'll help ya."

Curran wound up doing most of the work. He got Nick's sweatpants over his leg brace and helped him with his shirt. Nick grumbled the whole time and dry-heaved again. He limped his way into the bathroom and proceeded to do a lousy job with his toothbrush. Fifteen minutes after Karen woke them Nick and Curran were making their way down the stairs.

Curran kept his pace slow and Nick appreciated the gesture. He had grown used to walking with the brace but this particular morning nothing was easy. He nearly lost it twice on the stairs and once for no apparent reason on the first floor. Curran was there every step of the way. He led Nick to one of the side rooms near the front entrance.

Nick cast a quick glance at the doors that led to freedom. Had he been his normal self he would have been through them before Curran could protest. As it was he could just about manage to keep his feet under him. Freedom would have to wait until he was in better shape.

His roommate led Nick into the meeting room. A dozen chairs were arranged in a circle. Most of them were occupied by their fellow patients. Nick noted without much enthusiasm the presence of the two women from the pool. They sat next to each other and sipped coffee and chatted amongst themselves. Curran assisted Nick in plopping down into a chair opposite the women and then took the seat next to him.

Nick's head swam. He had been this bad before but not often. He tried to fight through the haze and remember the last time he found himself in such bad condition. He had an image of himself lying on the floor in Angie's apartment but he could not remember the context. When he tried to picture Angie's face he drew a blank. He put his face in his hands and did what he could to steady his breathing.

Curran was talking amicably with the young man seated next to him. Nick concentrated on their voices to the exclusion of all else. They discussed the Mets game from the night before. Apparently David Wright hit a bases-clearing double in the eighth to salvage the last game of their series against the Marlins. The guy next to Curran seemed quite pleased with this. They kept up their chatter until Buckley arrived.

"Good morning, everyone," she began. "And how are we today?"

Buckley's voice was far too loud. Nick peeked at her through his fingers. She wore a pantsuit of a different color than the one he saw yesterday. She held a clipboard in one hand and a cup of coffee with the other. She took the last remaining empty seat in the circle and placed her coffee mug on the floor. She surveyed her patients before her eyes settled on Nick.

"How are you feeling?"

Nick dropped his hands and squinted at the harsh fluorescents in the ceiling. Buckley looked at him expectantly. From the corner of his eyes he could see the other patients looking at him, as well. He drew himself straight in the chair and folded his hands in his lap. "Okay," he lied.

"I want you all to meet Nicholas Wade. He's our newest patient."

Several people said, "Hello, Nicholas." He nodded and smiled and snapped off a half-assed salute.

Buckley took attendance, making each patient answer with, "Here," as she called their name. With each declaration she checked off a name on her clipboard. It was ridiculous and Nick knew it. There were ten patients at Springbrook and Buckley knew damned well everyone was present. It had to be either a state law that attendance must be taken or else it was Springbrook's policy. That she would go to the trouble against all common sense grated on Nick's nerves. He was with it enough to know that such a display would have bothered him even if he was not going through withdrawal.

She made him address the group with the circumstances that landed him in Springbrook. He kept it as perfunctory as possible. (*You just remember Santos.*) Buckley prodded more information from him, making him repeat most of what he told her the day before. (*Santos got whachoo need.*) His dislike of the woman continued to grow.

When he was finished she moved on to another patient. It was the younger of the two women he had seen at the pool. He got that her name was Patty but he tuned out for most of her time on the floor. The meeting could not end quickly enough for him.

When it did eventually end Nick glanced at the clock on the wall. The meeting had lasted forty-five minutes. It felt to him like forty-five days. The patients filed out of the room slowly. Some of them headed outside, cigarettes in hand. Curran took him to the small cafeteria, insisting that he had to get some food in him. It was the last thing Nick wanted but a stern look from Buckley squashed any protest he could mount. He allowed Curran to lead him.

He selected a meager portion of scrambled eggs and a small juice box with a photo of perfect oranges on the cover. His stomach threatened to mutiny at the smell of the eggs but he managed to get through breakfast still in command of the ship.

Curran was heading back to their room, but Nick informed him he needed some air. Curran obliged and followed him out the sliding glass door which led to the fenced in backyard. It was no surprise to Nick that most of the patients had made it there and were engaged in chitchat in small groups. Patty and her friend sat in loungers by the pool and smoked. Two other young women sat with two of the guys and one older man. Nick found he could not remember any of them from the meeting. Had he really been that out of it? He did not think so but he was hardly in a position to trust his memory.

Curran guided him to the same picnic table at which he sat the night before. The man with whom Curran had discussed the Mets sat there and nibbled on an English muffin while reading a book. Curran sat across from him and pounded the table with open palms. The man jumped a bit.

"Goddamnit, John, would you knock that shit off?" He sounded genuinely annoyed.

"Just seeing if you're awake is all," Curran replied with a smile. "Can't have anyone isolating now, can we?"

Although Nick had never heard that expression before something in Curran's delivery made him believe the man was imitating Buckley. Curran drummed his hands on the table as Nick took the spot next to him.

"Isolate my balls."

"God already done that, motherfucker." Curran laughed, then said, "Pedro, Nick. Nick, Pedro."

"Hi."

"Hi back," Pedro replied. He stuffed the rest of the English muffin into his mouth and returned his attention to his book.

"He ain't the friendliest guy you'll ever meet but he ain't so bad once you get to know him," Curran continued. "Especially considering he's a Mets fan."

"You don't know me," Pedro said. "And at least my team doesn't have to buy their World Series rings."

Curran continued as if Pedro had not spoken. "Those dudes over there are Ricky, Richie and the old guy is Phil. The two girls with them are Jenna and Sarah." He hitched a thumb over his shoulder at the two women by the pool. "And those two are Patty and Jessica." He turned to Nick with a wolfish smile. "Rumor is they're more than roommates, if you know what I'm saying."

Nick knew but he found he could not care less about what Patty and Jessica did when they were alone at night. It should have mattered, should have produced at least a stirring somewhere south of his bellybutton, but it did not. If they had some H, well, *that* would make a difference.

"I'm sure I'll get to know everyone eventually." It was a lie. He would be over the wall long before that was a possibility.

In fact he surveyed the wall which surrounded the property and cut off the outside world. It was tall, at least ten feet high, and made of stone. Its façade was stucco, not much good for hand- and footholds. Scaling the wall would be a bitch, but not impossible if the climber was motivated enough. And Nick's motivation grew by the minute.

He remained seated at the picnic table with Curran and Pedro bickering about the merits of the Mets vs. those of the Yankees. Nick ignored them for the most part and sat with his eyes shut and the sun on his face. It felt good but it was not nearly enough to overcome the restlessness that threatened to send him over the wall or simply out the front door.

The only thing that stopped him was the memory of Rebecca when she dropped him off the day before. There had been pain and hope in her eyes. She would be disappointed, crushed, if he left Springbrook. It was this knowledge alone that kept him seated at the picnic table.

He knew—*knew*—it would not be enough to keep him there for much longer. But it was enough for now and that would have to do.

Joseph J. Christiano

Chapter 4

The Void Around Her

It had been a shitty flight and Melanie Allen was happy to have her feet on the ground again. She had had her share of such flights before, perhaps more than her share, but this was one for the ages. All she wanted to do was get back to her apartment and hit the sack. Dan would be horny, as he always was after she returned home after a few days. *Not tonight*, she thought. *I'm way too fucking exhausted for that.*

She hit the locker room and changed into her civvies. There were a couple of other flight attendants there and they chatted amongst themselves and nodded in her direction but took no further notice of her presence. That was fine with her. She had spent the last eleven hours doing nothing but talking and she was grateful for the chance to rest her vocal cords.

She kept going back to the man in 6-C. She had known he was trouble the moment she saw him. Overweight, white-knuckled, heavy-drinking trouble. And she had been proved correct before the wheels even left the ground. He had singled her out as his own personal valet and his constant demands for everything from an extra pillow to more vodka monopolized most of her time. When Chrissy volunteered to take him off her hands the man in 6-C protested and demanded Melanie. He had not made enough of a scene to warrant the captain's intervention nor even that of the anonymous sky marshal who was certainly present. Melanie did not know whether to be relieved or disappointed. In the end she simply did what she could for the asshole and tried her best to imagine him being blown out the nearest window, preferably into one of the engines on his way out.

But now the man in 6-C was out of her life and that was just fine with her. She thought about her warm bed with Dan lying next to her in the dark. The image made her smile, the first time she had done so since she first saw the man who would make the flight from Honolulu to Newark her personal version of purgatory. But her bed and Dan would have to wait. What Melanie Allen wanted more than anything in the world at that moment was a drink. There were numerous options in that regard at Newark International. It was the one saving grace of having it as her home base. She knew the bartender at the Silver Lining the best so it was in that direction she set off.

The place was packed, as it usually was, as all airport bars usually were. Rodney was not manning the bar, much to her disappointment, but she got over it rather quickly. Who poured the vodka mattered much less to her than the size of the glass into which it was poured.

A seat at the far end was open and Melanie parked her wheeled carry-on next to it. The bartender took her order and she helped herself to a couple cashews from the dish while she waited. The bartender wore a nametag but Melanie did not bother to read it. When her drink arrived she downed it with one gulp and ordered a replacement. She was nursing the second tall glass when a chubby man in a loud sport coat took the barstool next to hers.

She had no intention of looking in his direction, let alone make eye contact, and she would have kept to herself had the man not placed a twenty on the bar and said, "Scotch." Then, to Melanie: "Buy you a drink, darlin'?"

Melanie regarded him for only a moment before she turned back to her vodka. "No, thanks. I got it."

"You most certainly do," he countered.

Melanie rolled her eyes. It would be nice (not to mention unprecedented) if she were able to enjoy a drink in an airport bar without men like Loud Sport Jacket trying to loosen her up.

The bartender arrived a moment later with his drink and asked if Melanie would like another. Melanie spared a last look at the man next to her and emptied her glass. "One more for the road." The bartender nodded and took her glass.

Melanie reached into her pocketbook and removed her cell. She called up her schedule even though she knew it by heart. She studied the small screen intently. Anything to avoid the portly man sensing an opening to start a conversation. She could not bear to listen to another inane pickup line from him or anyone else. And she especially did not want to hear it in the man's too-jovial voice. She remained that way, eyes focused on her cell, until the bartender returned with her third and final drink.

She wanted to take her time with it but the presence of the man next to her caused her to drink it as quickly as she was able. No more than two minutes had passed between her drink being delivered to her replacing the empty glass on the bar. She took a few singles from her wallet and placed them next to the glass. Then she was gone.

"Nice talkin' with you," the portly man called to her. Melanie did not look back.

She walked quickly through the terminal, her wheeled carry-on bumping along behind her. The vodka was doing its job rather sooner and with more force than she expected but that was okay, too. She was not drunk, not by a long shot, but she was feeling good and that was all that mattered.

A moment later she was pressing the elevator call button. As she waited she realized she had the elevator bank to herself. Melanie raised an eyebrow. She could not recall a single instance, in any airport, where this had occurred. *Who cares? Just means I won't have to stop at every fucking level before I get to mine. Sometimes things* could *go your way, honey.*

A flickering light caught her attention and she turned. The ceiling fluorescents winked on and off rapidly for a few moments before returning to normal levels. It made her head throb. Melanie closed her eyes and listened to the buzz of the fluorescents and wished the goddamned elevator would arrive.

The doors opened suddenly and silently and Melanie resisted the urge to run inside. Once across the threshold she spun and hit the appropriate button. The doors closed as silently as they opened and Melanie leaned back against the wall. The throbbing subsided and was gone by the time she reached P4.

The man from 6-C popped into her head, just as most of the pain in the ass passengers did from time to time. She pushed him away only to have him replaced by Loud Sport Jacket. She banished him, too. Melanie sighed and allowed herself a wry smile. *Get lost, losers. It's just me and Dan for the next three days.* Dan and that warm, familiar bed. With luck and light traffic she would be home in thirty minutes, forty, tops.

She exited the elevator into almost complete darkness. One or two of the overheads flickered and it seemed the parking garage was experiencing the same electrical problem as the main terminal level. "So much for good luck," she said aloud. She remembered the level on which she had parked her red Volvo, but she could not for the life of her remember which section. Not that it would matter because it was too dark to read the signs posted on the support columns.

She took her keys from her pocket and thumbed the alarm button on the fob. She heard and saw nothing. "Come on." She walked ahead a few steps and tried it again. The elevator doors behind her closed and she was plunged into complete darkness. She could make out the dimensions of the garage through the open areas along the walls but that was all. "Just fucking great." She considered recalling the elevator and locking it on her level but that would just piss off anyone waiting for it. She swore again and picked a direction.

The wheels of her carry-on squeaked and jostled along the oil-soaked concrete. She might have been walking too fast but she did not care. She just wanted to find her Volvo and get home. She held her key ring out in front of her and continued to press the alarm button. After a few more tries she heard the telltale beep from somewhere ahead and to her right. A pale yellow light flashed on and then off. Melanie smiled and headed in that direction.

She hit the alarm button again when she was closer. Her car obediently beeped and the parking lights winked at her. She smiled again and reached her car. The carry-on went inside the trunk and a moment later she was behind the wheel and turning the key in the ignition. The headlights came on automatically when the engine started and for the first time since the elevator she could see. She put the Volvo in drive and pulled out of her spot.

She turned onto the ramp which led to level three when the ceiling lights on that level winked out in front of her. Melanie hit the brakes and swore. She peeked through the windshield at the dead lights and paused. "What the hell is this?" She made her way through the darkened garage and turned onto level two. The rolling blackout continued to outpace her; level two was plunged into darkness in front of her.

Melanie hit the gas pedal a little harder than she expected and her tires squealed through the turn. She felt her heart racing and sweat had sprung out on her forehead. She followed the curves of the garage as fast as she felt she could control the Volvo.

She approached the turn for level one, the ground floor, when her headlights suddenly went dark. Melanie slammed her foot on the brake pedal. The Volvo screeched to a halt and the front end swerved and nearly clipped the rear of a parked pickup truck. She reached for the headlight switch on the arm poking out from the steering column and turned it. The dashboard lights turned off and then on again, but the headlights remained dark. She tried it several times before she swore and gave up.

She could not pull onto the Turnpike with no headlights. Forgetting for a moment it was not safe, the first trooper who saw her would pull her over. If he smelled alcohol on her, or even if he didn't, he might give her a breathalyzer. She was not drunk but the breathalyzer might disagree. And then where would she be? Calling Dan from the nearest trooper barracks and asking him to bail her out. That would go over about as well as a fart in church. And then she would have to deal with the airline and their fucking standards board. It was simply not worth taking the chance.

Probably a fuse, anyway. That did nothing to help. She knew nothing about the fuses or even where they were located. She would have to call Dan. But not from here, the middle of the parking garage. The concrete structure was notorious for blocking reception, in any case. *Just clear the garage. Then we'll call in the cavalry.*

She craned her neck and could just make out the ramp to level one. The lights there were still on. "Okay, okay." She turned the wheel away from the pickup and eased her foot off the brake pedal. The Volvo obediently moved forward slowly. She advanced like that, her foot hovering over the brake pedal and the car crawling slowly toward the next level.

She reached the ramp the same instant level one vanished into darkness.

Melanie mashed the gas pedal without thinking. The Volvo surged forward. Her tires squealed again and she took the turn much too quickly. The dashboard lights winked out, but she did not care. Level one and the gate were just another turn away. The breaks squealed a bit and the car rocked on its suspension when she brought it to a sudden stop. The garage exit was directly ahead.

Melanie took a deep breath. It took a conscious effort to release her grip on the steering wheel. Her knuckles creaked as she did so, her heart thudded away inside her chest. "Calm down, calm down," she told herself. She squeezed her eyes closed and willed her heart to slow down. It took several deep breaths, but her heart finally obeyed and slowed its heavy metal beat. Melanie opened her eyes again.

There was complete darkness in front of her. Somewhere beyond the garage she could make out the sounds of airport traffic. She reached into her pocketbook and removed her cell and hoped she was close enough to the outside to get a signal.

Something moved outside her windshield. It was pitch black but she saw something move within the darkness. Her hand fumbled for the window switch. Her window glided down with its customary electric *whirr*. She poked her head out the window. "Hello? Anyone there?" Christ, she hadn't hit someone, had she? There had been no impact, but she had been jacked up on adrenaline when she took the corner.

She heard nothing, saw no one. "Hello? Are you all right?" She could hear the sounds of traffic outside and in the distance a plane took off. The garage itself remained silent. Melanie unlocked her seatbelt and opened her door. She stepped out of the car and looked about.

There was no sign of anyone; even the usual foot traffic was absent. Level one appeared deserted. She returned her attention to her phone and activated the screen. She held it in front of her and eyed her surroundings with her makeshift flashlight. The weak blue light revealed no one.

"For fuck's sake, get it together, girl." She got back into her car and buckled her seatbelt.   She reached for the gearshift and paused, realized how lucky she had been. Better to react to nothing than to have someone injured. It would look very bad for her and the airline if she had plowed over someone after a few rounds at the Silver Lining, blood-alcohol level be damned. She smiled and laughed and the act of it released all the tension in her body. She took a few deep breaths and felt better. "Okay." She put the lever in drive and moved slowly toward the exit.

There was a tremor through the steering wheel and Melanie knew it had originated at the back of her car. She gasped and stopped again and looked in the rearview. There was nothing but darkness behind her. She stuck her head out the window and craned her neck but she could see nothing. "Goddammit, what the fuck!" She threw her door open and half-stepped out before the seatbelt pulled her back inside. She swore again and clawed at the clasp when she caught movement to her left. She looked up, screamed.

She could not see the man clearly, was not at first certain it was a man. He was tall, taller than Dan, and thin, nearly anorexic. He wore a long, dark coat that seemed to undulate around him. His head was impossibly shaped and elongated; it took her a moment to realize he was wearing a hat. A top hat? He was enveloped in shadow, as if the darkness had given birth to him. His arm moved quickly, too quickly for her to follow in the void around her. Melanie felt sudden and intense pain in her left shoulder. She screamed again.

Her foot slammed down on the gas pedal and the Volvo's engine raced. The breath caught in her throat and she pawed clumsily for the gearshift.

The man swung again and she felt something hot and wet on her arm. Her fingers closed around the gearshift and she threw it into drive.

The Volvo shot forward and to the left. Her door slammed shut at the same moment her Volvo collided with the rear of a compact sedan. The airbag deployed and for a brief moment she was blind. The Volvo's horn began beeping loudly at her; the sound echoed off the concrete walls of the garage. Her hands tore at the airbag and after a moment she managed to clear it from her field of vision. She spun the wheel hard to the right and the Volvo cleared the mangled sedan. Her vision clouded and she realized her eyes were wet with tears. She blinked them away and steered for the exit.

It came into view with the security booth and its wooden arm blocking the way out. The old man inside the booth waved his arms frantically at her. Melanie stomped the gas pedal the last inch or two to the floor and shot straight through the security arm. Splintered wood flew past the windshield.

She reached the outside and the area seemed flooded with light. Melanie yelped and threw up a hand to shield her eyes. After the primordial darkness of the parking garage the outside area seemed made entirely of light. She squinted through her fingers and piloted the swerving Volvo toward the Turnpike. She alternately wiped tears from her eyes and squeezed the wounds on her arm and shoulder. Blood seeped between her fingers and ran in rivulets down her arm. Her shirt sleeve was soaked through. She did not look at the wounds, did not dare. Her eyes darted between the road in front of her and the garage behind her.

The garage and the airport were receding rapidly in her rearview. Her eyes, accustomed to the darkness of the garage, were nearly blind with the lights of the airport and its traffic. She could see no sign of the tall, thin man, but her eyes were glazed and she did not trust them. Melanie continued to split her attention between the Jersey Turnpike and her rearview mirror until she pulled into the emergency room parking lot in East Orange.

****

Nick sat up too quickly in bed and tumbled off the side. He landed hard on his backside and yelped. Pain shot up his leg and into his back. He had just enough time to mumble, "Oh no!" before he felt the bile rise up his throat. He vomited onto the hardwood before he had any chance to stop himself. When he finished emptying his stomach his arms gave out and he collapsed onto the floor. He had the presence of mind to roll off his bad leg, but little else.

He heard Curran mumble something and then he heard his roomie get out of bed. Nick felt Curran's footsteps as he crossed the room. Then, "Shit. Hang on, bro, I'll get Carol." And he was gone before Nick could protest.

Nick spat the last of the bile and his dinner onto the floor. He had felt this way before, usually when he was forced to go without. But this was worse; this was hell.

He lost all tack of time, but it could not have been more than a few moments before he heard Curran return with Carol. Between the two of them they managed to get him back into bed. Through lidded eyes Nick watched Carol pull her walkie-talkie from her pocket and call the night custodian to clean the former contents of Nick's stomach from the floor.

As Carol wiped at the vomit on Nick's lips and chin he heard Curran make a snide remark about the smell of vomit in the room. Nick did not smell vomit. Nor did he taste it. His mouth and nostrils were filled with something else. It made him think of working on cars in his mother's driveway. Oil? Yes, oil and something else, something beneath that. The clouds covering his mind parted just long enough for him to identify the smell and taste as car exhaust. It followed him down into darkness when he passed out.

Joseph J. Christiano

Chapter 5

A Bad Way

Nick felt like shit and he did not want to get out of bed. Karen and Curran helped him into the bathroom where he dry-heaved a few times. He managed to brush his teeth and empty his bladder without collapsing onto the floor so that, at least, was something. His arms and legs shook as he slipped on a shirt and his sweatpants. He was tempted, so very tempted, to lay back down and shut his eyes, but he did not. He knew he would pass out and miss morning meeting and then he would have to deal with Buckley. Not that he gave a shit what she would have to say. He was simply certain he was close to death and he did not want the last thing he heard to be her voice as she chewed him out. So he kept close to the wall and made his way slowly out of the room and down the stairs.

He was the last to arrive at morning meeting. He took the only empty seat, between Pedro and Sarah. Nick put his head down and closed his eyes and tried to stop the shaking in his arms.

Pedro leaned into him and whispered, "Deep breaths, man. That's how I did it."

Nick barely heard him; he did not respond.

Buckley came in and greeted everyone. Most of the meeting was a blur to Nick. It seemed most of the time was taken by Phil, the older man, who apparently had a pretty serious addiction to crack. His voice sounded to Nick like bees buzzing around a nest. After a while it grated on his nerves and he would have paid the man to shut the fuck up if only he had any cash on him.

Nick perked up a little when Sarah took the floor. She looked to be a little younger than Angie and she even resembled her a bit if you pictured her dark brown hair as jet black. She still bore the telltale trademarks of a heroin addict. Her eyes were sunken, her features gaunt, but they were not nearly as severe as Angie's had been. What interested Nick the most was Sarah speaking about her addiction to heroin. Nick did not give a shit about what she said so much as he listened intently to her tone. She was dying for a hit. He could hear it as plainly as if she said as much. She droned on about how much she used and what her addiction had done to her family and blah blah blah. Nick watched her hands, which shook when she squeezed them together, and paid close attention to her feet, which kept a thrash metal beat on the carpet. She was close to going over the wall, he knew it as surely as he knew he would go with her. She might be someone he should (*use*) get to know.

When the meeting concluded Buckley stopped him by saying, "Nick, could you hang out here for a few minutes, please?"

Nick nodded and stood by his chair and tried not to let her see the tremors in his arms and legs.

Curran clapped him on the shoulder and said, "See ya outside," as he walked out.

When they had the room to themselves, Buckley said, "I heard you had another incident last night."

Nick nodded and looked at the floor.

"It's okay, you know. Detox is very difficult, especially for heroin addicts. You don't have to be ashamed and you don't have to hide it." She smiled and she probably thought it was reassuring. "Besides, it's pretty tough to hide vomit. It tends to announce its presence whenever someone enters the room."

"Yeah."

"And you're not the first patient here to have an incident in the middle of the night. Believe me, it happens frequently. We just don't want you to feel embarrassed about it."

"Gotcha."

"From now on, though, if you make a mess you clean the mess. That's the rule here. I don't want Peter spending all his time mopping up vomit and urine and whatever else the patients produce. One of the things we try to teach here is responsibility. Everyone cleans up their own messes. So, next time, you'll be the one doing the mopping. Understood?"

Nick nodded.

"At least you had the presence of mind not to do it in the bed. That would have been messy."

"I fell out of bed. I had a—" He stopped. For the first time he caught an image of the dream. He tried to put it into context but it pulled away from him. "A dream." He closed his eyes and tried as best he could to recall it. An image had come to him but it was gone now. He tried for several moments before he gave up. "I can't remember it now. Must have been pretty bad to knock me out of bed."

Buckley made a notation in his file. When she spoke again her voice was a monotone. "Would you like me to set up an appointment for you with Dr. Piccochi? She's a psychiatrist who has a lot of experience working with addicts. She could probably help you."

Nick waved her off. "I'm okay. It was just a dream. No big deal." *Don't put yourself out*, he added silently.

Buckley scribbled something. "Okay. If you change your mind just let me know. She's here a few times a month. It wouldn't be any trouble."

"I'll let you know. Thanks."

Buckley smiled her fake smile again. "Go get something to eat. And we'll see what we can do about helping you keep it down."

Nick forced himself to return her smile, but it was a weak attempt. "All right." He left the room.

He made his way straight past the cafeteria and went outside. His fellow inmates were sprinkled about the area. Patty and Jessica were in their customary area by the pool smoking their customary cigarettes; Curran and Pedro were again debating the Mets and Yankees. Nick could do without another one of those conversations. Phil and another man (Ricky or Richie, and how the hell was he supposed to keep those two straight?) were having an animated conversation that was as interesting to Nick as the men themselves. He spied Sarah sitting at one of the picnic tables, finishing her breakfast and chatting with Jenna and Richie/Ricky. He walked to them.

"Mind if I join you?"

The girls said nothing, but the man slapped the bench. "Sure." Nick sat.

"I wanted to tell you," the man said and cleared his throat, "what you said yesterday in meeting was pretty fucked up. About your mom, I mean. But it ain't like that never happened to anyone else. I guess what I'm saying is you're not alone. And you're definitely among friends here."

"Thanks." Nick did not mean it, did not care at all for the man's sympathy or supportive tone. He wished he would just go away and take Jenna with him. It was Sarah he wanted to talk to, not some crackhead who fancied himself a counselor. "That means a lot."

"Richie's right," Sarah added.

Nick's attention level rose; listening to Sarah might pay off.

She continued. "The first time I got high I was twelve. My friend dared me to steal one of my dad's cigarettes. What I didn't realize was it was a joint I pulled out of his cigarette pack. We got so fucking wasted. My dad recognized the signs when he saw me. And he was cool with it if you can believe that. I smoked with him all the time from then on."

"Wow." Nick hoped he sounded sincere. He glanced at Jenna and Richie and saw the knowing, sympathetic looks they wore. He tried to ape their shared expression.

"From there it was a hop, skip and a jump to alcohol, coke, and then heroin. The funny thing is I don't drink anymore, haven't touched coke in years except for the occasional speedball. It's all about heroin for me."

Nick nodded. "Me, too." In this he was sincere.

Jenna, a meth addict like Richie, added to the conversation but Nick tuned her out. He wished with all his heart the broad and Richie would leave so he could get to the real reason he sat at this table. The three of them carried on for some time and Nick listened only enough to answer any questions directed at him.

He received half his wish when Jenna announced she was going to join Patty and Jessica at the pool. Nick crossed his fingers under the table that Sarah would not go with her. But the dark-haired woman seemed content to remain where she was, much to Nick's relief. After perhaps ten more minutes of droning conversation he began to despise Richie. The fucker seemed to have nothing better to do than keep talking. It was all Nick could do to stop himself from strangling the asshole.

He was relieved of his burden when Curran approached them. He held a badminton racket in one hand and a birdie in the other. "Me and Pedro want to get a game going. Anyone want in? Richie?"

Nick was thankful for the first time for the brace on his leg. He just hoped Sarah was not a fan of the activity. He was even more thankful when Richie agreed and Sarah waved off the offer with a polite, "No, thanks." Richie stood and followed Curran toward the net. Nick scanned the backyard and saw that Pedro was trying to recruit Phil and Ricky.

Nick's heart began to beat faster. For the first time since he walked through Springbrook's front door he saw light at the end of the tunnel.

"So where are you from, Nick?"

Nick gave Sarah his full attention. "AC, originally. Moved around a bit since then. Been in Philly now for, let's see, six years."

Sarah treated him to a sad smile. "Yeah. I guess our disease doesn't lend itself well to stability."

It was not much of an opening but Nick could wait no longer. He leaned forward and folded his hand together. He lowered his voice conspiratorially. "You got anything?" He watched her intently, his bullshit detector at full power and focused completely on Sarah.

Sarah blanched and recoiled a bit. "No. God, no." Her expression turned angry. "I'm here trying to get better."

"You want it as bad as I do. I can smell it coming off of you." He tried to keep his voice down, his tone level. "Just tell me you got a stash somewhere."

"Well, I don't." Her voice rose in volume, but fortunately no one seemed to hear her. Most of the other patients were absorbed in watching or playing badminton. She must have realized it herself because she looked about before she returned her attention to Nick and lowered her voice. "Look, I know why you're asking. I do. The first three weeks I was here I asked everybody that same question. But you're never gonna get better if you don't accept how serious this is. We're in a bad way, Nick. Both of us. All of us." She swept her arm through the air. "And frankly, one person using puts everyone here at risk."

"Yeah, yeah, yeah." Nick made a dismissive gesture with his hands. "But c'mon, where are you hiding it?"

Sarah shook her head slowly, sadly. "I'm sorry, Nick. All I can tell you is, it gets a little easier every day. Have faith in that."

It was the last thing Nick wanted to hear. He had heard enough of the healing power of faith and God to last him the rest of his life. He slammed his palms onto the tabletop and that drew looks from everyone watching the game. "Fuck you." Nick stood and ambled away from the table. He stopped midway to the door and half-turned back to Sarah. "I know you have something. You're just a selfish twat. Go fuck yourself." He moved as quickly as his throbbing leg would carry him into the building.

He slowed his pace somewhat when he passed the administration door. He did not want anyone to see him like this. He kept his pace casual until he made it up the stairs. He paused on the second floor landing and looked up. The third floor was empty. He could perhaps find Sarah's room and locate her stash before anyone discovered his presence. But he would not put it past the bitch to tell Buckley even if it meant she would be thrown out, as well. That had a satisfying air about it, he had to admit. With the threat of being tossed out of Springbrook removed from their lives he knew without a doubt he could take up with Sarah and use her contacts to keep himself in H for the foreseeable future.

If Buckley called the police, though, that would not do. And he wouldn't put it past the bitch to do just that. Spending a few days in a cell would just make the withdrawal worse. He almost mounted the steps anyway, just to spite the selfish bitch holding out on him.

In the end, however, Nick did not go to the third floor. He returned to his room and crawled under the covers. He remained there until Karen entered several hours later and told him to get ready for dinner.

He made his way downstairs alone. He was getting the hang of negotiating the steps with his bum leg. It still hurt like a son of a bitch every time he descended another step but he could deal with that. More deflating to him was the knowledge that Sarah had not been lying.

He was too excited, too hurting, at the time to read her tone and her body language. Enough time had passed that he knew now she had been truthful with him. She had nothing hidden away for a rainy day. Oh, she laid it on a little too thick with her air of being offended by the question, of that he was certain. She was hurting and the idea of getting her hands on some H was more than appealing to her. He had no doubt that if he offered some to her she would jump on it with no hesitation. But she was telling the truth about being dry. And that sucked.

He was the last to arrive for dinner. The meal consisted of French bread pizza with penne pasta and somehow he managed to keep it down. He sat with Curran and Pedro and Ricky. He did not pay much attention to the conversation. Two tables over Sarah sat with Richie, Jenna and Phil. Nick kept his eyes on Sarah for most of the thirty minutes. He hoped he was wrong about her. He watched her closely for any sign she was high. She did not appear to be under the influence of anything and that confirmed his suspicions. Nick's shoulders slumped and he picked at the rest of his meal. *Fuck her*, he thought. *Fuck her in half. I'll find whoever's holding in here. And when I do I'll smoke up right in front of her. A nice parting* Fuck You *before I head on down the road.* She looked up and caught him staring at her. She offered a sad, comforting smile. Nick looked away.

It was movie night and Nick found that attendance was required. Peter, the night custodian, revved up the old VCR and inserted an equally-old tape of *Saving Private Ryan*. Nick sat in the back row with Phil and paid no mind to the movie. He stared daggers into the back of Sarah's head.

After the movie he was the first to leave the room. He ambled up the stairs and got back to his room ahead of Curran. He washed up and brushed his teeth and was in bed by the time his roommate appeared.

Curran plopped onto his bed and turned on the television. "Anything you wanna watch?"

Nick shook his head. "Nah. Whatever."

Curran settled on a *Mad Men* marathon on AMC and tossed the remote onto the nightstand.

Nick stared at the ceiling. He filled his head with images of smoking up as Sarah watched and licked her lips and asked him to pass it to her. He imagined the thick, creamy exhale he would send her way. She would close her eyes and inhale but it would do little good. She needed a direct hit and he would deny her that.

It did not occur to him until that very moment that he missed the smell and the taste of the white smoke. He had been so focused on the feeling of the powder that he had forgotten about all else. He found he missed that smell almost as much as he missed the euphoria associated with it. He ground his teeth together as he reached for the covers.

He tried to focus his attention on the TV, but his skin crawled. He glanced out the window. The tree blocked most of his view, but he knew what was out there. Santos was out there, and Santos got whachoo need.

Nick made up his mind. Tomorrow morning he would go over the wall. In twelve hours he would be in bliss with no reason to hide the fact. Staci would hook him up like she always did. One more night in this shithole and he would be free.

He smiled and closed his eyes.

Chapter 6

Close Enough To Philly

Nick did not go over the wall the next day. In fact, he made it out of bed only twice. Both trips were to the bathroom. The first time he vomited up the remains of the previous night's dinner. The second time, about two hours later, he dry heaved until he thought he was going to die. That time he lacked the strength to stand or even crawl. He remained on the cold tiled floor until Karen came up to check on him.

Once the nurse returned him to his bed he lay there and did not move. It was a big enough deal, missing morning meeting, that Buckley herself made the journey to the second floor. She took his temperature, his blood pressure, and subjected him to a few other tests. Nick lay in bed like a dead fish, unable to respond to any questions beyond moaning a "yes" or "no." Buckley apparently agreed he was in bad enough shape that he could forego the day's schedule and remain in his room. It was a one-time deal, she told him. After this he would not be allowed to miss any more meetings.

Nick barely heard her. The doctor and nurse left with a promise from Karen that she would be back to check on him shortly. When Nick opened his eyes again the sky outside his window was transitioning from dark blue to purple. It was not Karen who entered the room shortly after he awoke, but Carol. Nick glanced at the alarm clock on the nightstand between the two beds. 8:19 PM it told him. Nick grumbled and sat up.

"How are you doing?" Carol asked.

Nick shot her an annoyed look but she simply smiled and walked around the bed until she stood in front of him. She held a small plastic cup in each hand. One of them contained two pills and the other was filled nearly to the top with water. "For you," she said with a smile.

Nick took the cup with the pills and upended it. He chased them with water and lay back against his pillow. The room spun, but it seemed to have bled off some speed from earlier. He felt nauseated but not enough to cause him to dash for the bathroom. Not that he could possibly have anything in his stomach, anyway.

"Glad to see you're still alive, at any rate," Carol continued. "You should get out of bed for a while, get out of this room, too. It's not good for you to isolate, Nick. That's a huge warning sign."

"Uh huh." Nick opened his eyes about halfway. Carol had not moved from her spot in front of him. She looked at him with what was probably genuine concern. Nick wished she would go away. Surely one of the other patients was in need of her services more than he. He opened his eyes the rest of the way and regarded her.

He had failed to notice it before, but Carol was quite pretty. Her black hair cascaded past her shoulders in loose curls. She smiled often, as she was smiling now, and it served to light up her features in a way that reminded him of old Hollywood actresses like Gene Tierney and Hedy Lamarr. Nick felt Carol could have given Tierney a run for her money had she been born six decades earlier.

It might have been the physical beauty in Carol he had not noticed before, or perhaps it was simply that he did not want a lecture from Buckley on the dangers of isolating. Whatever the reason Nick pushed himself into a sitting position again. The room spun around him but it seemed to be on its last legs, a merry-go-round grinding to a halt. *Let's hope it's closing time at the ole carnival,* Nick thought. *No more kiddies tonight. Can't deal with 'em.*

He swung his legs off the bed and Carol stepped back. "That's better," she said in an approving tone.

"Uh huh. I have to use the facilities. I'll see everyone downstairs."

Carol's smile widened. "Glad to hear it." She turned and left the room.

It took Nick about fifteen minutes to get himself together enough to leave the room. He stayed in his sweatpants and Nirvana tee-shirt, figuring he would be in bed again within the hour. The stairs sucked, as they always did, but he managed them better than before. He found everyone in the parlor watching a VHS copy of *Titanic*. Curran waved to him. Nick took the only open seat available, on the love seat next to Pedro. He sat back and watched a young Kate Winslet spit in Billy Zane's face before tearing off in search of her doomed lover. The ladies present voiced a subdued cheer. Nick rested his chin on his hand and tried to stay awake.

His eyes kept returning to Sarah. She was seated on one of the sofas, between Jenna and Richie. He was still angry with her, still planned to smoke up in front of her, but a crack had appeared in his plan. He knew it was not her fault. He even believed she was dry. He was less convinced of her sincerity about getting better but it was possible she believed it. They would find out together, and soon enough. All he needed was to identify the person in the room who was holding. Then he would see just how committed she was to sobriety.

Carol appeared over his shoulder with a small plate in her hand. Her presence startled Nick but his reaction was subdued enough that he did not draw attention to himself. He looked at the sandwich on the plate. Carol smiled and handed it to him.

"It's just peanut butter and jelly. The kitchen's been closed for a while now. It's all I could find."

"Thanks." Nick took the plate and set it on his lap. Pedro glanced at it before he returned his attention to the movie.

"You're welcome." Carol smiled at him and left the room quietly.

Nick was not hungry. Nevertheless he took a bite of the PB&J and it tasted fine. He chewed and watched the movie and thought about blowing smoke in Sarah's face.

Roughly ninety minutes later Nick found himself making his way down the corridor toward the stairs. Pedro and Curran walked with him, slowing their pace so he would not have to rush. Not that he would have, anyway. He was feeling queasy and his stomach had started performing Evel Knievel-like stunts around the time old Rose was reunited with her dead lover on the *Titanic*'s Grand Staircase. He felt he could keep the PB&J down, but it was an effort.

First Patty and Jessica, and then Jenna and Sarah walked past the men on their way upstairs. The first pair giggled and held hands and Nick could imagine what was going to take place after lights out. The second pair smiled at them and said good night and continued on their way. Nick shot Sarah a foul look but she did not see it.

A few moments after that he was in his room again. Curran let him use the bathroom first. Nick did not vomit, a pleasant surprise, considering the way the peanut butter-and-jelly sandwich was sitting in his stomach. He brushed his teeth and washed up. By the time Curran exited the bathroom after his turn Nick was sound asleep once more.

For the first time in a long time, he remembered his dream that night.

****

He feels sick, even in the dream. Distantly he hopes this isn't his mind's attempt to communicate with him that he is, indeed, vomiting all over his bed. Fuck Buckley and her rules; there is no fucking way he is cleaning up vomit. Nick decides he does not care. His dream has taken him away from Springbrook and that's just fine with him. He does not know where he is but anywhere is better than the shithole he left behind with its too-pleasant nursing staff and the zombified, whipped patients who can only repeat the mantra of clean living and act as if they wouldn't kill for a hit.

He takes a moment to breathe the free air. It stinks of car exhaust and old oil, but that's okay. It's still better than the antiseptic Lysol corridors wherein he left his physical body. Far away he can hear the unmistakable roar of a jet engine. Okay, I'm at an airport. I just gots to find me a big ole jet airliner and get the fuck outta P-A.

He is not in the airport proper. He looks about and finds himself in a parking garage. The place is packed with cars. He briefly considers jacking one; he used to be quite good at hot wiring. But that was a long time ago and he is out of practice. He decides to try his luck at playing on people's sympathies and try to hitch a ride. Anywhere. Direction is meaningless.

He hears a telltale beep *and knows the elevator has stopped at this level. Nick can hear two voices chatting and laughing and they are getting closer. A man and a young woman enter his field of vision, clearly a father/daughter combo. The father is hefting a rather large bag over his shoulder and his daughter is dragging a wheeled carry-on behind her. Nick wants to wave to them, but instead he ducks behind a convenient pickup truck with Jersey plates.*

He can't make out their conversation, although he hears the daughter mention the word Phoenixville. Close enough to Philly, *he thinks. He wants to approach the two travelers but he finds himself unable to stand. Too sick. No, not sick. In fact, he feels pretty good. What, then? It takes him a moment to come up with a more accurate descriptive term.* Weak. *Why he should feel weak is beyond him but he cannot deny that his arms and legs feel like wet spaghetti.*

*He can pick up their conversation now, at least, part of it. The man says something about the lack of lighting and seems to have a hard time navigating the garage, almost as if he is blind. Maybe he is, because Nick can see just fine. The man and his daughter walk past without seeing him. He aims his key fob at a maroon Chevy Equinox and the SUV beeps and flashes its lights obediently. Nick crawls (*slithers*) along the floor of the garage toward the vehicle. The daughter had a bit of trouble finding the back door but she has it open now and she has tossed her carry-on inside. Nick will try to sneak in before she closes the door. It's a ridiculous plan; he is not invisible but for some reason both the man and the young girl seem to have trouble seeing clearly. It probably won't work but he tries, anyway.*

It might be luck, but the girl's father calls to her from the other side of the Chevy and draws the girl's attention away at exactly the right moment. Nick slithers silently into the backseat and lays across the floor while the girl is distracted. He hears the door close, then the front two open up, and then the man and his little girl are in the car.

Nick can't believe his luck. Somehow they have failed to see him. All he has to do now is keep still and quiet and perhaps he can make it as far as Phoenixville before they notice they have a passenger.

Their chatter is inane as they exit the parking garage. Nick is thankful when one of them turns on the radio and drowns out much of their conversation. The car makes several stops at traffic lights. Nick remains motionless. When the driver guns the engine Nick knows they have reached the highway. He allows himself a peek out the window. It is dark but the green sign is easily seen: New Jersey Turnpike South, *it proclaims. Beneath that, in smaller letters,* Camden, Philadelphia.

Perfect. All he has to do is keep quiet and hope no one looks in the backseat and he'll be home free. From Phoenixville he can get to the Harrowgate neighborhood and pay a visit to Santos. Because, even in a dream, Santos got whachoo need.

Nick settles in for a long, relaxing ride.

****

The digital clock on the nightstand read 4:27 AM. Nick blinked at it, rubbed his eyes. He forgot how disorienting it could be, coming out of a dream he could actually remember. It had been some time, after all. He thought he could still hear the song on the radio (something by Never Shout Never, indicating it was the daughter who chose the station) and feel the bumps from the road coming up through the floorboards. It took him several moments to return fully to his room inside the Springbrook Healing and Recovery Center.

It should have felt like a letdown. He had been free only a few moments before.   Breathing free air, hitching a ride into Philadelphia's Badlands, just a few hours away from Santos and all the H he could afford. And being that it was a dream, he would have been able to afford an awful lot.

But he was not depressed to find himself back in his room, Curran snoring from the next bed. If anything he felt safe, as if he had just managed to avoid something unpleasant. He did not know what he had avoided, only that he felt relief in having done so.

Nick rolled onto his back and his eyes found the ceiling. He knew—*knew*—that something bad was about to happen or already had. His thoughts turned to Rebecca. She was the only person he truly cared for and thus was the only one about whom he worried. But Rebecca lived in a safe world where drug addicts and gang bangers rarely ventured. She was never stupid enough to associate with such people nor would she cross into their territory. No, Rebecca would be safe, as safe as possible, in any case. So why was he worried? Scared, even?

The ceiling of his shared room in West Philly provided no answer. Nick remained awake the rest of the night.

He was out of bed and showered before Curran even awoke. He felt none of the sickness from the day before and for that he was honestly thankful. He was still not himself, not by a long shot, but he felt a little better. Nick rifled his roommate's hair on his way out the door. Curran mumbled something Nick was sure was an insult directed at his mother and made his way downstairs.

He found Richie and Phil in the parlor watching the morning news. Both men sipped coffee and nodded in his direction when he entered. Nick poured himself a cup and negotiated his way carefully to the unoccupied loveseat. He sipped his coffee and caught the day's weather (sunny, high-eighties) and the traffic report and thought of Rebecca.

"Earth to Nick."

Nick blinked and looked at Phil. "Huh?"

Phil shared a knowing smile with Richie. They both laughed before Phil replied, "I said, do you have anyone coming next weekend? You know, the family and friends visit."

Nick shrugged and shook his head. "I didn't even know about it."

Richie finished off his coffee and placed the empty cup on the end table. "It's the one weekend a month where our families can come and be all judgmental on us. Buckley loves it." He guffawed and nudged Phil with his elbow.

"That she does," Phil agreed. "So, you planning to invite anyone? They have to have an invite and be approved by Buckley. She can't have just anyone show up and pass off any illegal substances to us."

Nick thought of Staci right away. Just as quickly he abandoned the idea. She may or may not have a criminal record, Nick could not remember. He also did not know her last name. All he had was an address and a phone number. That would surely be a warning sign for Buckley.

His thoughts turned to Rebecca. The dream had made him afraid for her. It was irrational in the light of day but he could not shake the feeling. He needed to see her again, and the sooner the better. "My cousin," he said after a moment. "I'd like to invite my cousin."

"Then put her on the list," Richie told him. "As long as she has no active substance abuse cases against her, or a lengthy record of said abuses, she should be approved."

"Who do I see about that?"

"Buckley," Phil replied. "Take it up with her after morning meeting. She'll probably be thrilled to see the new guy falling into step with the rest of us losers." He laughed again. "Or Amanda in reception can take the info and pass it along. Either one will get the job done."

Nick cracked a *faux* grin and resumed watching the news. For the first time since he arrived at Springbrook he could not wait for the morning meeting to start.

The stars of the meeting were Richie the Methead and Jessica the Cokehead. Nick did his best to look interested with their respective stories of woe but he could barely contain himself. He needed to speak with Buckley about next weekend. He tapped his foot on the floor and typed a novel on the loveseat's armrest.

Richie's story was short and to the point and Nick was thankful for that, at least. Jessica, on the other hand, went into vivid detail about how cocaine had ruined her life and the lives of everyone who knew her. Tossed out of her house at seventeen, sneaking back in when no one was home and stealing anything she thought would bring her enough money for another hit. Nick had heard this same story from any number of people both inside and out of Springbrook and he tuned out most of it. She wrapped up her tale by expressing her gratitude to the fine staff at Springbrook as well as her roommate and new best friend, Patty. The girls clutched hands and Patty gave her a reassuring smile. Nick knew beyond doubt their relationship had turned sexual. *Well, why not? Someone around here should be having a little fun.*

Buckley brought the meeting to its end with the Springbrook Sobriety Mantra. Nick recited it as best he could, meaning he mumbled a few words and lip-synced the rest and hoped Buckley would not catch on. He had never really listened to it before, and he spent no time reading or memorizing it since his arrival. When everyone started to file out of the room Nick went straight for the doctor.

Ten minutes later, having given Rebecca's contact information to Buckley, Nick entered the cafeteria and secured himself a second cup of coffee. He joined Curran and Pedro at a small table in the corner. Nick sipped his coffee and smiled to himself.

That night, as Nick lay in his bed half-watching the Phillies get pounded by the Indians in interleague play, the nausea returned. He threw the covers off and made it to the bathroom just in time to throw up that night's ziti dinner. The sickness passed rather quickly. Curran came in and helped him to his feet and supported him all the way back to his bed.

Nick lay there thinking of how much he needed a hit, just one hit, and all this bullshit would go away. No more sickness, no more vomiting, no more dashes to the bathroom with his brace slicing its way into his skin and sending lightning bolts up his spine. Curran replaced his covers but Nick kicked them off with his good leg. He was burning up. His skin crawled. In that moment he would have happily strangled everyone in the building for *just one hit*.

He needed his cell, locked away in the nurse's office. He had Staci's number in there. He thought he could convince her to pick him up and bring him home. *Her* home, of course. Even the thought of being her sex slave, which would probably be his fate, was okay with him. Anything to stop this fucking sickness that seemed to have no end.

He got as far as sitting up in bed before he stopped himself. He was weak and his arms and legs shook. He would never get close to the nurse's office, let alone get through the door and find his cell. The reception area was locked up so that was not an option, either. *Just make it through tonight*, he told himself. *Tomorrow's a new day. You can escape then.*

Nick did not so much fall asleep as he passed out. The sounds of the ballgame on TV grew soft and indistinct and then faded away altogether. Nick felt the sensation of floating in darkness. He greeted it with much enthusiasm.

The last thing of which he would be aware was a voice. It was familiar, somehow, although Nick lost consciousness before he could identify it. The voice did not belong to him, that much he knew. It was deep and gravelly, a child's idea of what a monster would sound like. It said only one word and then it was gone and Nick was left with nothing but darkness.

The word was *soon*.

Chapter 7

A New Experience

Nick woke up early and with the goal of retrieving his cell from the nurse's station. He cleaned up and dressed quietly while Curran snored in his bed. In the corridor he could hear the shower in the next room and across the hall the sounds of Richie and Phil arguing about last night's game at Citizen's Bank Park. Good. He should have several minutes to achieve his goal, assuming Karen was prepping the meeting room.

His hopes were dashed as he ambled down the stairs. Sarah and Jenna caught up to him easily. "Morning, Nick," Jenna greeted him. "Sleep okay?"

Nick hid his disappointment well. Most addicts became quite adept at hiding their true feelings. It would not do, for instance, for a relative to suspect the real reason they were asking to borrow money. In this Nick was no exception. "Yeah, pretty good. You?"

Sarah responded but Nick did not listen. Outwardly he was open and perhaps even friendly; inside he was raging at the women for screwing up his plan.

"It'll get better, Nick," Sarah added. "I'm speaking from experience."

Her eyes matched the sincerity in her tone. She seemed to have gotten over his tirade from a few days before. Her concern certainly appeared genuine and Nick could see none of the signs of deception he knew so well.

"Uh huh."

The women could have outpaced him easily but they slowed their progress down the stairs, an inclusive gesture Nick could have done without. It was most likely an honest attempt at treating him as one of their group; Nick could not help but feel they knew the reason for his early appearance and were purposely blocking him from accomplishing his goal. He hated them for it.

Nick eyed the nurse's station as they passed it. Sure enough Karen was not at the window. The door was certainly locked but he thought he would be able to get past it if only Sarah and Jenna would disappear. They did not. Instead they kept pace with him all the way into the meeting room. Nick risked one last look over his shoulder at the unoccupied nurse's station and silently cursed his two unwanted companions.

Karen was indeed in the meeting room. She had moved the furniture into its customary circle and was arranging some paperwork for Dr. Buckley when Nick and the two women entered. She greeted them with a smile and a happy "Good morning!"

Nick took a seat in a single chair. Sarah and Jenna took the loveseat and talked amongst themselves. Sarah tried a few times to engage Nick in conversation, but she gave up after a few curt replies. His eyes wandered out the door and across the hall to the nurse's station. Karen was there now and she was organizing the morning meds. Nick hated her, too.

The rest of the patients began to arrive in pairs. Curran was the last to arrive, walking in behind Jessica and Patty. They chatted amicably with each other, all except Nick, who stared daggers at

Karen working quietly and no doubt efficiently behind the counter across the hall. He broke away from her only when Buckley entered, clipboard in hand.

"Good morning, everyone," she said and took the center chair. "How are we today?"

Nick hated the morning meeting, but he especially hated this part. Buckley did not make small talk; she did not move on until every patient informed her how they were feeling. Nick made his by-now rote response of, "Doin' great here," just to move things along.

Then the tall woman who never seemed to run out of pantsuits made her way down the roll call, waiting for the obligatory "here" after each patient's name was called.   When Buckley received a satisfactory answer from everyone she traced her finger down her clipboard and announced, "Today we'll be hearing from Pedro and Nick. Who would like to start?"

Nick rolled his eyes. He nodded in Pedro's direction. "All yours, m'man."

Ten pairs of concerned eyes turned in Pedro's direction. Nick looked at his slippers.

He caught that Pedro was an alcoholic, but little else. The man droned on about how his arguments with his wife became physical and how his wakeup call was seeing her in the shower covered with bruises. Blah fucking blah. This was another story Nick had heard before, from so many of the people he hung around with since he moved out of his mother's house. He remembered being shocked the first time someone confessed to beating his wife, but by the tenth or twelfth time it ceased to have much meaning for him. In truth he could not remember hearing a single original story at these meetings. Every addict had the same experiences, the same tales of violence and broken hearts. Would somebody, anybody, change the fucking record, please? Nick looked up a few times, saw the sad, knowing expressions on the faces of the group. Most of them nodded in sympathy. Nick just wanted the meeting to be over.

"Nick? Your turn," Buckley said.

He looked up again. She was staring at him. So were the others.

Nick had thus far avoided sharing anything more than the broad strokes of his story with the group, but he had realized shortly after his arrival that he would eventually have to come clean about his past. He was dreading it. But now that the moment had arrived he found himself cool and calm. He laced his fingers and glanced about the room before he began.

****

"My father was an addict. I heard a rumor that his father was, too. Heroin, just like me. I never knew my grandfather because he was dead before I was born. But I caught little snippets of conversation between the adults when I was a kid and I'm pretty sure ole granddad was into the powder. So I guess that's at least three generations in a row, right? Some fathers hand down heirlooms to their sons. A baseball autographed by Robin Roberts, or some old muscle car or maybe even something like a watch. Us Wade boys, we do it right."

Knowing nods from around the room. Nick ignored them.

"My father died when I was fifteen. He overdosed in the parking garage at Newark International. They found him slumped across the front seat, needle still in his arm. I remember when the cops showed up to tell my mom. She didn't cry. She nodded her head and thanked the cops for letting her know and she closed the door behind them and she never cried. Even as a kid I thought that was weird. Then again, I didn't know him the way she did. I know what I've done and if my father did some of those same things then my mom was probably relieved he was out of the picture."

Nick shrugged. Curran approached with a cup of water. Nick thanked him and downed the contents of the cup with one gulp.

"A few days later, before the dirt had even settled on the coffin, my mother called me down to the kitchen. She had a syringe all loaded up and ready to go. I remember being nervous about the needle. I always hated the fucking things whenever I had to get a shot at the doctor's office. I had never seen one in the house. My father, as much as he was hooked on that shit, he never did it in front of me. This was something new."

"So your mother used, as well," Buckley said. Her voice remained neutral. Nick wanted to punch her. She knew this already, had gotten it out of him his first day here. If she was dead-set on making him relate the story again, in front of his fellow losers, the least she could do was keep her mouth shut. Instead he nodded slowly.

"Yeah, she did. But this is gonna sound weird and maybe I'm wrong, but I honestly believe she had never touched the stuff before he died. I remember my father being high all the time. My mother was never like that. I know the signs now. In fact, I'm kind of an expert on the subject. And I think the first time she ever shot up was that night in the kitchen of our home on Wallace Street. I can still see her expression when she pushed that needle home. She didn't know what to expect."

"She had probably been trying to shield you from the reality of her addiction," Sarah suggested.

Buckley nodded approvingly. "Very good, Sarah." She returned her attention to Nick. "I think Sarah has a point. It's unlikely your mother would decide to take up such a habit when her husband had just passed away from exactly the same thing."

Nick chewed on his lower lip. "Like I said, I might be wrong. But the impression I got at the time, and the one I still have now, is that that night was the first time my mother ever used heroin."

"Tell us how you started, please, Nick."

Nick's right hand moved to the sweet spot his left arm. He massaged it slowly as he spoke. "It was that same night. My mother told me to sit and she wrapped a piece of rubber tubing around my arm and she shot me up. It hurt like a motherfucker, too. But the pain didn't last long, as some of us know." He glanced at Sarah. "Then she fixed herself. We just sat there in the kitchen, melting into the chairs. The first time you do it, I don't care if you have experience with other shit or not, it fucks you up. And I was a narcotics virgin at the time. Oh, I'd stolen some of the old man's cigarettes a time or two, but I never tried anything illegal, not even weed. This was a new experience for me."

Patty, seated closest to him, leaned over on the sofa and placed her hand over his. It was clearly meant to be comforting; it was all Nick could do not to rip his hand free. He smiled benignly at her in his best "It's all good" expression. It would have worked on a non-addict. Patty obviously saw through it instantly and frowned. Nick shrugged again.

"Anyway, we shot up together a few more times, but like I said, I hate needles. So my mom introduced me to smoking it. That's been my preferred method ever since."

He paused and looked around the circle. Everyone was watching him, paying attention to his story. Some of his fellow addicts regarded him with outright horror, Sarah included.

"Your mom got you into it?" She could not hide her surprise or her revulsion.

Nick's first instinct was to defend his mother, but he stopped himself before he uttered a word. He had never given much thought to it, most likely because he had never been sober for this long, but perhaps the expressions of horror were justified. He knew plenty of addicts, but he had yet to meet anyone who had begun that life under the tutelage of their own parent.

"Yeah," Nick said after a moment. "Yeah, I guess that is kinda fucked up, now that I've said it out loud."

"Oh, Nick." Sarah's voice dripped sympathy.

For the first time since he accused her of holding out on him he saw something other than pity or disgust in her eyes. Perhaps it was the sobriety or the fact that for the first time since his arrival at Springbrook he did not feel like his skin was crawling off his bones. Whatever the reason Nick noticed Sarah for the first time. She was quite beautiful when you got past what the disease had done to her features. He caught a glimpse of the woman she might have been had she never caught the dragon. Or perhaps he was seeing the woman she would become when she finally beat her addiction. Either way he felt honest affection for her, something he had not felt for anyone else in years. He smiled at her, the first genuine smile he had used in longer than he could remember.

"Anyway, she died a couple years ago. OD'd, as you probably guessed. Not that we were close by then, anyway. The day they put her in the ground I was on my girlfriend's couch high as a kite. I've pretty much been that way every day since." He cast a sideways glance at Buckley. "Well, except since I've been here."

People started to clap. Nick had seen this strange phenomenon at just about every morning meeting and he did not understand it. Now they clapped for him and most of the expressions of horror had been replaced by smiles. Pedro whistled through his teeth and

Jenna shouted, "Bravo! Bravo!" Patty and Richie, seated closest to him, clapped him on his shoulders.

"You did well for your first time, Nick," Buckley said. Her expression was neutral. "Good job. You, too, Pedro." She led them in the Sobriety Mantra and dismissed everyone for breakfast.

Nick was the last out as he usually was. Most of the patients made for the backyard, Jessica and Patty in the lead. Curran clapped him on the back as he walked past. Only Sarah remained, walking beside him.

"That was very brave, what you did in here," she said. "We all have that first time where we don't know what to say or even if we should talk about it at all. You're the first person I've seen come clean about everything since I've been here. It makes me think you have a real chance at beating your disease."

"We'll see," Nick replied. He eyed the nurse's station as they followed the stragglers of their group outside. Karen looked like she had everything ready for when the patients came back in. Nick thought about his cell phone, but only for a moment.

****

Nick spent his time outside seated at one of the tables with Sarah and Jenna. The conversation was pleasant enough but he wished Jenna would go away. Sarah looked truly beautiful with the morning sunlight behind her. She had bummed a cigarette from Jessica ("I smoke about a pack a year," she explained) and the smoke played in the sunlight and wreathed her head in a bright corona. Jenna, unfortunately, did not leave them alone and so all Nick could do was watch Sarah and talk about whichever mundane topic came up.

The patients went inside as a group and ate breakfast and still Jenna would not disappear. Nick felt some of the old impatience starting to rise and he did his best to squash it down. *Life was so*

84

much simpler when I was high, he thought. He would have had little trouble telling Jenna to get lost if he were still using.

They lined up for their morning meds. Karen handed them out efficiently and quickly. When it was Nick's turn at the window he thought again of his cell phone and how Staci – and all the H he could handle – was one call away. He nearly asked for his cell but he stopped himself. Karen looked expectantly at him, clearly wondering what he wanted to say, but Nick simply offered her a forced smile and walked away.

The rec room was populated by Curran, Richie, Sarah and Jenna. The TV was tuned to the local news. Nick took an empty chair and faced the television. He watched Sarah from the corner of his eye. She spoke softly with Curran and smiled and laughed quietly at something he said. Nick frowned, as much at Curran as at himself.

Why should he care how Sarah got on with his roommate? Or anyone else, for that matter? What was she to him? She was clearly nothing more than yet another junkie in his orbit. She was no different than his mother, or Staci or Angie.

His breath caught in his throat. Angie. He was surprised and ashamed to realize he had given no thought to the dead woman since the night her Mustang careened off the road and into the wooded area on Route 30. He had never loved Angie, but he did like her. She was a genuinely nice girl who had taken him in and fed him and kept him happy and high. She shared with him her apartment, her bed, her heroin and her life. He had been too preoccupied with his present circumstances to even give her a passing thought. For the first time in more than a decade Nick felt ashamed. His cheeks were warm and he found he could not bring himself to look at Curran and Sarah and their private, funny conversation. He would have stood and left the room if not for a sudden wave of dizziness that caused his head to swim. Nick closed his eyes and waited for the room to stop spinning.

He lost track of time, but he could only have been that way for a few minutes. When he felt stable enough he opened his eyes. Curran and Sarah were still engaged in conversation, Richie was reading an old issue of *Rolling Stone* and Jenna was watching the television with a horrified expression. Nick's eyes traveled to the small flat screen, anything to avoid having to look at Curran and Sarah.

There were two photos side by side on the TV. One was a man who appeared to be in his mid-forties; the other was clearly his daughter. Nick was too far away to hear the reporter but he could read the caption beneath the photographs: FATHER/DAUGHTER FOUND MURDERED IN PHOENIXVILLE   .

Nick's breath caught in his throat. He could not remember every detail from the dream, but he was pretty sure the two with whom he hitched a ride looked an awful lot like the people staring at him from the flat screen.

"Turn that up," Nick said.

Jenna fiddled with the remote and the volume increased. The image returned to the anchorwoman from Six ABC Action News. Nick's face fell when he heard her read the intro to another story.

"What was that about?" he asked Jenna.

The young girl shook her head. "Not sure. Some asshole killed a guy and his daughter in the garage of their own home. TV said the cops are investigating, which probably means they won't find shit. I hope they catch that asshole."

"Yeah."   Nick felt suddenly sick to his stomach. He stood on unsteady legs and headed for the stairs. "I'm gonna lay down," he announced over his shoulder.

"Need a hand?" Curran called after him.

"Nope, got it."

Nick negotiated the stairs as quickly as his injured leg would allow. He made it into his room and into the bathroom. He remained hunched over the bowl, ready to spew his breakfast, for some time before he realized he was not going to vomit. His forehead was coated with sweat and his hands shook but for the first time since he arrived at Springbrook Healing and Recovery Center he knew it was not due to withdrawal.

Nick returned to his bed and lay there and looked alternately at the ceiling and out the window where the blue sky and sunlight promised a gorgeous day. Nick would remain in bed until Karen showed up and told him to get ready for dinner.

Chapter 8

Blacker Than The Darkness

Nick sat between Curran and Ricky at dinner and ate his spaghetti and garlic bread quietly. He had avoided the television since the morning's news story but he was starting to feel foolish. The murder victims in Phoenixville could not be the same people from his dream. It was im-fucking-possible and he knew it. Nick believed in a lot of things, mostly what he could see and touch; he had never been one of those pathetic losers who believed in the supernatural or the existence of a higher power watching over them. Leave that bullshit to the Jesus freaks and the con artists who will read your fortune for fifty bucks. Nick would have none of it. That included precognitive dreams.

Angie used to love that shit. A typical night consisted of them smoking up and watching something on TV. If Angie had the remote he was forced to watch shows where ignorant red necks hunted Bigfoot or someone doing their best Rod Serling impression would talk about ghosts or the afterlife. Her favorite was something called *The Cemetery Game*, which focused on psychic twins who spoke to the dead. Nick feigned interest only to keep Angie happy. He would have gladly thrown the TV out the window instead of wasting time watching that nonsense.

So for the second time in a day Nick felt ashamed. This time it was because he had allowed himself to get caught up in something ridiculous. *This is the face of sobriety*, he thought. *Stop using drugs so you can believe in some* really *weird shit. Say what you will about heroin, but at least it didn't have you believing you could see future murder victims in your dreams.*

Nick could not argue with that. Maybe it was time to say goodbye to Springbrook and shack up with Staci again. Sobriety, it seemed, was not agreeing with him.

After dinner it was Patty's turn to pick the movie. She selected *Bridesmaids*, much to the delight of the women present, less so the men. Nick watched the first fifteen minutes before he had seen enough. He went out back and sat near the pool.

The night air was cool on his skin and it made him feel better. He watched the small ripples in the pool water caused by the filter and thought about Angie and then Staci. He remained alone until the movie ended and Jessica and Patty came out for their usual before-bed cigarettes. Nick wished them a good night ("Don't worry, it will be," Jessica replied with a knowing glance at her roommate) and walked back inside.

A few minutes later he was in his bed again. Curran had the TV tuned to the Discovery Channel and some rather large sharks were swimming across the screen. That program gave way to one which focused on life above the Arctic Circle. Nick closed his eyes. It was a few moments later when he smelled it.

Nick was never a big fan of weed, but he had smoked it on occasion. Its unmistakable aroma reached his nostrils and he opened his eyes and looked at Curran. The man was not smoking anything, nor was there any sign of smoke in the room. Curran, in fact, was watching the television with half-lidded eyes.

"What are you doing?"

Curran did not look away from the television. "Huh?"

"You can't smoke in here. Buckley will kill you."

Curran looked at Nick with his brow furrowed. "What the hell are you talking about?"

"I can smell it, man." He may have been wrong about Sarah holding out on him but he was convinced his roommate was doing just that. Weed was not Nick's first choice or even his fifth and he could not believe Curran was going to risk getting bounced for something so stupid and meaningless. "If you're gonna do that shit at least be more careful."

Curran looked at him as if he had two heads. "Nick, you're not making any sense. I don't have anything here." He held up both hands. "You see me smoking anything?"

"I can smell it clear as day."

"Smell what?" Curran sniffed the air loudly and theatrically. "I don't smell anything."

"Weed," Nick said a bit too loudly. "If it ain't you then it's someone in the next room."

Curran took the remote and lowered the volume on the TV. "Nick, no one is smoking weed in here, believe me. It's probably Carol outside smoking a cigarette. She has a place out there below our windows she thinks no one knows about. But I guarantee you no one is getting high. Not in here, anyway."

"It's not a cigarette. You think I don't know the difference? Someone in here has some shit." He sat up and limped to the window. He scanned the darkness below the window and came up empty. He turned back to Curran triumphantly. "Carol's not out there. Neither is anyone else. It's coming from in here."

Curran did not quite roll his eyes, but he came close. "Whatever, man." He returned the TV volume to its former volume.

Nick started to protest but it was clear Curran wanted nothing more of the conversation. Nick put his head back down on the pillow. The smell was so strong he knew Curran was covering for someone. It was most likely Pedro and Richie in the next room. He could hear nothing on the other side of the wall, but he knew what they were doing.

Better not get caught, idiots. When Carol makes her rounds she'll smell it and then we'll see who isn't here come morning.

Nick rolled onto his side and looked out the windows. He could still smell it and it reminded him of Angie again. When they were unable to procure any H she would settle for weed. There were times when the smoke was so think inside the apartment he could barely see the TV. That was something else to which he had given no thought since his arrival. *Amazing how quickly you can forget the details of someone else's life, isn't it? You should seriously rethink this whole sobriety thing, m'man.* Nick agreed. He fell asleep smelling marijuana smoke and thinking of Angie.

****

Miki MacKennedy closed the door to her son's room and made her way downstairs as fast as her feet would carry her. It was hell getting Dylan to go down with so many people in the backyard and the volume of noise coming from outside would ensure the boy would be awake well past his bedtime. She could talk to her husband about it but she could hear his answer already. "Occupational hazard," he would say. And he would be correct.

Miki made it out the sliding glass door in the kitchen and reemerged into the backyard. She counted heads and came up with eleven. She and Ryan rarely had such a large number of people over at the same time, but they had just found a new source and the price was worth celebrating. She found her husband at the glass patio table, organizing dime bags. His brother, Pat, sat next to him hitting his bong. Everybody in their backyard was smoking and she watched clouds of illegal smoke swirl in the floodlights before vanishing into the night sky.

Her eyes went to the house next door. The O'Briens were an older couple and a constant pain in the ass. Anytime Miki or Ryan had friends over, or customers, the old fucks would peek at them from behind their curtains. Sometimes they called the cops. It never amounted to much. The Manayunk PD had bigger things to worry about than a few people smoking weed in their backyard. But their constant vigilance annoyed Miki even more than it annoyed Ryan, and Ryan was plenty annoyed with the O'Briens. Miki breathed a sigh of relief. The O'Brien home was dark and she could see no one peeking at her from any of the windows.

She reached the table and Pat offered the bong. Miki took it and fired it up and felt the green smoke fill her lungs. She nodded and smiled and handed it back.

"You two picked the right night to do this," Pat said. "Couldn't ask for a nicer night."

"I heard that," Miki replied as she exhaled her own cloud of smoke toward the floods. She lit a cigarette from her husband's pack and eyed the small bags on the glass tabletop. "How are we doing?"

Ryan did not look up from his work. "Cost us 600, we should clear well over 1,100 by the time this is gone."

"Whew!" Miki raised her arms in triumph. "That's what momma wants to hear. Good job, babe."

Ryan remained focused on his work. Miki smiled at Pat and worked her way toward the small crowd near the pool. She knew some of them, had sold to most of them, but there were a few strangers there. Miki found Shauna, her friend since junior high, standing by the pool with her boyfriend and a man she did not recognize.

"Good stuff, honey," Shauna coughed to Miki, holding a joint in her outstretched hand as if inviting Miki to inspect her rolling skills.

Shauna's boyfriend, Steve, nodded his agreement. "Yeah, this is good shit. Thanks for having us over."

"Not at all, not at all," Miki assured him. "Glad to see you guys here." She regarded the man standing next to them, the one she did not recognize. She held out her hand. "Miki."

The man took her hand and shook it. "Ray. Nice to meet you. Nice place you have."

Miki took in the backyard at a glance. "Yeah, we like it. Thanks for coming."

"Thanks for the weed," Ray replied.

Miki managed to hide her frown until she walked away. *Fucking freeloader. Must be sponging off Shauna and Steve. Buy your own shit, loser.* She said none of this, of course, but the thought repeated itself in her head. She and Ryan had little patience for people who didn't buy their own supply. It was not just because they made no money on such people; Miki felt the same way even before she and her husband set up shop.

She visited another group of people standing around and chatting in the corner where the fence separated their yard from that of the O'Briens. She was introduced to the two strangers by her co-worker Angela as Stephanie and Orlando. Miki greeted them and accepted their compliments on the new product. Her last stop was the young couple from down the street, the Cables, and their son, Dave. Miki spoke with them and took a hit from Jacki Cable's pipe and eventually made her way back to the patio where Ryan at last seemed finished arranging the dime bags.

Miki counted sixty and she found it difficult to contain her excitement. She hugged Ryan when he pushed himself away from the table and stood. "All right," he said to everyone in the yard, "come and get it. No need to rush, plenty for everyone." He laughed and slapped a high five with his brother.

Miki put her cigarette out in the ashtray and watched with satisfaction as her friends and customers began to make their way to the patio. Most had cash in hand already or were reaching for their wallets. Miki scooped up Pat's bong and took another hit.

Shauna gave her a hug after her boyfriend paid for four dime bags. "Thanks again, babe."

"You're very welcome," Miki replied. She shook Steve's hand as he walked past.

The procession was slow and she caught a few off-color jokes from Ray, the newbie, and Tom Cable. Ryan came back with a few of his own. Miki glanced up at Dylan's window. The light in his room was on, but thankfully he was not peeking outside. *Reading comic books*, she thought. That was fine with her, so long as he did not get curious enough to look out his window and see or hear what was happening on the patio.

The floods flickered. Miki redirected her eyes at them. They flickered again, went out, and then came back on. "What the hell now?" she asked no one. She looked at Ryan. "Think there's a blackout coming?"

"Who cares?" her husband replied. He continued to hand out dime bags while his brother accepted money.

Miki frowned and hoped the power stayed on. It had been a hot day and it was still muggy. Trying to sleep without the AC would be hell.

"Who's that?" Pat asked.

Miki followed Pat's gaze.

Someone stood in the corner of the yard. He was alone and wrapped completely in shadow. Miki could barely make out the man's outline. He wore a long coat that was far too warm for the weather. And was that a top hat? A chill that felt very out of place in the warm night air worked its way up her spine.

"Ryan," she whispered.

"Hang on," he replied. Angela, Stephanie and Orlando were next in line. The Cables were already around the side of the house and on their way home.

The man did not move, simply stood in the corner of the yard. Miki could see nothing more than his dark shape, but she knew he was staring at them, staring at *her*. "Ryan."

"Don't worry," Pat said. He handed his fistful of cash to her. "I'll see what his story is."

Miki reached out to stop her brother-in-law, but she moved too slowly. Pat was off the patio and making a leisurely pace toward the corner.

Angela and her friends had paused to watch what was happening. Ryan finally looked up.

"Yo, Slash. You here to buy?" Pat asked as he neared the stranger. "Because if you ain't then you'll have to leave. So what's it gonna be?" Pat stopped a few feet away from the man in the corner. He planted his hands on his waist, a gesture Miki recognized as Pat's famous "shit or get off the pot" stance.

"Who is that?" Ryan asked. He got to his feet and walked around the table until he stood next to Miki.

Miki shook her head. "I don't—"

The floods winked out and the yard was plunged into complete darkness.

Miki gasped and took a startled step back. She heard something from the corner of the yard, a sound that suggested a scuffle. Ryan heard it and must have thought the same thing. He shouted, "Pat!" and all but leaped off the patio.

"Ryan, be careful!" Miki shouted. She wanted to run into the house and call 911. It was a foolish notion; there was weed and all sorts of paraphernalia all over the place. Also, whoever the man was, even if he was here to rob them, he was alone. Ryan and Pat would be more than enough to handle him. Her husband vanished into the darkness. The sounds of a scuffle increased in volume, but only for a moment. No more than ten seconds after she lost sight of her husband Miki could hear nothing.

"Ryan?" Her heart pounded inside her chest. Sweat trickled down from her hair and stung her eyes. "Honey?"

She caught movement on her right side. Angela, Stephanie and Orlando were retreating slowly toward the driveway. Their eyes were locked on the dark corner. They said nothing, made no eye contact with Miki. Angela's eyes were loaded with fear.

A shadow blacker than the darkness flashed in front of Miki's eyes. She yelped and fell back, landing hard on the patio stones.

Angela shrieked, but only for a moment; her scream ended abruptly. Miki could still see nothing but she heard a loud *thud* from where she had last seen Angela and her friends.

Another scream, undoubtedly from Stephanie. Something hot and wet splashed across Miki's face when that scream, too, was cut off. Miki wiped at her eyes, her mouth. She tasted hot copper sliding wetly down her throat.

"Oh Jesus," she whispered. She tried to get to her feet, failed. She managed to back up on all fours, but that was as fast as she could move.

A man's scream this time, close, much closer than the two women. Something large and heavy landed on the patio next to her. Miki's hand trembled as she reached into the darkness. She felt cloth, a man's shirt; it was saturated with what she prayed was water. Inside the shirt was Orlando and her fingers found wide grooves gouged into his flesh.

Miki would have screamed but she had no breath. It took her several moments to realize nothing had happened since Orlando crash landed next to her. She could still see nothing, and she became aware she could hear nothing. Slowly she regained the ability to breathe. Her breath sounded loud in her ears, the only evidence she had not indeed gone deaf.

She turned over slowly, still on all fours, and looked into the blackness that was the corner of the yard. "Ryan?" she whispered. She strained her ears, but she heard no reply. "Ryan." Her husband did not answer. "Ryan, goddammit, *answer me!*" This was a shout, and the sudden increase in volume startled her.

Slowly, all her senses dialed to ten, Miki pushed herself to her feet. Her legs shook and she felt something wet and warm trickle down and pool in her sandals. *Pissed yerself, luv*, she thought in her best British accent, the one she reserved for role playing night with Ryan. *Not a good example for—*

Miki's eyes started the slow trek up to Dylan's window. She got sidetracked when she caught sight of the Cables' house a few doors down. Light spilled from several windows. She could even see Jacki's silhouette standing within of one of them. How could they have power?

Miki pulled her eyes from her friend's house and refocused on Dylan. It took her a moment, but she found the vague outline that was the widow to her son's room. She saw something contained within the window frame, something small that looked down on her.

Something hard and sharp slashed across her abdomen. Miki drew in a sharp breath and she felt her knees buckle. She landed hard on the patio stones. Her hand went reflexively to her side and she felt something hot seeping between her fingers. There was no pain, not at first, and she had time to wonder why.

Something rose within the darkness in front of her. She could not see it, nor could she hear it, but she knew it was there. The man in the coat and top hat.

Tears spilled down her cheeks. She pulled her hand away from her wounded side and held it in front of her. Blood dripped in fat drops and thin streams from her fingers. "Please, I have a son." Her voice was little more than a whisper. "Please don't kill me." Her eyes went to where the table should be. "Take it all, I won't tell. The money, too. Just don't kill me, please."

Something slashed across her chest, an inch or two below her throat. Miki was thrown back by the impact. Her head connected solidly with the patio stones and for a brief moment she forgot where she was. Blood welled up from the new wound and saturated her tank top. Her hand moved weakly to the spot and felt the new, deep tears in her flesh.

"Dylan," she whispered. Her eyes went to the window again. She could still not see her son, but she got the distinct impression he was looking down at her. Numbly, Miki raised her arm toward her son.

The shadow that was blacker than the darkness loomed above her. It remained stationary for a moment, as if studying the dying woman at its feet.

Miki shook her head. "Please."

The shadow descended.

****

Nick Wade screamed and flailed his arms. The movement was so sudden, so violent, that he succeeded in throwing himself from the bed. He landed on the floor between his bed and the wall and stifled a second scream as a lightning bolt shot up his wounded leg. He clutched the appendage with both hands, tears in his eyes and his arms and chest coated with sweat.

"Jesus Christ," he gasped through gritted teeth. "Holy shit. That hurt." He waited several moments for the pain to subside. He noted with some guilt his scream seemed to have awakened Curran. His roommate propped himself up on one elbow and reached for the nightstand light with his free hand.

"What happened?" he asked as he shielded his eyes from the harsh light.

"Nightmare," Nick replied. "Sorry." His leg still throbbed, but the pain was already dull and distant. *At least you didn't break it again*, he thought. *Small favors and all that.*

He threw one arm onto the bed and started to haul himself up. Curran kicked off his bed sheet and stumbled in his friend's direction. "I'll do it, I'll do it," he mumbled. "Don't hurt your leg again."

Nick waited patiently for his roommate to hoist him onto the bed. Nick lay back, breathing heavily. He rubbed his leg above the sore spot and said, "Thanks."

"You okay? Need me to get Carol?"

Nick shook his head without opening his eyes. "No, I'll be okay. Just need a minute."

"You sure?"

"Yeah."

Curran waved at the camera and gave it a thumbs up. Nick did not know if Carol was watching at that moment but if she were she would know it was nothing serious.

A minute later Nick felt a little better. His leg still hurt but he had managed to slow his breathing and he was no longer sweating.

He rubbed his eyes and opened them. Curran was propped up on one elbow and watching him. "What?" Nick asked.

"You look like shit is what," Curran replied.

"Go fuck yourself," Nick said. He laughed weakly.

Curran joined him a moment later. "Must have been some nightmare."

It came back to Nick just then. He stopped laughing and closed his eyes. He could almost see the house and the backyard and the dead people he had left behind. Almost. Unlike the dream with the father and daughter at the airport, this one was fading quickly. Nick tried to find a detail, any detail, and to hold on to that. Everything slipped through his fingers. By the time he opened his eyes a moment later he had only the vaguest sense that something bad had happened.

"I can't remember it."

"Well, maybe that's for the best. That's probably an attempt by what passes for your brain to save what little sanity you have left." Curran laid back and laughed.

Nick would normally have voiced a smartass comeback, but not this time. He tried to remember anything about the dream. He felt it was important, even if he did not know why. Several moments later he decided it was a lost cause. He reached over and turned off the light and lay flat on his back. His eyes remained open and he stared at the ceiling. It would be another ninety minutes before he was able to return to sleep. As consciousness finally left him, Nick whispered a single word. He was aware of it only in a dim corner of his mind and he would not remember it for another two days. By then he would realize its significance.

The word was "Dylan."

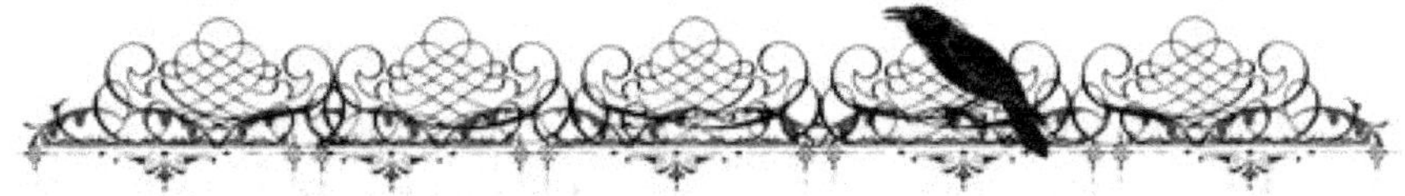

Chapter 9

The Withdrawal

Mike Connelly sat at his desk and scrolled through last night's reports. There was certainly no shortage of reading material; West Philly did not lend itself to quiet, uneventful nights. No murders, which was good, if somewhat rare. Twenty-four drug busts, six prostitution charges, a few weapons charges and seven assaults. The new cases either did not require a detective or already had one assigned. *Looks like a patrol day*, he thought.

In truth he did not mind it. Driving around the precinct looking for trouble had always appealed to him. There was something he enjoyed about catching someone in the act. It was not something he got to do very often these days; "A detective's job isn't to make arrests for jaywalking," was a favorite saying of his captain. But Connelly enjoyed getting out from behind his desk and hitting the streets. It reminded him of his rookie year and that had been a good year, indeed.

His first week on the job he stopped a carjacking and saved a young mother and her child from the strong-arm thief. That same week he made sixteen additional arrests, all on narcotics-related charges. It only got better from there. By the end of his first year he had received three official commendations and the medals to go with them. From there he progressed through the department until he received his gold shield at the tender age of twenty-nine. He had led and assisted in a number of high profile cases since then, everything from first-degree murder to the theft of the Philly Phanatic costume before a game against the Mets. Before the ninth inning the costume was returned and the mascot was on the field, much to the joy of the little ones in the stands. Connelly had watched and smiled from the owner's box as the children cheered the beloved goofball.

All good memories, but what he really enjoyed was being in the patrol unit and seeing what was happening on his streets in real time, not responding to a crime after the fact. And it looked like today would be a good day for that.

He refreshed the screen one more time, more out of habit than any desire to see new updates. Another assault charge from just two hours ago, two more minor narcotics arrests, and a bulletin from Manayunk. He nearly read past that last item before he caught the term *sextuple homicide*. That was rare enough even in West Philly; in the burbs it was unheard of. Connelly sat up and leaned in closer to the screen.

There was only one crime scene photo. It was of someone's backyard in what appeared to be a residential neighborhood. Three bodies lay presumably where they fell, already covered. There was quite a bit of blood on the patio and around the bodies. What looked to be dime bags of marijuana were scattered around the scene. A large amount of cash lay in neat piles on the glass table. *See how long that lasts*, he thought. *Won't be long before that vanishes mysteriously.* There was very little in the way of information in the report. Connelly checked the time stamp and realized the crime scene was new. At the bottom of the preliminary report was a note from the detective-in-charge. It read, *Possible same MO as homicide X2 in Phoenixville.*

Connelly had read the report of the murder of the man and his young daughter. He had not given it much thought and still did not. Phoenixville and Manayunk were far enough away that even the captain had made little mention of it.

"Good luck, gents."

He stood and walked to the duty sheet and updated his status to ON PATROL. He exited the room.

****

Everyone was present at the morning meeting. Nick scanned the faces of his fellow patients and tried to spot the guilty party, the one who had smoked up the night before. He was quite good, an expert, in fact, at spotting the signs of recent usage. Addicts always had a tell, no matter how practiced they were at the art of concealment. Nick was willing to bet the signs would be even easier to spot in a rehab, as the guilt normally associated with drug use was most likely multiplied to a degree not seen on the outside. This ability had served him well in the past; he was always aware of who was holding out on him. It led to more than a few arguments, and a few busted relationships, but it also led to Nick getting a fix and that was what mattered.

He looked at each of his fellow patients in turn. He grew more irritated the closer he got to the end of the circle without locating the culprit. He finished his rounds and sat back in his chair, disgusted. Someone was very good at concealment, better even than Nick was at smoking them out. *Fine*, he thought. *Keep your shit. I'll catch you eventually, or Buckley will, and that'll be the end of you.* Nick sat and waited for the meeting to start.

After the meeting came breakfast and then the usual sojourn outside. He sat with Sarah, Jenna and Curran and the conversation was friendly enough, but Nick's mind wandered. His leg still throbbed a little from his fall the night before. He wished he could remember the dream even as he was grateful he could not. It was probably more of the same that occupied his thoughts during the day, anyway. Angie in her Mustang on what turned out to be her final night on earth, smiling and laughing and without a care in the world. The view of the Schuykill outside the window, the sound of squealing tires and her sharp intake of breath just before the scream. It was the only thing Nick could come up with that would explain him ending up on the floor. The only other subject that occupied his thoughts was escaping Springbrook and getting his hands on some H and he knew the dream had nothing to do with that. That would have been a happy dream, certainly not capable of dumping him out of bed.

He realized the conversation at the table had ceased. Nick looked up and saw his companions were focused on something across the yard. Nick followed their eyes.

Richie and Phil stood toe to toe with one another, their noses about an inch apart and spittle flying from their lips. They shouted at each other with enough volume that Nick could make nothing of what they were saying. Both men gesticulated wildly with their arms and Nick knew they were seconds away from coming to blows.

Jessica and Patty realized it, as well. They stood and walked quickly away from the two men. "So much for the nice morning," Jessica said as she walked past Nick's table and into the building.

Curran stood, as did Pedro and Ricky, who sat at the next table.

Richie shoved Phil with both hands. The older man stumbled back with a yelp, arms pin-wheeling. Richie charged forward and shoved him again. Phil lost all semblance of balance and fell into the pool.

Pedro and Ricky ran to Richie and pulled him back. Richie still shouted at Phil and struggled against the two men. Curran ran to the pool where Phil was treading water and rubbing the back of his head. Curran knelt by the pool and offered his hand. Phil took it.

Dr. Buckley and Karen rushed outside. Buckley said something and pointed to Phil. Karen moved in that direction. Buckley slowed her pace and walked the last few yards to where Richie was still struggling to break free of Pedro and Ricky.

"What is this?" Buckley asked. Her tone was stern, demanding, but somewhat sad, that of a teacher who has just witnessed her star pupils cheating on a test. Her eyes, however, told a different story. She was livid, nearly incredulous that anyone would have the nerve to disrupt the routine tranquility of her little kingdom. Her eyes drilled into Richie's.

"I can't take it here anymore," Richie shouted. "I hate that cocksucker and I hate this fucking place and I hate *you*! I'm getting the fuck out of here and you can't stop me!"

By now Curran had succeeded in pulling Phil from the pool. The older man stood on shaky feet and dripped onto the concrete. He massaged the back of his head and mumbled something to Curran.

"If you want to leave, Mr. Bruno, that's your right," Buckley replied, her voice borderline calm but her eyes flashing rage. "I think you should take some time to think it over. But you'll have to do it in quarantine. You know the rules around here."

"Fuck your rules," Richie snarled. He shrugged and freed himself from Pedro and Ricky. They remained close enough to grab him should he try to renew his fight with Phil, or even take a swing at Buckley. Richie did neither. He threw his arms in the air, shouted, "I'm out!" and made for the back door.

Sarah and Jenna stood and moved farther away from the doorway as Richie approached. Nick stood with his hands curled into fists behind his back, just in case.

Richie paused when he reached them. "If you're smart, you'll leave, too. Fuck this place."

"Richie—" Jenna began.

Richie disappeared inside. Nick could hear him stomping loudly in the direction of the stairs.

It was silent for a moment. Nobody seemed willing to speak. Then, Buckley said, "We've all seen this before. Let's hope he comes to his senses before he does anything he'll regret." She turned to Phil. "Are you okay?"

Phil nodded. "Been better, been worse."

"We'll have Karen take a look at you."

Phil smiled at the young nurse. "My pleasure."

Karen guided Phil inside. Buckley followed them. Pedro and Ricky joined Nick and the others.

Curran shook his head. "Bad shit."

"What was that about?" Nick asked.

"That? That was nothing," Ricky said. "People have slugged it out big time around here. The withdrawal, y'know? Some people just can't take it."

"No shit," Pedro added. He rubbed his left shoulder. "That skinny little dude was stronger than he looked."

"And he pulled this shit the day before Family and Friends Day," Jenna noted. "Guess we won't be seeing his wife this time around. Too bad. I liked her."

"Maybe he'll get his shit together," Nick said. "You never know."

No one replied. Nick returned to his seat and rubbed his eyes. Maybe Richie Bruno was right. A bit too theatrical for Nick's taste, perhaps, but correct nonetheless. This place *was* shit, and so was Buckley. Part of him envied the man. In a matter of hours he would probably be high as a fucking kite and loving life and his reclaimed freedom. Perhaps it was time for Nick's own Declaration of Independence from Springbrook. He gave the matter some thought.

****

Connelly returned to the precinct house at 3:15 PM. It had been a decent day, not great. He managed three drug busts, including a very stupid hand-to-hand transaction right in front of him, and a domestic disturbance where an old man had been stabbed with a hairpin by his even-older wife. The wounds were more laughable than serious and the husband had even told Connelly he had no intention of leaving his wife. Connelly felt a twinge of guilt when he slipped the handcuffs onto the old woman. She had been calm by then, at least, which was fortunate. There was no way to struggle with such a person and come out looking like anything other than a dick. After that he hit a few bad neighborhoods but came up empty. He was surprised to find his shift was ending and it was with some reluctance he drove back to the station.

He sat at his desk and wrote out his reports and filed them. He was about to log out when he decided to look at the day's reports. He scrolled through until he got to the murders in Manayunk. The report had been updated and there were now eight pages of details. Connelly sat up and skimmed the report.

Six dead, including the two homeowners. Twenty-nine total ounces of marijuana recovered as well as six thousand in cash. *Was probably more like seven or eight*, he thought. *Some flatfoot is going to have a fun weekend.* Several neighbors interviewed denied hearing or seeing anything. Naturally. The braver of them would be on the news later explaining how the MacKennedys were such a wonderful family and never bothered anyone. The only survivor was a four-year-old male, the son of the two homeowners. He was listed as a witness.

Connelly shook his head. "Christ, I hope he didn't see too much," he whispered.

But the boy had apparently seen something. He had given a statement. Connelly read it. And read it again. His mouth opened, but he found he could not speak.

He was, however, able to think. *Son of a bitch.*

****

"Most of us have seen it before. It happens," Buckley said that night in a special group meeting. She probably tried to sound consoling but to Nick she sounded simply annoyed, as if Richie's defection would look bad on her record.

The patients were seated in their usual circle. Nick's eyes lingered on the empty chair. He thought of Richie Bruno and the anger he had seen in the man's eyes. Nick had indeed seen that before, in an endless procession of friends and girlfriends, roommates and casual acquaintances, and in the mirror, as well. He had even seen it once in Angie when they were going through a particularly bad time and it seemed the whole fucking city was dry. Every addict had times like that. But this was his first experience with it at Springbrook.

If he was honest about it, the episode with Richie had shaken him. It was not the screaming, not even the violence, not really. It was the idea that anyone could snap like that at any time, himself included. Richie had gathered his things and stormed out of Springbrook and was probably hitting a meth pipe even as his former prison mates sat in a circle listening to Buckley tell them it wasn't the end.

Nick took a moment to look at every member of the circle. They were as shaken as was he, although most of them were good at hiding it. Sarah's feet shuffled and Jessica and Patty held hands. Curran licked his lips. They were all upset and it seemed any one of them could follow Richie out the door. *So much for having a handle on your disease. If that's all it takes we're doomed.*

Nick had pondered following Richie out the door for perhaps a full twenty minutes. At one point he even stood and started inside to pack his things. He stopped himself. It was not inner strength, something Buckley harped on in their meetings. It was simply the image of Rebecca standing at the curb and watching him make the long trek up the walk to Springbrook's front entrance. She looked scared but hopeful. How might she look when she found out Nick jumped ship? The pain he imagined in her eyes stopped him and made him sit back down. He still wanted to join Richie, but he wanted to avoid hurting Rebecca even more. For now, anyway.

"Just don't forget the progress you've all made," Buckley continued. "That's the important thing. It hasn't been easy on any of you and you've all proven how strong you are and that you can beat your disease. Think about that tonight when it's lights out. You're all stronger than you know and you'll come through this."

Nick wondered how many times Buckley had given this speech and if she still believed it. No, she could not be that foolish. She was playing them, hoping she would still have patients, and a job, by morning. Nick would not have minded going over the wall that night if they all left as a group. It would be worth any relapses if it got the bitch fired. Except there was still Rebecca. For the second time in as many hours, the young girl kept him within the walls of Springbrook.

"And don't forget about tomorrow. We have quite a few people showing up. I think the timing of this is excellent. It'll remind us all why we're fighting this fight." She smiled her most reassuring smile before she dismissed the group.

"That was a load of shit," Nick said after they were in the corridor and out of earshot of the doctor.

Ricky nodded. "You just know Richie's out there right now high as a motherfucker." He sighed. "I wouldn't mind being with him."

"Me, too," Jenna agreed.

"Not me," Curran said as he joined them. "I've worked too goddamned hard to make it this far. I ain't letting some asshole screw that up. I got a wife and a kid and I'll see them tomorrow. Might be best if you all forgot about Richie. At least for now."

"He's right," Ricky said. "Just concentrate on tomorrow."

Nick watched Sarah follow Jessica and Patty outside. Nick limped after them. He found all three women at the first table. They were nervous, that much was obvious. Sarah looked the worst. She fidgeted and it took her several attempts to light her bummed cigarette. She inhaled and exhaled slowly and looked a little better. Jessica and Patty lowered their heads and smoked in silence.

"Who do you have coming tomorrow?" Nick asked Sarah.

She puffed nervously on her cigarette for a moment. "My brother," she said, her voice barely a whisper. "My brother, Scott. I asked my mom, but she said no. She doesn't want me around anymore."

Nick placed his hand on hers. "Well, that's her loss. She'll come round, I'm sure." Nick did not believe that for a moment. He could see the need in Sarah's eyes. In a few days, a week at most, she would follow Richie out the door. *Let's see how much your mom wants you around after that.* He stayed with the girls for another fifteen minutes before he went back inside and up to his room.

Curran was already in bed, laying on top of the covers with the remote in his hand. Unlike the girls outside he seemed none the worse for wear after the episode with Richie. He scrolled through the channel guide nonchalantly.

"You seem okay," Nick said.

"That's because I am," Curran replied. "I meant what I said down there. I'm doing this for my wife and my kid. I'm not gonna let some dickhead's meltdown screw this up."

Nick shrugged. "I guess that's one way to look at it." He removed his shirt and tossed it on the floor between his bed and the wall.

Curran dropped the remote and regarded him. "You know how long it's been since my last drink? Seventy-two days. You know how long I've been here? Sixty-eight. Do the math. I didn't drink for *four days* before I got here. Before that I couldn't go four *hours*. That's how serious I am about this. What happened out there,"—he gestured in the direction of the backyard—"that's Richie's problem. It ain't mine." He picked up the remote again and leaned back against the headboard. "You shouldn't make it yours, either."

"Sound advice." Nick went into the bathroom and washed up.

A few minutes after that he was in bed. Curran had settled on the local news but Nick did not watch. His thoughts were of Sarah. He could see her, one floor up, lying in her bed, staring at the ceiling. It was all she could do to resist the urge to pack her things. She needed it bad, maybe even as bad as Nick himself. He lay in bed and wondered if he would see her again.

He surprised himself by hoping the answer was yes.

Joseph J. Christiano

115

Chapter 10

An Understanding

Nick woke up feeling queasy. He was experienced enough to know he would not vomit so he made no dash for the bathroom. He lay in bed and waited for his stomach to quiet down. He became aware of the growing dizziness in his head. It set up shop behind his eyes and radiated backward. "Oh, no," he whispered. He rubbed his eyes but even that movement caused his stomach to threaten mutiny. "Not now."

He had felt this way before, many times, in fact. He was quite well-acquainted with his personal set of withdrawal symptoms. He had not experienced them in some time. They were present his first few nights at Springbrook but in a much reduced and manageable form. The methadone had done its job. By the time Buckley toned down the dosage it seemed they might be gone for good. Now he thought they had merely been taking a break, building their strength for an all-out attack. Before Springbrook it had been some time since his last bout with them. At least a year, if he remembered correctly. However long it had been they were back with their familiar assault. He would not get physically sick, as long as he did not attempt any big movements, at least; his withdrawal did not work that way. But he would be dizzy and unable to stand until they passed.

He put his arms at his sides and concentrated on his breathing. He listened to his heartbeat and tried to think of a song with the same cadence. It was something his mother had taught him the first time she had been unable to find a supply and they both had to ride it out. It might have worked then, he could not remember; it did nothing for him now.

His thoughts turned to Sarah. He wondered if she was still upstairs in her room or if she had gone over the wall. Sarah, shaking so badly she was nearly incapable of even lighting a cigarette. He read her eyes and knew what she was thinking. He had certainly seen that look enough times in others to know the score. Nick was again surprised to find himself hoping she was still upstairs. If pressed he would have been unable to articulate why the fate of some junkie he barely knew, and with whom he had never smoked up, should matter to him. All he knew was that it did matter.

Suddenly not knowing if Sarah was still under the same roof bothered him. Without thinking he sat up and kicked at the covers. A wave of dizziness crashed over him and knocked him flat on his back. Nick's breathing quickened until he was gulping air. Slowly, too slowly, he felt the dizziness subside. *Don't try that again*, it warned him. *That was just a warning shot. Do it again and it'll be a direct hit. Believe it.* Nick did believe it. He lay in bed and did not move for another hour.

By the time Curran exited the shower, towel wrapped around his middle and water dripping from his short hair, Nick felt better. He eased himself into a sitting position and waited for the dizziness to strike. It did not, although he still felt lightheaded. And he needed a hit. God, did he need a hit.

You just remember Santos. Santos got whachoo need.

"Yeah, I remember," Nick mumbled.

"Say something?" Curran asked. He was running the towel through his hair.

"Nah, just talking to myself."

Curran laughed. "Then you're a crazy motherfucker, because you definitely ain't rich."

"Fuck you," Nick said, and offered a weak smile. He pushed himself off the bed and steadied himself. His legs shook and it took him a moment to be sure they would not buckle. He made his way into the bathroom and turned on the water in the shower.

His body was covered with gooseflesh despite the faucet dial being turned all the way to the left. The tremors returned to his hands for the first time since his arrival at Springbrook. He leaned his head against the shower wall below the nozzle and tried to control his breathing. He had not felt this sick in some time, even without the vomiting. Nick pounded his fist against the wall and silently commanded his heart to slow its heavy metal rhythm inside his chest.

He lost track of time. He might have remained in that position for hours for all he knew. Slowly, the symptoms started to subside. His breathing slowed, his legs and arms stopped shaking, the tremors in his hands subsided. When Nick was sure the sickness had passed he stood up straight and opened his eyes. He could see nothing through the steam. The water suddenly felt hot, scalding. He turned the dial and relaxed his muscles. It did not take long before he felt better. Cleaner.

He was out of the shower a few minutes later. He toweled off and found Curran had already left the room. Nick dressed slowly, still not trusting his body not to revolt again. He thought of Santos and the long, narrow stairs that led to his apartment. Santos got what he needed, all right.

Nick began to stuff his clothes into his duffel bag. Fuck Springbrook and the sad losers within who mumbled through their insipid Sobriety Mantra and entertained fantasies of living clean. Each and every one of them would be back on the shit as soon as they were outside these goddamned walls. He knew it and they knew it. Buckley probably knew it, too, which made her the worst of them. "Job security, that's all we are, right?" He very nearly put his fist into the mirror above his dresser but that would gain him nothing except a broken hand. Instead he tossed his duffel bag onto the bed and made for the door.

He was down the stairs in record time and headed for the nurse's station. Once he had his cell he would be out the door, waiting for Staci to pick him up. Part of him hoped Karen or even Buckley would put up a fuss about his leaving, if only so he would have one last opportunity to tell them exactly what he thought of their recovery program.

Nick was nearly to the nurse's station when he saw Sarah standing outside the door to the conference room, talking with Curran. She wore a yellow-and-pink sundress and she had put on makeup and done something with her hair. She smiled and then laughed at something Curran said.

She had not left, after all. And more than that, she looked beautiful. Her anxiety from the day before had vanished. Nick thought this was how Sarah would have looked every minute of every day if she had never gotten involved with heroin. Her smile was warm and it reached her eyes and her laughter was genuine.

Nick's thoughts turned to Santos again, but this time the long, narrow stairs looked decrepit, even dangerous. He could not imagine making the trek up those stairs, nor did he want to think about what would transpire after he reached the top. The white smoke still appealed to him and his heart picked up the beat when he thought about it, but somehow the need felt less urgent than it had a moment before.

Nick changed course from the nurse's station and instead joined Sarah and Curran at the doorway. Sarah was in mid-laugh and she looked even more beautiful up close. How could he have never noticed before? Was it just the makeup? That might have been part of it but Nick knew it was deeper than that. She was a beautiful woman and he could not believe he had never seen it before now. *Well, you really weren't thinking straight, were you?* No, he wasn't. He probably still wasn't, not completely straight, anyway. But enough to see her for how she should have been, and maybe how she would be again.

"Hey, Nick," she said.

"Hey, yourself."

"Holy shit, is that a smile?" Curran leaned in closer to Nick's face, as if examining a phenomenon heretofore unknown to science.

"Shaddap," Nick replied, although he continued to smile.

"Today's the big day," Sarah said. "I can't wait."

Nick nodded. "Family Day."

"You have anyone coming?" she asked.

"Yeah, my cousin, Rebecca." He inclined his head in the direction of the front door. "She's the one who drove me here."

"My brother Scott will be here," Sarah replied. "Haven't seen him in a month, since the last one of these." Her eyes grew dark. "I wasn't in great shape the last time. We fought, I said some pretty nasty things to him."

"He'll forgive you," Curran said. "He already has, I'm sure. Or else he wouldn't be coming."

Sarah's eyes brightened and she looked up again. "I hope so."

Her smile returned and Nick felt a thump from within his chest. It had been some time since he had felt anything like it, years, in fact. He had not felt it with any of the women with whom he shacked up over the years, not even with Angie. Nick tried to remember the last time he felt this way and he came up empty. It excited him in a way usually reserved for when he scored a big bag of H. His legs felt weak again, but he knew it was not from withdrawal. Not this time.

"Shall we?" Curran extended an arm into the conference room and Sarah stepped across the threshold. Nick was quick to follow her inside, stepping in front of Curran as he did. Curran stopped to avoid a collision in the doorway and laughed. He clapped Nick on the back and followed him into the conference room.

Nick sat next to Sarah on the loveseat, keeping a few discreet inches between them. She did not seem to mind; she even allowed him to drape his arm across the back of the loveseat. He did not attempt to put his arm around her, but being even this close unsettled his stomach and made him lightheaded. This time he welcomed the dizziness.

The rest of the patients began to file inside the room. Nick watched them each in turn. They were all dressed nicely and the girls had put on some makeup and the men had shaved and combed their hair. The meeting might have been in an office in some high rise downtown instead of a rehab hidden in the wilds of West Philly.

He found himself excited, and not just because he was sitting next to Sarah. The thought of seeing Rebecca again appealed to him. He had certainly gone longer without her in his life, but that was someone else, a lowlife son of a bitch who managed to alienate his entire family except for one sweet girl. Maybe it was time to do something about that.

Nick sat next to Sarah and enjoyed the proximity and waited for Buckley to show up. He could not stop his eyes from wandering to the clock and calculating the minutes until Rebecca arrived. For the first time in a long time, he was looking forward to something that wasn't white powder.

****

Connelly knocked on the door to Captain Calabrese's office. Through the translucent glass window he could barely make out the vague outline that was his boss, seated behind his desk, possibly on the phone. He waited patiently for a reply. It came a moment later, in his boss's usual, gruff, "Enter."

Connelly swung the door open. "Cap," he said.

Calabrese was indeed on the phone. He indicated one of the empty chairs in front of his desk.

Connelly normally had little use for the captains in the PPD. He considered most of them to be soulless bureaucrats who had long since lost the ability to think like real cops. Calabrese was the lone exception. The bald man in his late-fifties was a cop's cop, one who would still get his hands dirty with actual police work if not for his bosses who insisted his place was behind his desk. Connelly actually felt a bit sorry for the bastard. Calabrese always appeared uncomfortable looking over reports and attending meetings with the city brass. He was an outdoor cat forced to live indoors. Connelly hoped he would fare better when his time came.

He took the chair and waited for Calabrese to finish his conversation. He resisted the urge to tap his foot or fiddle with his fingers. The captain ended the call a few moments later with a simple, "Yes, sir," and hung up. He scribbled something on the notepad in front of him and then looked up. "What's up?"

Connelly had to force himself not to blurt out everything at once. Surely Calabrese would know it was something big; Connelly's body language would have told him that much. The captain sat with his hands on his desk and his fingers laced. A hint of curiosity played across his features.

"That homicide case in Manayunk, you heard about it?"

Calabrese nodded. "Uh huh. I read the preliminary report yesterday, and the official report today. I assume you've solved the case already?"

The deadpan delivery threw Connelly. He stuttered for a moment. "Um, no. But I did a little research on it last night. I assume you caught the similarities in the wounds on the victims there and the man and his daughter in Phoenixville?"

"Naturally." Calabrese hit a few keys on his keyboard and looked at something on his computer monitor. "*'The pattern of the wounds is identical, strongly indicating they were inflicted by the same person. Forensic analysis indicates an assailant at least six-foot-nine-inches in height and with great upper body strength. Weapon remains unknown.'* That's what Manayunk PD had to say."

Connelly shrugged. "Okay, I guess you did read the report." He reached into his back pocket, pulled out a folded piece of paper. He held it up triumphantly. "Did you see this? Two of the victims in Manayunk, Ryan and Miki MacKennedy, had a son who survived unharmed. He not only saw what happened, he drew a picture of the guy who did it." One of Calabrese's hands rebelled against the other and separated. He drummed his fingers on his desk. "Okay, Detective, I'll bite. Who are we putting out an APB on? SpongeBob SquarePants or Dora the Explorer?"

Connelly bit his lip. He might have been offended if he felt he would have reacted differently had their positions been reversed.

He knew he would not. He placed the folded piece of paper on the desktop and slid it toward Calabrese. "Take a look, Cap."

Calabrese snapped up the paper and unfolded it. He regarded it for a moment before he turned it back toward Connelly. "Is this a joke?"

The image drawn by young Dylan MacKennedy was colored mostly in black. It was a hulking figure with bulging shoulders and thin legs. Its arms ended in hands that might have been talons. The figure's head was covered with black except for two small slits that could be nothing other than eyes. It wore a top hat.

Connelly shook his head. "No joke, Cap. I think he's back."

Calabrese refolded the paper and slid it back to Connelly. "You're serious about this? The child is how old? Four? Five? He watched his parents and four other people get torn to pieces in front of him. I think it's safe to say he didn't have a clear head when he drew this. And remind me to call Chief Leonard in Manayunk and tell him he's stupid for letting a clearly-traumatized child draw him a picture instead of at least having a sketch artist do it."

Connelly took the paper back. "I am serious about this. He was never identified and never found. I think the MacKennedy kid came pretty close to what the perp looked like."

Calabrese pointed to the paper in Connelly's hand. "That's a picture of the boogey man. I wish that's what the prick looked like. He'd be pretty easy to spot."

Connelly stuffed the paper into his back pocket. "Why is it so hard to believe? The Shadow Man murdered twenty-one people back in '99 and then he up and vanished. He could be making a comeback."

Calabrese held up both hands. "I remember the case. Hell, every cop and detective working back then followed it. How could we not? And I always hated that name, by the way. The Shadow Man. That was something the fine folks at some newspaper in Jersey came up with because—"

"He always killed at night and managed to surprise his victims. There was never a reliable description from witnesses, not that there were many. Yes, I know."

"The usual sensationalized bullshit from the media."

"I'll give you that," Connelly replied. "But what if he is back? I'm already doing a search on convicts in the Northeast who were locked up around the time the Shadow…the murderer vanished and last week when the man and his daughter were found. I should have something within the hour."

Calabrese laced his fingers again. "Did you ever stop to think we might have a copycat? That I might be willing to swallow."

Connelly nodded. "That's a possibility, yes. I kinda hope not, though. That'll make him tougher to track down."

Calabrese sighed his resignation. He leaned back in his chair and rubbed his eyes. "Okay, Detective, do your search and let me know what you find out."

Connelly sprung from the chair. "You got it, Cap."

He was halfway to the door when Calabrese stopped him. "Mike? Do yourself a favor. Look up the Shadow Man on the internet. Do a Google search, whatever. Tell me what you find."

Connelly nodded. "Yes, sir." Then he was out the door.

****

Nick paced back and forth in the media room. The television was on but he paid it little mind. He had the room to himself; everyone else was out back visiting with their friends and family members. He had been introduced to Curran's wife and young son. He met Phil's son and daughter-in-law. Sarah's brother seemed nice enough but he regarded Nick with open suspicion.

Nick could not blame the man; he was, after all, a drug addict. Nick was pleasant to all of them, at least, he hoped he had been, but all of that seemed a distant memory. It was 12:16 and Rebecca was a no show.

Nick fidgeted with his hands before he rubbed them on his jeans. Christ, why was he so anxious? Even the withdrawal gnawing at him had taken a backseat. He wanted to see Rebecca, perhaps he even *needed* to see her. So where was she? Had she changed her mind? Written him off like the rest of the family? No, not Becks. His thoughts turned to the girl's mother, his Aunt Noreen.

Noreen was a right bitch in every sense of the term. She had never liked Nick, not even before the heroin. He knew she disliked her daughter spending any amount of time with him. There was a time her fears were justified. About ten years ago Nick had tried to persuade Rebecca to try heroin with him. He even used weight loss as a benefit of the drug, and he was not entirely incorrect about that. "C'mon, Becks, it'll help you lose some weight," were his exact words. How Rebecca had managed to restrain herself from smacking the shit out of him he would never know. She turned him down, in no uncertain terms, and that was that. Nick had never made the attempt again. Aunt Noreen need not fear Nick's bad influence on her daughter. There was no way Rebecca would touch the stuff and that was a fact. But that did not mean Noreen hadn't succeeded in keeping her daughter away from Springbrook on this day. He could even picture the woman standing in her kitchen with her arms folded across her chest and insisting Rebecca remain home. That would certainly explain her absence.

Nick swore. The certainty that Aunt Noreen had kept Rebecca from visiting upped the wattage of the withdrawal. He plopped himself down of the sofa and just as quickly bounced back up. His leg barked at him but he ignored it. He was thankful, at least, that none of the staff were around to see him. He had a feeling Buckley would have him on more methadone in a minute and he would be back in his room alone and in the dark.

Nick's moth was dry. He ambled to the water bubbler and drank a little and felt no better. For the second time that day he decided to leave Springbrook. He turned in the direction of the vacant and locked nurse's station.

"Nicky?"

He froze at the sound of Rebecca's voice. He was momentarily nervous, as if turning around would reveal no one there. When the voice repeated itself, Nick turned slowly.

Rebecca stood in the corridor leading to the media room. She wore a knee-length skirt and a bright pink sleeveless top. Her hands were folded in front of her. She looked nervous, timid, even. She stood in place and looked expectantly at him.

Nick broke into a grin and he moved as quickly as he was able. At last he embraced her. Her arms encircled him and he heard the breath hitch in her throat. "Becks!" He pulled her tighter to him. Her hair smelled of peaches and felt smooth as silk on his cheek. He might have remained that way for some time if she did not pull away slightly. He ended the embrace and held her at arm's length.

She wiped tears from her eyes. "It's so good to see you."

"You, too," he said. He was probably grinning like an idiot but he did not care. Seeing Rebecca, being able to hear her and touch her, he felt like a drowning man who had just been thrown a lifeline. "I'm so happy to see you," he told her. "You have no idea."

"I'm happy to see you too," she replied. "You look good."

"Liar." He laughed when he said it. "I didn't think you were gonna make it."

"I almost didn't." She looked over her shoulder. "My mom gave me a hard time."

So he had been correct. He thought of a thousand mean things to say about Aunt Noreen but he held back on all of them. It would accomplish nothing but to upset Rebecca and that was the last thing he wanted to do. All he said was, "I guess I can see her point. I've been nothing but bad news for a long time. I'm sure she only wants to make sure you don't turn out like me."

Rebecca shook her head. "You don't understand. It's not that she didn't want me to come here. She didn't want me to come here *alone*." Rebecca half-turned and Nick followed her eyes. Standing in the foyer and looking at him was Aunt Noreen.

Nick could not remember the last time he saw her. It had to be ten years, at least. Her hair was just as short and well-coiffed as he remembered. It was the same dark shade of auburn as it had been back then, as well, nearly as auburn as Buckley's. Aunt Noreen had always dressed and carried herself as if she were a politician constantly running for office. The smart business suit she wore reinforced the image in Nick's mind.

"Hello, Nicholas," she said. She started toward them slowly, a general about to inspect her troops.

Nick stuttered a moment before he acknowledged her. "Aunt Noreen. Been a while."

"Indeed." She closed the distance and stood before him. "I have to say you look better than I thought you would. This place must agree with you."

Nick raised an eyebrow. He glanced at Rebecca before he returned his eyes to his aunt. "I don't always agree with it, but yeah, so far, we're getting along."

"Glad to hear it."

"So you're doing okay?" Rebecca asked. "No drugs since you got here?" Suspicion and guarded hope competed in her voice. Her eyes were large and wet and searching his for the truth.

"No drugs," he assured her. "I can't say it's been easy. In fact, it's sucked pretty much since I walked through the front door. But so far, so good."

Rebecca hugged him again. Before he could return the gesture the girl's mother cleared her throat. Rebecca pulled back self-consciously. She swallowed and looked at the carpet.

The three of them were silent for a long moment. Finally, Nick said, "There's food and drinks out back. Non-alcoholic drinks, obviously. My fellow inmates are out there already. Wanna grab some chow?"

"Maybe something small," Rebecca answered. "Mom?"

Aunt Noreen waved her off. "I'm okay. But yes, by all means, let's join the party."

Nick extended an arm in the direction of the backyard. "Ladies."

Noreen and Rebecca stopped at the threshold and took in the scene in front of them. A few people were in the pool, splashing each other and laughing. Pedro was dancing with a little girl who had to be his daughter. The child whirled and clapped her hands in time with the music coming from the boom box someone had brought along.

Curran sat with his wife and son. Their conversation appeared quite personal. Curran made slight gestures and kissed his wife on the cheek. His son, no more than three- or four-years-old, waged battle with a cheeseburger.

Phil and his family and Sarah and her brother were seated at the largest table. They talked pleasantly and ate their burgers and dogs. Karen stood near them and laughed and smiled. Sarah saw Nick in the doorway behind Aunt Noreen and Rebecca and she offered him a subtle smile.

Jenna sat with her legs dangling in the pool and her parents on either side of her. Her father draped an arm across her shoulders and Jenna leaned against him Jessica and Patty were in the pool. There were a couple people the same approximate age as the girls swimming around with them. Friends, most likely, or siblings. Buckley stood nearby, observing the interactions. Her expression was neutral.

Ricky and a man Nick did not know worked the grill. At first Nick thought the stranger was one of Ricky's friends but when the man gave Ricky a peck on the cheek Nick saw the truth of their relationship. Noreen did, as well; she scowled in their direction.

In fact, Noreen scowled at everyone. She stood stiffly in the doorway with her lips turned down and her brow furrowed. She clearly did not approve of the atmosphere and she did little to hide her disdain. Rebecca looked hesitant. Nick realized just how alien this environment must be for her. Unlike her mother, she did not appear offended, simply unsure of what to do or how to act. Nick let her off the hook.

"This way." He indicated the only empty table and led the way. When the women were seated Nick asked Rebecca what she would like.

"Maybe a dog. Mustard and ketchup, if you don't mind. And a Coke, if they have one."

"I'm sure they do," Nick replied. He turned to the girl's mother. "Aunt Noreen?"

"Nothing for me, thanks." She smiled at him, but it was forced. She looked about as uncomfortable as Nick had ever seen anyone.

"Okay. Be right back." He weaved his way through the people in the yard and made for the grill. A few minutes later he returned with Rebecca's food and two Cokes. He sat and drank in silence while Rebecca nibbled at her lunch.

"Quite a place," Noreen said.

She may as well have added, *For a bunch of fucking losers who can't get their shit together.* She did not say it, of course, but Nick knew it was foremost in her mind. She was clearly having a difficult time hiding her disdain for everyone within her field of vision. She squirmed in her seat and continually readjusted her blouse.

"Yes, it is," Nick agreed. "The staff here isn't so bad. They seem to genuinely want to help us beat this disease, so it has that going for it."

"You mean a self-inflicted disease, don't you?" Her lips pulled back in a bad imitation of a smile. She spread her hands. "What I mean to say is, you all brought this on yourselves, right?"

"Mother…"

Noreen held up a hand to silence her daughter. It worked; Rebecca returned her attention to her food and looked uncomfortable.

"I suppose so." Nick's voice was flat.

"Calling it a disease seems like a copout to me. It makes it sound as if you're all a bunch of innocents who just happened to catch a bad break, like getting cancer or something. Like it's not your fault. But it is, isn't it, Nicholas? It is *your* fault you got hooked on heroin. Am I right?" Her smile remained in place.

Nick shrugged. What he wanted to do was slug the old bitch. She had seen Nick's father, her own brother, deal with this exact thing. She knew what it could do to a person, to a family, and still she had no sympathy, no compassion, for anyone, least of all him.

She sat and smiled her fake smile at him and Nick felt his blood pressure climb quite rapidly. His hands curled into fists and it was all he could do to keep them under the table and out of sight. If not for Rebecca's presence he might have reached across the table and strangled his aunt in full view of everyone. Instead, he said, simply, "I guess so."

"And you haven't had any drugs since you got here? Is that correct?" As much as her fake smile angered him the poisoned honey of her tone was worse. She had apparently reached levels of condescension heretofore unknown to mortal man. He was surprised to find he was not physically burned by the venom behind her words.

His hands shook. The tremors worked their way up his arms and into his shoulders. In all his life he had never wanted to throttle someone as badly as he did at this moment. It was not Rebecca's presence that stopped him; he knew if he actually did it Buckley would throw him out and his aunt would have him arrested. As bad as Springbrook was, it was still preferable to prison. Noreen, however, seemed to be doing her best to change Nick's mind about that.

"That's one-hundred-percent correct," Nick replied. He kept his voice even. *I'd like to thank the Academy for this Best Actor Award...*

"And do you think you'll stay clean?"

"I hope so."

Noreen leaned forward slightly. She studied him the way an entomologist might examine a new species of insect. She held his stare for only a moment before she returned to her original position. "You do, don't you? I can tell. You're honestly trying to get clean."

Nick shrugged again. "What can I say? Maybe I've finally had enough of that shit."

"See, mom? I told you." Rebecca looked hopefully at Nick. Her smile, unlike her mother's, was honest and venom-free. "He's gonna do it."

Noreen patted the back of her daughter's hand. "We'll see, honey, we'll see."

"It hasn't been easy," Nick said before he was aware he was going to speak. *Where the hell did that come from?* The voice sounded suspiciously like his own but he seemed to have little control over it. "In fact, this is the hardest fucking thing I've ever done. You think this is a fucking country club? Every night I lay in bed and think about getting the fuck out of here. I even went so far as to start packing. A few times I would have done it but I was so goddamned sick I couldn't move. I still think about it. Just a few hours ago I was planning where I was gonna go and who I was gonna look up when I made my great escape. Oh, yeah, I still know plenty of dealers and they'll hook me up without a second thought. Hell, they'll welcome me back with open arms. The only thing that stopped me was you." He pointed to Rebecca. "I don't wanna disappoint you, Becks. I keep seeing you the day you dropped me off here. I remember the look in your eyes, the tears. I don't wanna be the reason you cry. So here I sit and here I stay until I beat this thing. *That's* why I'm still here." He turned his attention to his aunt. "So drop your fucking holier-than-thou bullshit attitude because it's not helping."

Nick froze. Had he really just said all that? He glanced nervously at Rebecca. She sat with her mouth agape, clearly unsure of what she should do. Aunt Noreen, on the other hand, regarded him with cold eyes. Her hatred of him was still there, but something had changed. Nick could not identify the new presence behind her eyes.

"Nicky…" Rebecca began.

"Honey, would you get me something to drink? Maybe some spring water, please?" Noreen's tone was suddenly casual, almost friendly.

Rebecca looked from Nick to her mother.

Nick nodded. "It's okay, Becks." Better this happen with Rebecca out of earshot.

"Um, sure." Rebecca sounded as if leaving the table was the last thing she wanted to do. Slowly, perhaps hoping one or the other would change their mind and clearly disappointed when neither did, she got up from the table. She walked in the direction of Ricky and his friend at the grill. She looked over her shoulder after each step.

Noreen watched her go. When she was satisfied her daughter was not about to reverse course, she leaned across the table. "Let's get to it, shall we?" Her voice was low, almost a whisper.

Nick leaned forward as well. "Yeah, let's."

Noreen placed both hands on the tabletop. "I didn't think you'd even get this far, Nicholas. Your father certainly never did. I think his record for sobriety was something like ten days. And those were the last ten days of his life, by the way."

"Mm hmm." Bringing his father into this would get her nowhere. Nick settled a little. If this was the best she could do…

"You probably don't know this, but the men in our family have had this same problem, this *disease*, as you call it, going back a bunch of generations. My brother wasn't the first, not by a long shot. Our father was hooked on heroin, and so was our grandfather. It might even go back further than that."

"And your point?" Her statement surprised him, just a bit, but he hid any reaction. His aunt would get no satisfaction from him.

"My point is I watched my father go through hell to beat this thing. He was sick all the time, vomiting and suffering through cold flashes every day. He'd throw us a beating for no reason at all. He cried, he screamed, he hit our mother on more than one occasion."

Nick held up both hands. "Whoa, look, I have never gone after Rebecca that way. I wouldn't—"

"Please don't interrupt me. There is a point to all this. I came here today fully expecting to see you bouncing off the walls and throwing up your guts."

Nick held her gaze. "The day is still young."

"There you go again, interrupting me. You're not letting me finish. Would you kindly let me say my peace so I can get out of here?"

"Anything that gets you out the door is fine with me. By all means, continue."

"Thank you." Her hands fidgeted nervously. "I believe you when you say you'd never hurt Rebecca. Not intentionally, anyway. I also believe you when you say you're going to beat your addiction. I can see that much in your eyes. But it won't be easy, like you said. There will be more nights when you're lying in bed too sick to move. I know, I watched my father go through that. I don't want you to have to do it, too."

She glanced to her right, toward the grill area. Nick followed her gaze. Ricky's friend rummaged around a large cooler while Rebecca stood to the side, waiting. Rebecca looked up and saw them. Noreen smiled and waved. "Wave to Rebecca, Nicholas."

Nick waved.

Noreen surprised him by taking his free hand in hers. He started to pull back but she wrapped her fingers around his and held him there. "I want to spare you the torture, Nicholas." She released her grip and retracted her hand.

Nick pulled back, utterly confused. "What—" He stopped. She had slipped something into his hand. Instinctively, as he had done since the age of fifteen, Nick dropped his hand below the table and peeked at its contents.

The ten-bag of heroin was smaller than the bundles Nick used to buy with Angie. The translucent green plastic of the bag turned its contents into jade crystals that reflected the weak light that reached under the table. Nick felt the bag, ran his index finger on its surface, turned it over and watched the crystals catch the light.

It was only when he felt an unpleasant pressure on his chest that he realized he was holding his breath. Nick exhaled and looked up. Aunt Noreen sat back with her arms folded across her chest and the ghost of a smile on her lips. It was the first honest smile she had produced since her arrival at Springbrook. She looked pleased, a parent who had just watched their child unwrap a much-coveted present on Christmas morning.

"I—I—"

"You're welcome, Nicholas," Aunt Noreen purred. "I just don't like the idea of someone in my family going through that kind of pain. Truly, I don't. Just put it in your pocket before Rebecca comes back. I don't want her to know I'm helping you."

Nick stammered. Without conscious effort he did as his aunt told him. He felt the slight bulge in his pocket. It seemed heavy, but he found its weight reassuring. He resisted the urge to touch it again, to take it out and make something with which he could smoke it right there with everyone watching. His mouth was suddenly full of the taste of the white smoke. Sweat sprung up on his brow. He did not wipe it away.

"How did you get this in here?" It was a stupid question and he knew it the moment he asked.

Aunt Noreen waved a dismissive hand. "Who's going to search an old lady? And what makes you think I'd stand for that in the first place?"

Nick blinked. It made sense. All she had to do was fix one of her withering stares at anyone who dared suggest she might be smuggling something inside. He would not have believed it himself if not for that wonderful rectangular object in his pocket.

She glanced to her right again and straitened. Nick looked and saw Rebecca was on her way back with her mother's spring water. She moved quickly until she saw they were not at each other's throats. She reached the table and placed the water in front of her mother. "Here, mom."

Aunt Noreen welcomed her with a smile. "Thank you, dear." She opened the water and took a sip.

"Everything okay here?" she asked.

"It's all fine, honey," Aunt Noreen replied. "We reached an understanding. Didn't we, Nicholas?"

Nick wiped the sweat from his forehead. He nodded mutely. They had, indeed.

Rebecca smiled as she sat. She regarded Nick and her mother with some suspicion. In the end she must have decided not to question their sudden lack of hostilities. She sipped her Coke and watched the other patients and their families enjoy the festivities.

Nick could not bring himself to look at her.

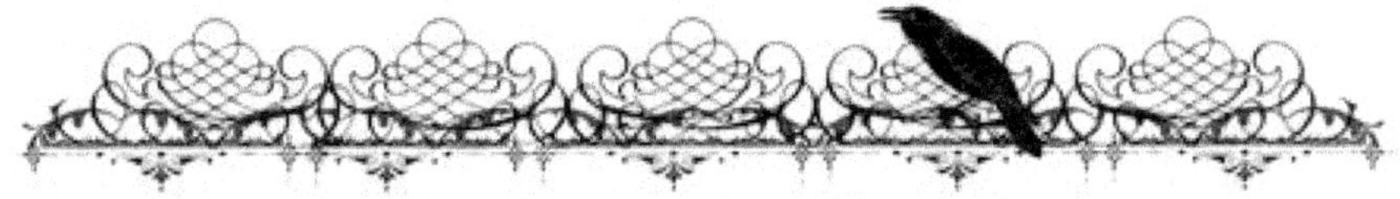

Chapter 11

You Just Remember Santos

Connelly leaned back in his chair and rubbed his eyes. He had found what Captain Calabrese wanted him to find. He resisted the urge to hurl the computer monitor off his desk. His eyes returned to the news story dated October 12, 1899. He did not read through the story again; there was no need to give himself a double dose of humiliation. He simply looked at the photograph that accompanied the story. It was grainy and indistinct but it was clear enough for Connelly.

The photograph was taken in a town called Glenwood, New Jersey. An ancient factory stood beside an equally-ancient section of railroad tracks. In the background of the photo stood a figure. It appeared slightly hunched as if it were under a heavy burden. The old photograph provided no detail; the figure was little more than a human-shaped blob of black ink. Connelly could discern that it was tall and thin but little else. The shape of its head suggested a top hat. Its resemblance to the image drawn by Dylan MacKennedy was unmistakable.

"Son of a bitch." He did not have the Shadow Man, after all. At least, not the original. It was possible they were dealing with a copycat, someone who had come across the old news articles and appropriated the trappings of the old killer. That brought him back to square one and dashed his hopes that the victims of the killer's last rampage sixteen years ago could have a bit of justice.

And Calabrese knew it. He had allowed Connelly to present his theory all the while knowing it would lead to nothing. Maybe if he had not been so excited at the idea of catching the bastard after all those years he might have picked up on what the captain had been trying to tell him. Connelly now felt like more of a fool than at any other time in his life.

His research had revealed other copycats since the murders in Glenwood. There were seven unsolved murders in Trenton, New Jersey in 1920, and the same number again in 1952. There were no eyewitness reports from that spree and no connection was ever made to the unsolved cases upstate. Years later an armchair detective had discovered the similarities in the Trenton killer's MO to what had transpired ninety miles to the north. It was a decent bit of detective work, Connelly had to admit. He doubted anyone, himself included, would have tied the cases together, not after a span of fifty-three years. It was nothing that would hold up in court, of course, but after more than sixty years, odds were the perp was dead now, anyway.

The next story was from Willingboro, New Jersey. The series of four unsolved murders ended in 1974. There was one eyewitness. He described a tall, thin man in black clothing and wearing a top hat. The same armchair detective noted the identical wound patterns on the Willingboro and Trenton murder victims. He lamented the absence of any autopsy records from the Glenwood victims but postulated they were likely the same as those from the other towns.

The internet cowboys came up with a single suspect from 1999, a man named Henry Wade whose death coincided with the end of the Shadow Man killings. Connelly read the guesswork done by the armchair detectives and found it ridiculous. For one thing, Henry Wade had an ironclad alibi for the first murder and the last two. This did nothing to stop the conspiracy theorists from naming him Suspect Number One. Connelly shrugged and continued his research.

The Google search even found a song titled "The Shadow Man" by a metal band in Connecticut. Connelly watched the short video of the band of longhairs playing the song on stage in a smoke-choked dive that reminded him of the seedier bars in Philly. The song lyrics helpfully scrolled across the bottom of the video as the lead singer, top hat in place, screamed into his microphone: *The Shadow Man rules the streets at night/Better lock your doors and hide inside. The Shadow Man rules his Kingdom Come/He lives for homicide.* "Charming," Connelly remarked to himself.

And now they had someone just down the road in Manayunk. It was still possible they were dealing with the same person who managed to slip away back in 1999 but Connelly would not hold his breath. His search of inmates with similar lockdown and release dates turned up nothing. It was unlikely the bastard had decided to come out of retirement after sixteen years, anyway. So they were dealing with someone new.

And, of course, it was out of his jurisdiction, in any case. So unless the murderer with the knowledge of history decided to set up shop in Philly, Connelly was finished with his personal and unofficial investigation.

He sighed and brought up the case files from the day before.

****

Nick lay in bed and stared at the ceiling. He replayed the scene from Family and Friends Day in his head over and over like a video clip. Aunt Noreen being just as vile as he expected her to be and then slipping him a ten-bag when no one was looking. And he knew everyone in the backyard was completely oblivious to what had transpired.

He looked over each person out there for a hint that he had been caught. They were too busy going about their day, enjoying their time with their family members and close friends, to pay any attention to what Nick was doing with the old lady. He expected Sarah or maybe Buckley to figure it out right away; neither gave a hint that they even suspected anything. He figured he could fool Buckley. She might be very well-acquainted with the signs, but she was not an addict. If she knew ninety-nine ways to spot someone holding, Nick knew three hundred ways to conceal the truth. Sarah was a different story. Addicts had a sixth sense when it came to knowing who was holding and who was not. But Sarah was around him quite often after the event was over and he caught no sign that she knew about the white powder in his pocket. Nick knew he was good at covering his tracks; he did not know until today he was *that* good. Or perhaps Sarah was simply out of practice. Either way…

He still could not believe his aunt did it, even with the evidence in his hand under his pillow. His fingers gently stroked the small green bag. He could feel its contents shift at his touch. The taste of the white smoke had stayed with him the whole day. He had even resorted to bumming a cigarette from Patty after evening meal just to get rid of it. Nothing worked, not even Curran's industrial-strength mouthwash. So he lay in bed and tasted the white smoke and fondled the little green baggie under his pillow.

He could not smoke it, of course, not without being caught and tossed out. He considering trying to palm a syringe from the nurse's station but he quickly abandoned that idea. There was simply no way he could get in there and grab one without Karen or Carol seeing him. That left him with one option. He disliked snorting the stuff. The few times he did it in the past it left him with a splitting headache that took hours to subside. But beggars could not be choosers, not in Springbrook.

So he would wait for Curran to fall asleep. A quick glance at his roommate told Nick it would not be long. The man's eyes were already half-lidded and the shitty movie playing on the SyFy Channel would not be enough to keep him awake. Wait for those eyes to close and sneak into the bathroom. Run the water to deaden the sound of him snorting the H and then stay in there until he was presentable. He did not know how long that would take. He had never gone this long without it and his tolerance might not be what it once was. However long it took it would be worth it.

Nick simply had to wait. He was good at that.

****

He stands in the middle of the street facing a dilapidated three-family house. It is familiar to him, but the absence of functioning streetlights in his immediate vicinity stymies his attempts to identify his location. Two of the windows on the second floor are lit up although the shades are drawn. The bottom and top floors are dark. He does not know the time, but he gets the impression it is not that late. He concludes the second floor apartment is the only one occupied. That is fine with him. That is where his business brings him this night, anyway.

Someone passes in front of one of the illuminated windows. He has no way of knowing who it is, but his heart picks up the pace.

He can tell something bad (wonderful) is about to happen. All he needs to do is settle in and enjoy the show.

Voices from down the street, getting louder. He turns and sees two people, a man and a woman, both in their late-teens, making their way in his direction. He moves silently back across the street and takes a position behind an old, beat-up Ford. There is no need to duck behind the vehicle; there is no light here and the two new arrivals will be unable to see him. He watches their progress.

They're chatting and laughing, not a care in the world. He can't make out what they're saying, but the woman lets out a loud, sharp bark of a laugh. The sound is unpleasant and Nick scowls. But only for a moment. The woman and her male companion can do nothing to darken his mood. He considers coming out of the shadows to greet them, but he decides against it. His business is not with them.

Or is it? They stop in front of the three-family house and mount the concrete steps leading to the front door. At first he thinks they are residents, but they ring the center doorbell. He looks up and sees someone cross in front of the second floor windows again. "It's Henry," the male says when he knocks again. The door opens a moment later. Henry and his female companion enter the structure and the door closes behind them.

Nick moves back into the middle of the street. It occurs to him he is no longer flowing across the ground like he did in the airport parking garage. He's walking now, one foot in front of the other. He should be sad, losing this marvelous and unfamiliar mode of mobility, but somehow it makes him feel better. He is stronger now than he was in Newark, or even Manayunk. That causes him to smile.

He observes the windows on the middle floor. Someone is silhouetted in the window and is then joined by a second person.

They are facing each other and talking. They make a gesture that looks like they're shaking hands, but Nick knows what's really going on. They're exchanging cash for little bags of white powder. Henry and his female companion are not friends of the apartment's occupants, they're customers. Nick's smile widens.

His feet are moving again. Up the concrete steps and to the front door. He reaches for the doorbell, but stops himself. This is a dream, after all, why bother? In fact, he doesn't need to use the door handle, either. Can he still use that flowing-across-the-ground ability? He thinks about it and it happens. Nick slides beneath the door and stands inside the first floor landing. What a wonderful ability to have, he thinks. He looks up the stairs. All is darkness, but he hears voices coming from the next floor.

He mounts the steps slowly. They are old and made of wood but they do not creak under his weight. They should, they did the last time he was here, the night Angie died. This time the sagging wood does not seem to notice his presence at all. That ability will certainly come in handy when he sneaks out of Springbrook tomorrow after he samples Aunt Noreen's unexpected gift.

Nick stops in front of the door to the second floor apartment. The voices are louder but he still can't make out much of the conversation. There's a TV on somewhere inside and it's making it difficult to follow what's being said. That's okay. The conversation taking place on the other side of the door is largely irrelevant. It'll stop completely when he walks inside.

But he doesn't open the door. He utilizes his favorite new trick and flows beneath it.

The apartment is a dive, exactly how one might picture it when seeing the house from the outside. The furniture is old and worn, the hardwood floors are pitted and lacking any kind of coating. The walls are bare of framed photos or posters of any kind.

Ashtrays filled to overflowing dot the floor, the counters and the single end table that looks like it might have been manufactured around the time Philadelphia still had two baseball teams. The television looks new, however. It's a Sony big screen HD and it looks totally out of place in these surroundings.

What draws his attention, though, is the coffee table in front of the decaying sofa. Its surface is covered with neatly-arranged bags of white powder of varying sizes. A scale coated with a light film of white stuff occupies one corner of the table. A woman who looks familiar sits on the sofa and watches the two new arrivals deal with the Hispanic gentleman holding a bundle of stamp bags in his hand. She looks bored, but Nick doesn't buy it; her hand rests beneath the pillow next to her and he has no doubt she has her finger on a very big trigger just in case Henry and his female companion try something stupid.

Nick plans to save them the effort.

He spreads his arms like a rock star emerging onto the stage. The reaction from the four people in front of him is immediate and dramatic.

The man with the bags retreats a few steps and reaches for something behind his back. Henry's girlfriend screams and throws her arms out. One of her hands finds Henry's arm and her fingers wrap around it like a vice. Henry yelps and backpedals a few steps. The wad of bills in his hand flutters in all directions. The woman on the couch springs to her feet and Nick sees he was correct; she has a handgun. She waves it around in front of her and screams, "Santos!"

It takes Nick a moment to realize the room's occupants have suddenly gone blind. Or perhaps the power went out. No, he can still hear the TV even if the screen has gone dark. And besides, he can still see just fine. He knows the rules of a dream allow for some pretty fucked up scenarios, but he never realized spontaneous and shared blindness is one of them. Well, so what? As long as he can still see...

"What the hell's goin' on here?" Henry shouts.

"They're pullin' some shit, Santos!" the woman with the gun shouts.

Santos is whipping his head about frantically. He, too, has drawn a gun. He's pointing it in every direction, aiming at nothing.

Henry's female friend is backing up slowly, in the direction of the door. She's tugging on Henry's arm, but he seems rooted to the spot.

"Everyone calm down," Henry shouts. "No one's trying anything, okay? We just wanna get the fuck outta here."

The girl is only a few feet in front of Nick, close enough to touch. He reaches out a hand and places it gently on her shoulder.

She screams and whirls.

Santos's girlfriend whips the gun around in that direction and fires. Her target and Henry both scream. The first shot hits nothing, but her second and third shots take the girl. One hits her in the chest and the other embeds itself in her forehead. Her knees buckle and she collapses in a heap in front of him. Quite a shot, Nick thinks, admiring the woman's marksmanship. Apparently blind but she still managed a head shot. Bravo!

The girl fires again and this time Santos joins her. They fire blindly and empty their guns. Henry is dancing about holding both hands in front of his head. He's trying to get to the door, but he obviously has no idea where he is. He's heading for the shaded window when one of Santos's shots finds his calf. Henry squeals and goes down, clutching his leg. Blood flows unimpeded from the wound.

The girl is still squeezing the trigger although she is out of ammunition. Santos is a bit more with it; he drops the spent clip and grabs for another in his back pocket.

"You picked a really stupid thing to do, Maricon," Santos shouts into the room. "No one plays me, got that?" He inserts the new clip with blind, practiced ease. He has no trouble locating Henry; the man is thrashing about on the floor and grunting. "Where you at, esé? Huh? You think you can pull some shit on me? Huh? Is that it?" He fires in the direction of Henry's whimpers. The bullet chews up some of the old hardwood, but doesn't come close to its target.

Henry knows enough to shut up. He stops moving. Nick can still hear him breathing, but Santos seems oblivious. He takes a few tentative steps in Henry's direction, gun held out in front of him.

"Did you get the fucker?" his girl asks.

"Quiet," Santos hisses.

It is all actually quite amusing to Nick. He remembers suddenly what he has stashed under his pillow back in the real world and he wants to get to it sooner rather than later. But he still has business here. And quite important *business at that.*

The girl is meaningless to him; it's Santos he wants. Santos, who hooked him up and probably shrugged—if he had any reaction at all—to the news of Angie's death. Even if the fucker dropped to his knees and screamed his grief to the heavens, here he is, still dealing the shit.

Nick glides across the floor with grace. His newfound dexterity allows him to sidestep the female corpse at his feet soundlessly. He comes to a stop in front of Santos's girlfriend. She must really be blind because he is no more than a foot in front of her and she has no idea. She's holding her useless gun in front of her, but she's aiming it at the floor, probably afraid of hitting Santos. Even if she had a full clip loaded and her finger on the trigger it would make no difference.

Nick watches his hand shoot forward. Fingers that end in sharp points close around her throat. She gasps, but is unable to produce any other sound. Instinctively she drops the gun and her fingers wrap themselves around the hand at her throat.

Nick lifts her from the floor easily. Not only can he do cool shit like slide under closed doors, he's also very strong. He has never felt more powerful or alive, not even after inhaling clouds of white smoke.

The girl's feet scissor the air. She lands a couple of feeble kicks but they barely register for him. It would be the easiest thing in the world to snap her neck, but no. For reasons he cannot articulate he wants more. *He digs his fingers (talons) into the flesh of her neck. Blood spurts out and she tries to scream. In a simple, savage movement, he tears out the front of her throat.*

Free of the hand holding her, the woman hits the floor hard. One hand wraps itself weakly around the empty space where her throat used to be. She produces feeble, pathetic gurgling sounds for a moment.

Nick drops the wet flesh from his hand. He turns his attention to Santos.

The drug dealer still has his hands on his gun and he's looking about the room. He must have heard the body land on the floor and he's trying to puzzle out what, exactly, has transpired. "Maria? Maria, where you at? Say something, babe."

It is not Maria who answers. Even dreams need some sense of continuity. So Nick does the honors himself.

"You just remember Santos," he says.

He is surprised by the sound of his own voice. It is low, guttural, the growl of a death metal singer.

Santos screams and fires blindly around the room. One or two of the shots find Nick, but he feels no pain. He has discovered yet another new ability. He smiles.

Santos fires the gun dry. He panics. He must have had only one spare clip on him. There are undoubtedly more stashed around the apartment. Someone like him would not stop at two clips when they had all this H and cash to protect. He stumbles back, into the television, and knocks it off its stand. The picture is still missing but Nick can hear some Spanish news reporter droning on about something. Santos puts his back to the wall.

Nick advances on him. He holds his position perhaps five feet in front of Santos. The man is nearly paralyzed. His eyes are wide and wild, darting back and forth. His breathing is fast and ragged. Nick can smell the fear radiating off his target in waves. He thinks he might be getting an erection.

"Santos got whachoo need," Nick whispers.

Santos screams.

Nick has the time of his life.

****

Nick awoke in time to feel his stomach about to purge itself. He kicked the covers off and dashed for the bathroom as quickly as his bad leg would allow. He did not quite make it. He doubled over and the vomiting commenced a few feet shy of the toilet. He had the presence of mind to crawl the rest of the way and get at least the end of it aimed in the proper direction. He clutched the sides of the toilet with both hands and threw up what little remained of the leftover cheeseburgers he had for dinner.

"Damn, man," he heard Curran say from somewhere behind him.

Nick lifted his head only when he was sure he was finished voiding his stomach. He looked at Curran through wet eyes and offered a weak smile. "Hey," he said, and drooled onto the bathroom floor.

Curran waved a hand in front of his face. "God*damn*, man. And you were doing good, too." He stepped around the vomit on the floor and got his hands under Nick's arms and hoisted him to his feet. "C'mon, if you're finished redecorating the bathroom I'll help you back to bed. Then I'll call for Peter with a mop and a bucket of sulfuric acid to get rid of that shit."

"I'm done," Nick said, weakly.

"You have no idea how glad I am to hear that. You know, though, it's your turn to clean up. House rules. The first one's on them, we clean up anything after that."

Nick allowed Curran to just about carry him back to his bed. Once he was down he heard Curran walk to the corner where the camera was. As his roommate called for the night custodian, Nick became aware of the small object in his right hand. He had enough strength to lift his head a few inches from the pillow and look down.

Cupped in his hand was the green baggie courtesy of Aunt Noreen. Nick had held onto it the whole time.

Chapter 12

Snow Melting Before His Eyes

Carol had accompanied Peter upstairs to check on Nick. She took his temperature, his blood pressure, all the usual nonsense. She even talked the old man into cleaning up the disaster in the bathroom. By the time Peter declared the bathroom to be habitable again, Carol had given Nick two Aspirin and watched him swallow them. She left with her usual, "Call me if you need anything," and then she was gone. Nick watched her leave and then turned his attention to Curran.

His roommate was lying on his side, a wide grin on his face. "I think you do that shit just so she'll come up here. I never notice you throwing up your guts during the day when Karen's on duty."

"Actually, I do it so you can spend time with Peter."

Curran laughed. "Go fuck yourself."

"It's more like luck of the draw. On the few occasions I got sick on the outside, it was always at night or first thing in the morning. That's what happens when a heroin addict doesn't get his fix."

Curran pursed his lips. "Well, I guess that means you're still clean. I'm impressed."

Don't be, Nick thought. *You have no idea what's in my hand or how it got there.* He said, "Well, I'm an impressive sorta guy."

"You impressed Sarah, that's for sure."

"Oh?"

Curran shrugged. "I might have overheard something she said to her brother earlier. Something about a certain man with a gimpy leg she thought wasn't a total douche. I wasn't gonna say nothin' on account of the rules here. But once you get out…"

Nick smiled and rested his head on his hands.

"Just goes to show she has shitty taste in men," Curran added.

Nick threw one of his pillows without looking. Curran laughed and threw it back.

The conversation trailed off and after a while Nick stole a glance at Curran and found the man fast asleep. Nick brought out the small green bag and looked at it. There was very little light so he hopped silently out of bed and limped to the window.

The nearest streetlight was some distance away but it provided enough illumination for him to watch the light play in the crystals. It occurred to him he had never done this. Whenever he got a new supply or was about to smoke up he had never stopped to admire the color and texture of the powder. It had always gone straight onto the foil and then straight into his lungs. He had never taken the time to actually *look* at it. *That was when the supply was limitless and so were the opportunities to use it*, he reasoned. *These days, not so much.*

Nick caught movement from below his window. He cupped the green baggie out of habit. Carol stepped away from the bushes and walked slowly toward the front entrance. He watched her take one last hit from her cigarette and then toss it into the caddy beside the doors. She disappeared inside.

Nick smirked. "I see you," he whispered. It was perfectly acceptable to smoke that shit, but not the contents of the green baggie. That had never made sense to Nick. "And you're a nurse, too. You should know better." He laughed and returned to bed.

For no reason whatsoever, his mind turned to his last night with Angie. Specifically, he thought of their visit to Santos's apartment. He whispered, "Santos got whachoo need." Then he was asleep. The little green baggie was once again under his pillow.

****

Connelly stepped out of his car and counted three other police units all parked in front of the three-family tenement. He walked up the concrete steps and ducked under the yellow police tape and entered the building. He could hear the activity on the second floor. He climbed the narrow, winding staircase with its strip of faded, worn carpet in the center and got his first look at the crime scene.

He counted five cops and four dead bodies. "Everyone out," he said. Five sets of eyes looked up. The officers' reactions ranged from relief to irritation, but they stopped what they were doing and filed through the door without saying a word. Once the room was clear Connelly shut the door and locked it.

He surveyed the bodies one at a time. One of the female victims died of one, possibly two gunshot wounds. He found two guns in the room and noted the place cards left by one of the officers, one beside each weapon. The other female was missing most of her throat and lay in a wide pool of her own congealing blood. One male was decapitated; the other's head was crushed, as if someone had stomped up and down on it. This last victim also bore a bullet wound in his left leg.

Connelly took notes and did his best not to contaminate the scene any more than had the beat cops before him. He avoided stepping into any of the blood on the floor, of which there were buckets, something else the beat cops had managed to do.

It was when he walked around the smashed TV that he gasped. A word had been scrawled across the back of the Sony flatscreen. Connelly leaned in and examined the flowing script. "Son of a bitch," he whispered. He snapped a couple photographs and continued surveying the room. All in all he spent two hours inside the apartment. When he was finished he drove back to the precinct house.

He made a few calls and received a few emails and even one fax. He organized it all and when he felt he had his ducks in a row he went downstairs to Captain Calabrese's office. He knocked on the door and waited. Calabrese told him to come in. Connelly entered and sat down and placed his paperwork on his lap.

"What can I do for you, Detective?"

"That quadruple homicide on Dikeman Street, I just came from there. Wondered if you wanted to see the report."

Calabrese extended his hand. Connelly gave him the paperwork and sat back. The captain flipped through the report, pausing here and there, and then placed it on his desk. "Not bad as far as preliminary work goes. What are you thinking?"

"I'm thinking we have a copycat Shadow Man is what I'm thinking. I'm thinking this is the same guy who did those people in Manayunk, too. And the two in Phoenixville. I tossed in a report of a woman who was assaulted at Newark Airport a week ago. I'll explain why in a minute" He saw the look from Calabrese and he held up both hands. "It's not that big a stretch, Cap."

"Plastic Man couldn't stretch that far," Calabrese replied.

Connelly rifled through the paperwork until he found the map he printed online. He held it up. Four locations were circled. He pointed to the first. "This is the airport. A woman named Melanie Allen was brutally assaulted by a man she could not identify because it was too dark. Her wounds were serious but non-life-threatening. Those same kind of wounds were evident on the two victims in Phoenixville." He pointed to the second circle. "According to the wife her husband had gone to Newark Airport to pick up their daughter from a trip to see her grandparents in New Mexico. I think our guy hitched a ride with them, most likely without their knowledge. I can't imagine this man giving a stranger a ride with his young daughter in the car. He probably snuck into either the backseat or maybe the trunk when they weren't looking. With me so far?"

Calabrese nodded noncommittally. "Go on."

Connelly pointed to the third circle. "The six homicides in Manayunk. A backyard pot party that went bad. Six dead, one survivor. A young child, the same one who drew that sketch I showed you yesterday."

Calabrese did not quite roll his eyes but he came close.

"Please, Captain, hear me out. I think I'm on to something."

Calabrese spread his hands. "By all means, continue."

"Even Manayunk PD knows that wasn't a drug hit. There was weed everywhere. And cash, too. What kind of drug dealer or gangbanger would leave that behind? So we're dealing with someone who doesn't give a shit about either." His finger traced a line from the third circle to the fourth. "Dikeman Street right here in West Philly. Same thing. This time the narcotics involved were even more valuable. There was coke, crack and heroin all over the place. And more cash, too."

"The media already made the suggestion there's a serial killer on the loose in Manayunk. It was on the news this morning. The chief is pissed." Calabrese leaned forward in his chair. "But none of what you've said so far proves it's your carbon copy Shadow Man, Mike."

Connelly shook his head. "It can't be the same guy we all heard about back in the day, no. I checked into that, like you told me to. The original Shadow Man murders took place in 1899 in North Jersey. Since then there have been various murders all over the Northeast. They go on for a time and then they just stop. There doesn't seem to be any rhyme or reason to when each killer starts and then ends his killing spree, unfortunately. I'd say this is someone who knows history and is using this story as window dressing. That's why he started at the airport. The one suspect from the 1999 murders killed himself at the airport. The murders seemed to stop at the same time. Now, that suspect was rejected on account of he had a pretty solid alibi, but it's still well-known to Shadow Man enthusiasts that he was a suspect. So I think our asshole is picking up where the previous asshole left off."

Calabrese raised an eyebrow. "Still not convinced, but what else ya got?"

"Not much, unfortunately. The investigators in Phoenixville and Manayunk are testing for DNA, see if they can ID the perp that way. Our own guys will get on that, too. If we can match this prick to someone we already know, we'll at least have a target."

Calabrese said, "Very well."

"There is one more thing, Cap." Connelly pulled the sheet of paper from his back pocket and handed it to Calabrese. "I took this photo with my phone at the Dikeman Street scene."

Calabrese unfolded the paper and looked at the photo. "'Wade.' Looks like it's written in blood."

"It is. There's no report of anything like this found at the other scenes, but I asked both Phoenixville and Manayunk to do another sweep. I'm guessing they'll find the murderer's calling card there, too."

"Assuming it's the same perp. What makes you think they'll find it?"

Connelly smiled. "Because that same name was written in blood at the crime scenes at least as far back as 1952."

Calabrese's eyebrows marched north. "That's confirmed?"

"Uh huh. It was kept out of the press but the police reports mentioned it. It happened in every suspected Shadow Man spree since then. Might have happened before that, too, but there's no way to confirm, unfortunately."

Calabrese nodded and pursed his lips. "I am officially impressed. Good work, detective."

"Thanks."

"Any idea who Wade is?"

Connelly shook his head. "Beyond the dead guy at the airport? No. Not yet. I'm working that angle, too."

Calabrese placed the folded paper atop the others and handed them back to Connelly. "If you're right about all this, and it's a still a stretch, we'll have to find this guy and quick. The last thing we need is a panic out there."

Connelly nodded his agreement. "I'll let you know as soon as I find anything." He took the papers and exited the office.

****

Around the time Connelly was pulling up to the three-family on Dikeman Street, Nick awoke feeling strangely refreshed. He had managed to fall back asleep after spotting Carol outside and this time he did not dream. He glanced over at Curran and found his roommate still asleep, snoring lightly. Nick glanced out the

159

window. The sun was already up and he could hear birds singing their morning anthems. The slight breeze wafting through the window smelled of late-summer. For the first time since his arrival at Springbrook, Nick awoke with a smile.

He ambled into the bathroom. After his morning piss he stepped into the shower. He kept an eye on the towel he placed on the vanity, just in case Curran needed an emergency trip to the bathroom. It would not do for his roommate to come in, move the towel, and find what Nick had hidden within its folds.

The hot water felt good on his skin and he breathed in the steam. His head was remarkably clear this morning, so much so that Nick at first did not know what to make of his heightened senses. He seemed able to smell and feel things much more vividly than usual. It made him think of Daredevil, the blind superhero whose adventures he read about as a kid. "I am the Man Without Fear," Nick whispered.

He exited the shower and toweled off. His eyes were fixed on the little green baggie and he made sure to stay close to the vanity just in case Curran or Karen came aknockin'. Once he was dry he wrapped the towel around his middle and stood in front of the mirror. The baggie was now in his hand. He looked at it, then at himself in the mirror.

It had been weeks since he last used. Was he really about to break that streak? Yes. Yes, he was. Nick opened the baggie. He held it beneath his nostrils and sniffed tentatively. The contents of the baggie smelled wonderfully familiar. It reminded him of when Angie would come home with a new supply and how excited he would be to see her.

In his mind's eye, Angie morphed into Sarah. Sarah, who had been offended (but not surprised) when he asked if she was holding. The same woman who seemed genuinely determined to quit her habit and lead what addicts referred to as the "civilian life." He and Angie spent years scoffing at those people. And now it seemed he would scoff at Sarah, as well.

Before Nick realized he was going to move he took a single step to his right. He upended the open baggie and watched its beautiful, magical contents spill into the toilet bowl. A voice that sounded suspiciously like Angie's screamed, *No! What the fuck are you doing? That was Grade-A shit*! Angie was followed by Aunt Noreen, who lamented, *You just can't do anything right. You know how much that shit cost me? Or where I had to go to get it? You ungrateful fuck!*

They were right, both of them. Good God, what had he done?

Nick dropped to one knee and nearly reached into the bowl before common sense intervened and stopped his hand an inch from the water. The white powder floated on the surface, precious snow melting before his eyes. He did not cry, but he was unable to stop a whimper from escaping from somewhere within.

Slowly his eyes moved from the dissipating white grains to the baggie in his hand. There was little left inside. Certainly not enough to get him high, but maybe enough to at least give him that old, familiar burning sensation he knew so well.

Nick lifted the bag to his nose.

Before he could snort the pathetic remains of his aunt's surprise gift he threw himself at the sink. He held the baggie under the tap and let loose the water. It filled and quickly overflowed the baggie. Thin white swirls swam within the green plastic. Nick kept the baggie in place. It seemed like an hour but was more likely ten or twelve seconds before there was nothing but water inside the baggie. Nick squeezed it and water spurted out. The tears did come, then. The tremors followed a moment later.

It took him some time but when he finally regained control of himself he tore the baggie and spiked its remains into the waste basket. He made it a step toward the door before he went back and retrieved it. He wrapped it in toilet paper and dropped it into the toilet and flushed.

Nick exited the bathroom.

He was the first downstairs, something that had occurred rarely during his tenure at Springbrook. He even managed to get down to the media room before Ricky. Nick needed to sit after the catastrophe in the bathroom. He plopped down on the sofa and scooped up the remote.

The TV was tuned to the local news. Nick almost surfed past it before he caught the scroll at the bottom. After a mention of local sports was the message: POLICE FEAR SERIAL KILLER AT LARGE IN MANAYUNK AREA. Nick raised an eyebrow. That was only about fifteen, twenty minutes away. He thumbed through his mental rolodex for anyone he knew in Manayunk and came up empty. He might have been there with Angie on one of her weed-buying excursions but he could not be sure. Nick shrugged and brought up the cable guide.

He quickly exited it when the corner image on the screen changed to a house Nick recognized. It was a three-family in a rundown neighborhood Nick had last visited the night Angie was killed. He leaned closer to the TV, as if proximity would show he was incorrect. He was not. Several police cars and a CSI van were parked in front of Santos's apartment building. Yellow police tape was stretched across the front porch. Several officers and people in white coats walked in and out of the front door. Nick fumbled with the remote and increased the TV's volume.

"Revisiting our top story, police have confirmed four persons are dead in West Philadelphia this morning. They have yet to comment beyond the basics of this active crime scene. Once again, in case you're just joining us, four people are confirmed dead in this house on Dikeman Street. Precinct Captain Matthew Calabrese has scheduled a press conference for noon today. We'll bring that event to you live."

Nick dropped the remote and studied the tenement. He knew the bottom and top floors of the home were vacant. There was no doubt the bodies would be in Santos's apartment. "Santos got whachoo need," Nick whispered. Except, well, probably not anymore. Nick had no idea how he knew Santos was one of the four victims mentioned by the anchorwoman, but he knew just the same. Santos was dead. So was that chickie he had with him, the one who had eyed Nick during his one and only visit to see the man. She had tried to look bored but Nick caught her several times stealing a glance at him. Her hand flexed beneath the pillow and he knew she had a gun aimed at him. He never caught her name, never asked. He simply did not care. And now she was dead, too.

The newscast had moved on. The image now was of the backyard of a much nicer home. More police tape stretched around the fence enclosing the yard. Nick had missed the transition to this story. He reached for the remote again but he froze when the scene was replaced by the photograph of a young child, a boy who smiled into the camera. It was obviously a school picture, taken during a happier time.

"...the only survivor of what Manayunk Police describe as a massacre, a drug deal gone bad. Four-year-old Dylan MacKennedy has been released into the care of his grandparents..."

"Dylan," Nick said. The boy seemed familiar somehow, even though Nick knew beyond doubt he had never seen the child before today. The child's photo vanished, replaced by the previous view of the home's backyard. The camera lingered on the back porch, where a glass top table stood among several knocked-over chairs.

"Her name was Miki," Nick whispered. "Her real name was Mikal but she went by Miki." Nick closed his eyes. He could almost see the woman standing on that porch. There were two men with her but their features were vague. He could not make them out. "One is your husband," Nick continued. "Not sure about the other one. Brother, maybe?" Nick's eyes snapped open. "Jesus Christ."

How did he know this? Even if this turned out to be the house Angie visited he had not gone inside. He stayed in the car and listened to a block of Nirvana on WMMR. He had no memory of Angie mentioning the names of the people who lived there. But Nick knew. Among those six dead people was a woman named Miki and her husband.

The news had moved beyond the slaughter in the MacKennedy backyard to something else. Nick tuned it out. He felt numb. The heightened senses he had enjoyed just a few minutes ago upstairs were now gone. He thought of the heroin he flushed and the torn and broken baggie that swirled inside the bowl before vanishing from his sight.

And he thought of a small child who had watched his parents torn apart in front of him. The murderer had seen Dylan, too, but he was uninterested in the child. He had to make his way to West Philly and take care of Santos. And then?

Nick did not know that answer to that. But he suspected he would before long.

Chapter 13

Something Worth Seeing

Nick kept mostly to himself during the morning meeting. Curran took his turn at the plate and eventually yielded the floor to Jessica. Nick listened to their stories and their proclamations of sobriety, but his heart was not in it. He thought of Miki MacKennedy and Santos. He thought of the heroin given him by Aunt Noreen that by now had made its way into the river, gone forever. He thought of his dreams.

In a horror movie, it would be revealed that Nick himself was the killer. That was ridiculous no matter which way he looked at it. He had dreamed of killing those people, that was true. But he had never left Springbrook, and it would be impossible to go to all those places with his leg in its present condition, to say nothing of flowing across the floor of a parking garage or slipping beneath a door. So how did he know so much about the murdered people? Nick had no answer.

After the meeting he sat with Sarah and Jenna. Nick pushed down his anxiety and honestly tried to enjoy the girls' company. The chitchat was lightweight stuff, bouncing between the next selection for movie night (*Sleepless in Seattle* was the frontrunner) to the results of last night's *American Idol*. Nick was entirely ambivalent about both topics but he could fake interest with the best of them.

After breakfast they went outside. Nick lucked out when Curran pulled Jenna away for something, leaving him alone with Sarah. As Curran stole her away, he looked over his shoulder and smiled at Nick. He mouthed, "You owe me."

Nick appreciated the gesture. Being outside had brought back some of the good feelings with which he had awoken. He did not feel quite as good as he had three hours before but it was still better than he had felt at any time since he first stepped through the doors of Springbrook.

And Sarah looked particularly attractive this morning. She wore a low cut top and cutoff jean shorts and the angle of the sun created a corona around her hair. She smiled at him and Nick felt his heart palpitate. He could not remember feeling this way for anyone before. Not Angie or any of his past girlfriends. This was unchartered territory as far as he was concerned.

"You look better, Nick," Sarah began. "I mean, not just better than yesterday or the day before. You look better than I've seen you so far. I think this place is finally starting to agree with you."

Nick shrugged. "About time, right?" *Plus, I flushed a ten-bag down the toilet this morning. How's that for progress?* He did not say it but it was on the tip of his tongue.

"You'll get there," Sarah replied. She placed her hand on his. Nick's heart picked up the pace. "We'll all get there. That's what this place is all about."

"Suppose so."

They sat in silence for several moments. Nick noted that Sarah did not remove her hand. It rested there as casually and naturally as if they were an old couple together for decades. He hoped the move was intentional on her part. Nick certainly had no intention of ending the contact. He knew she had left her hand there on purpose when Karen emerged through the sliding glass door and Sarah pulled her hand back quickly.

Nick smiled despite his disappointment. *She knew. If Karen hadn't come out...*

"I heard Buckley is planning another field trip for the week after next."

Nick raised an eyebrow. The thought of being somewhere other than Springbrook, especially in Sarah's company, appealed to him. "Any idea where?"

"Not a clue. Buckley likes to spring shit like that on the patients. But I have to admit, most of the field trips have been fun, so it might be something to look forward to."

Nick was already looking forward to it.

"My last fieldtrip with the fine folks of Springbrook," she said, placing her hands behind her head and lacing her fingers.

Nick started. "Huh?"

"I thought you knew." Sarah bit her lip. "Um, I'm done here in three weeks. Then I get my first taste of freedom in ninety days."

Nick's mind raced. She was leaving? *Now?* He stuttered but regained his composure quickly. Sarah had probably noticed his reaction, but she gave no sign. "Well, um, that's fantastic. Good for you." He managed a smile.

"Thanks." She smiled and reached for his hand. Then she must have remembered Karen was prowling the backyard and she pulled it back. After a moment of silence, she said, "Rumor has it we're getting a new inmate tomorrow," Sarah said.

"Oh?" Nick did not give a shit. His head swam with images of Sarah walking out the front door for good.

"Well, when Richie…When Richie left, there was an open bed. Buckley wants an even number of patients here at all times. Everyone has to have a roommate. I can see her point."

Nick nodded. He still did not give a shit. "Uh huh. Any idea who?"

Sarah shook her head. "No. But it'll be a man. That much I know. So it looks like Phil will be getting a new roommate."

Nick glanced at the older man in the lounge chair by the pool reading the paper. "Well, good luck to Phil."

"Whoever the new guy is he can't be any worse than you were when you got here."

Nick turned on her quickly, but his guard dropped when he saw the smile. In a moment he was smiling, too. "Okay, okay, you got me. I guess I was kinda a dick."

"There's no 'kinda' about it." Her tone was playful, her smile, genuine. She laughed then, an honest laugh that Nick found very attractive.

After a moment, despite the bombshell she had dropped on him, he joined her.

****

Connelly stood in the break room with his arms folded across his chest and watched Captain Calabrese's press conference on the TV mounted to the wall. The room downstairs was packed with reporters outshouting each other. The questions were coming fast, and not for the first time Connelly hoped he would never be promoted and find himself behind that lectern. He had little patience for chaos, and that was the perfect word to describe the scene on TV.

Calabrese was doing his best. He appeared uncomfortable to Connelly, but the signs were subtle and he doubted anyone else would pick up on it. He hoped not, for Calabrese's sake. Once the reporters sensed a crack in the captain's armor, they would be all over him.

Connelly regretted the unfortunate timing of the press conference. As Calabrese was stepping into the conference room and the flashbulbs were going off, Connelly had received an email from one of the investigators in Manayunk. They had found the name "Wade" written in blood beneath one of the chairs on the MacKennedys' back porch. They photographed it and emailed him the image. He had yet to hear from anyone at the Phoenixville P.D. but he suspected they would find the same thing somewhere in close proximity to the dead man and his daughter. Even if they did not, Manayunk had confirmed his suspicions.

Unfortunately for Connelly, he knew no one with that name. Oh, there was that asshole who had survived the one-vehicle collision a couple months ago, but Connelly had already checked. He was in rehab with his withdrawal symptoms and an airtight alibi. Not that he suspected the man. His impression of Nicholas Wade, fleeting as it had been, was that he was mostly harmless, if not to himself. Connelly considered that a dead end.

He was missing something and he knew it. Whatever it was would have to wait. He needed to report the information from Manayunk to Calabrese. Connelly tapped his foot impatiently and waited for the press conference to end.

****

The rain started around 2:30 that afternoon. Nick and Sarah were back at their table after lunch but this time Jenna was there, stymying Nick's attempt at more alone time with Sarah. Against his will he found himself resenting Jenna's presence. Sarah was here for only another three weeks; Jenna was her roommate and she could spend every night with her. Nick's time with Sarah, on the other hand, was extremely limited. Some of the old hostility attempted a comeback, but Nick squashed it. The last thing he wanted was a confrontation with Jenna. It would do nothing but alienate Sarah, and that was something he was unwilling to do.

Their table was the only one under cover of the awning. He entertained thoughts of remaining outside even as everyone else rushed past them. His hopes went sideways when both women stood and made for the door. Sarah looked over her shoulder. "Coming inside, Nick?"

Nick stood. "Yep." He followed them through the door.

They wound up in the media room. The TV was on with several patients seated and watching. Nick stood behind Sarah as Jenna claimed an open seat next to Patty. Pedro, taking up two spaces on the sofa, stood and extended an inviting arm at Sarah and Nick. "Please."

Sarah waved him off. "It's okay, Pedro, we don't wanna take your spot."

"Nonsense," Pedro exclaimed with exaggerated chivalry. "My fat ass has sat enough today." He looked at Phil. "Let's hit the gym, m'man. We could both stand the workout."

Phil looked like a workout was the last thing on his mind. He frowned but held out his hand and Pedro grabbed it and hauled him to his feet. Pedro clapped him on the back; the older man winced and looked as if he wanted to plant one on Pedro's jaw. Instead they began their trek to the Springbrook gym.

Nick guided Sarah to the open spot of the sofa. When she was seated he plopped down next to her. He paid little attention to the television, opting instead to simply enjoy Sarah's proximity. She, on the other hand, seemed riveted to the TV.

Nick reluctantly followed her gaze.

A bald cop in dress whites was giving a press conference. A text box below read: POLICE CONFIRM KILLINGS IN MANAYUNK AND WPHIL SIMILAR.

"You believe this?" Curran gestured at the TV. "Not enough crazy shit in this city. Now there's a fucking Charlie Manson on the loose."

The press conference was replaced by the footage Nick had seen that morning. It was the backyard of the MacKennedy residence, then Santos's building. After a moment a map came up showing the two locations circled and their proximity to each other.

"Chief Calabrese would not elaborate except to say the department is working on several leads at this time," the reporter's voiceover informed them. "He reiterated his warning for residents to be aware of their surroundings. Do not let anyone into your home you do not know, do not give rides to hitchhikers, and above all, be vigilant. If you see anyone suspicious in your area you should contact the police department immediately."

"Don't let anyone into your house," Curran said with disgust. "No shit, really? Well, there goes my plan for Friday night."

Ricky laughed. Nick did not.

Nick realized Sarah had placed her hand within his. He glanced up at her.

"That doesn't sound good at all," she told him.

Nick had no reply. He had done his best to forget about the morning's news and how it seemed to match his dreams. He felt his good mood leave him; even holding Sarah's hand did not bring it back.

"They'll catch the bastard," Curran assured her. "Don't you worry about that. Gonna be some crackhead or something, you watch."

I don't think so, Nick thought. *I don't think so at all.* He patted Sarah's hand. It was feeble as far as comforting gestures go, but it was all he could manage.

****

Connelly sat at his computer. He scrolled lazily through old reports and tried his best to stay awake. He was close, he could feel it. The old familiar rush of excitement he felt every time he broke through a case was on the fringes of his consciousness, flitting about, narrowly out of reach. He knew the answer was right there, but somehow it continued to elude him. He had felt this way for the last hour, when Phoenixville finally sent him an email with a photograph of the name "Wade" scrawled in a young girl's blood inside the glove box of her father's car. The news had come far too late for Calabrese's press conference but it served to show Connelly he was on the right track. Not that it seemed to be doing him any good.

He was missing something. Something obvious, he knew. He kept returning to Newark Airport. It was nothing to do with the two victims from Phoenixville or the woman who escaped with deep lacerations on her arms and shoulder. It was something else. Worse, it was something he had already read. He had all the pieces right in front of him and yet the fucking puzzle refused to materialize.

The airport. The goddamned airport.

He was right at the edge now. Tumblers in his mind started to fall into place. Not the victims from the last two weeks.

Go back further.

Connelly nearly sprung from his chair. He rifled through the paperwork on his desk. Pages went flying and drifted slowly to the floor. He got to the bottom of the pile and came up empty. He returned his attention to the computer. Where had he read it?

172

He scrolled through his history file until he found the correct link. He clicked on it.

April 1999. Henry Wade, the favorite suspect of the keyboard detectives, is found dead in his car inside the parking garage at Newark International. A syringe with heroin residue rested in his hand. A single eyewitness reported seeing someone standing beside Wade's vehicle. The witness was unable to provide police with a description of this person. Their explanation was simply, "It was too dark."

Connelly scrolled to the end. The victim's next-of-kin was listed as Margaret Wade, his wife of nineteen years. And their son, Nicholas, aged fifteen.

"Whoa." Connelly smiled.

****

The rain let up a little by nine that night. Richie Bruno noticed but only in a vague sense. He had not noticed much in the three days since he made his great escape from Springbrook. He had spent nearly all of that time tweaking.

After leaving behind the losers and pretenders at Springbrook he made his way to his cousin's house in West Philly. He remembered waiting for his cousin to answer the door and wondering what Buckley would think if she knew he had gone only four blocks from her bullshit house of horrors. Once his cousin let him in and hooked him up with some high quality crystal, he ceased thinking about Buckley at all. The past seventy-two hours had seen him not straying far from his cousin's couch. He ate little, drank even less. He watched TV through a haze of smoke and listened to the wall clock tick off the seconds.

The hallucinations were few and far between. In fact, he experienced only two. The first was a parade of cats that marched through the living room, oblivious or ambivalent to his presence.

The second was far less pleasant; it involved one of his cousin's friends sodomizing him while the rest of the meth heads in the room laughed and cheered him on. This second hallucination continued past its initial unpleasantness the first time he used the bathroom. But it was a small price to pay, imagining such negative things. His lungs were full of crystal smoke and his head drifted free of his body and he flew, far above the shitty little apartment and the lowlifes who called it home. He suspected his cousin of spiking the meth with something, PCP, maybe. There were always hallucinations, but rarely were they so vivid. Richie decided to enjoy the ride.

The bugs returned, as they always did. It was the one thing he would change about crystal, if he could. It always brought out the bugs. They crawled along his arms and legs, his neck and face. They were sneaky little fuckers, too. They were always there, but they only revealed themselves when he was tweaking. He clawed at the bastards but they always managed to get away. He had long since accepted the bugs as part of the experience but someday he was going to find a way to kill them all. He could guarantee that.

He would still be there in that apartment if one of his cousin's less-than-friendly cohorts hadn't slammed him across the jaw for no reason whatsoever. That had hurt enough to snap Richie out of the fog. He massaged his jaw and blinked back the tears and felt betrayed. Maybe more than that. Maybe violated. The son of a bitch who hit him told him to get out, his cousin wanted nothing to do with him and if he didn't leave *right now* something very bad was going to happen to him. So Richie left. He stumbled out the door wearing nothing but his underwear and socks.

It would have been impossible not to notice the rain, but he refused to let it bother him. There were a few more places he could go, a few more couches he could crash on, if only for a night or two. It just so happened the nearest of those couches took him past the Springbrook Healing and Recovery Center.

The rain had stopped completely by the time he reached the correct street. Richie could just make out the top floor of the rehab about a block away. Light spilled from some of the windows and he saw one of the girls walk past, silhouetted briefly in the warm light within.

"Hey, Jess," he called. His voice was harsh, froggy, something that happened every time he smoked meth. He had forgotten about that side effect until this moment. He waved, but there was no one at the window now. Richie frowned. "Stuck-up dyke."

She was probably getting ready to jump into bed with Patty. It used to bother him, lying in bed and staring at the ceiling and wondering what was going on in the room above. He used to picture all sorts of scenarios. And when Phil was asleep Richie would fix his eyes on the ceiling and beat off, imagining himself the meat in that lesbo sandwich. He always knew the first thing he would do when he got out was to get laid. Somehow that had not happened. He made a bee line for his cousin's door instead of Arlin Street where the working girls hung out. So here he was, three days out of that hellhole and still not fucked. But those two…

Richie was suddenly in the mood for some good old fashioned shouting. He staggered down the street. His eyes remained fixed on those windows, hoping to catch a glimpse of one or both of them. Whatever they were doing when he got there, they would stop soon enough. They would come to that window and look down and he would tell them everything he thought of them. And he would do it loudly enough so that Carol and Peter and whoever else was around would hear him and know what was going on above their heads. "There's a no-sex policy," he slurred, still fifty yards from the building. "And if I can't get any, you can't either."

He stumbled and went down on the sidewalk. He picked himself up slowly and surveyed the damage. Both knees were scraped and bloody, and his left hand throbbed. He shook it and resumed his march.

At last he stood in front of the main walk leading to the front doors of Springbrook. Christ, how he hated this fucking building. Why couldn't he hallucinate a bomb going off and blowing the shit out of the place? *That* would have been something worth seeing. The icing on the cake would be Buckley's burned and mutilated body landing on the sidewalk at his feet. He could almost see her scorched features staring at him, her thick makeup melted to her skin, her dead eyes pleading with him for help. His bladder was probably just full enough for him to help put out the flames consuming her flesh. The image made him smile. Instead the building stood as it always had, and probably always would. And an endless procession of sad assholes would pass through those doors with delusions of cleaning up and getting their shit together. But not tonight. Tonight there was something new on the activity board. Tonight they were gonna learn something.

He took a deep breath but stopped short of beginning his tirade by a simple word spoken in a kind voice.

"Richie?"

Richie looked about, confused.

"Is that you?"

Richie turned in the direction of the voice.

Carol stood near the bushes and shrubs that decorated the front of the building. Richie smiled. He always liked Carol. She was about the only person within those walls he could stomach for any length of time. He waved, and the act nearly caused him to fall over. "Heeey, Carol."

Carol pitched her cigarette into the street and approached him. "Richie, what are you doing here? Are you coming back?" She reached him and looked him over. "Jesus, do I even want to know where your clothes are? You're gonna get pneumonia, you know."

Richie smiled again. "Nah, I'm good. I haven't felt this great in a long time."

"Yeah, you look it." Carol frowned.

Richie's opinion of the nurse slid a little. She sounded a tad judgmental. Maybe not quite as much as Buckley or Karen, or even Phil, but enough to get his attention. "I'm great!" he exclaimed loudly. He spread his arms and twirled about. He nearly went down again, but this time Carol got her arms around him and steadied him.

"Oh, Richie." She sounded disappointed, disgusted. "C'mon, let's get you inside. I'll have to keep you in quarantine, but lucky for you, Dr. Buckley picked tonight to work late. We'll see what she can do for you." She put her arm around his shoulder and guided him gently in the direction of the walkway.

"I like you, Carol." He belched and nearly vomited.

"I like you, too," she replied.

The streetlight behind them winked out. Carol half-turned and Richie followed.

Something big and black descended out of the darkness and settled atop Carol's head. Her body went rigid, except for her arms; the one previously around Richie's shoulder flew up, its twin whipped about blindly. Carol shrieked and clawed at the massive hand. Her fingers tangled in her hair. Richie went down on the sidewalk again, crying out when his bruised knees impacted the pavement.

"Ow!" He got himself into a sitting position and rubbed his bruised knees. He heard someone nearby gasp. He looked about until his eyes fell on Carol.

The nurse stood only three feet from him. Something that looked black sprayed from her head. The young woman's expression was frozen; eyes wide and looking straight ahead, mouth agape in a mute scream. The black fluid poured into her eyes and mouth and flowed down her cheeks. Her feet staggered forward, slowly, the world's most horrifying drunk. She made it five or six steps down the sidewalk. Something in the darkness loomed behind and above her, something big, but Richie could not make it out. It might have been a man, probably was, because he could not imagine any other animal that big wearing a top hat. Whatever it was, it matched Carol step for step, a shadowy puppeteer walking behind his gruesome marionette.

It lifted its hand suddenly and rapidly. Carol's body jerked sideways. She managed one last sharp intake of breath as she turned. Richie could see the top of her head was crushed, her dark curls now soaked in that black fluid and flattened against what remained of her skull. The rivers of blood that flowed and spurted from the top of her head like an obscene crimson river covered her eyes completely. It stained her scrubs, the baby blue fabric turning black in the meager moonlight. Carol staggered toward him, one arm outstretched, blood-soaked eyes pleading.

Richie began to laugh.

She went down directly in front of him. The remains of her head impacted the pavement with a sick, wet sound. Blood and bits of brain spurted from the crushed remains of her head, some of it landing on Richie's naked chest. Her fingers curled into a fist and then she was still.

Richie sat on the sidewalk and looked at her. It was cool as far as hallucinations went, but he would have much preferred the part of the victim be played by Buckley. It only reinforced his suspicion that his cousin had spiked that last dose of ice.

Richie's eyes travelled up from Carol's imaginary corpse to the imaginary man with the top hat. He loomed above him. Richie could not see the man's face, so dark were the shadows around him, but he felt (*knew*) the man was looking down on him. Richie smiled and held up his hand. "Help a brother up?"

The Shadow Man helped him up.

Chapter 14

A Mass of Pure Darkness

Nick sat on the sofa in the den with Sarah. They had the room to themselves tonight, and that was fine with Nick. Curran had left a few moments before, dragging Phil along with him. The older man was oblivious as to why, and that was also fine with Nick. He doubted Phil was the tattling kind, but he still did not want anyone to glean what was happening between him and Sarah.

What was going on was still not well-defined, even to him. He knew he liked her, just as she liked him, but they were in a bad spot. If Buckley got wind of anything there would be a problem, a big one. And so they sat on the same sofa but with enough room between them for another person. They did not hold hands although Nick wanted to, and so did Sarah, if her body language was any indication. But they played it cool, especially with Buckley uncharacteristically still on premises.

Sarah was morose after watching the news. Her mood persisted until dinner, when she started to snap out of it. By the time the patients retreated to the backyard for their after-dinner downtime she was almost back to her usual self. He even succeeded in making her laugh a few times. Her smile and her honest laughter made his heart ache. It was at that moment he realized he honestly liked her. Until then he did not trust himself. His infatuation could easily have been his usual technique of ingratiating himself to someone in order to shack up and provide a home base for when the H started to roll in. But now, Nick realized he truly liked her. It was a bizarre experience for him. He could not remember another woman for whom he felt honest affection. Not unless he counted Rebecca, but that was a different type of affection entirely.

Nick listened to Sarah's plans once she walked through Springbrook's front door a free woman. She planned to take up nursing, possibly drug counseling, so she could help others beat their disease. He nodded and smiled and offered words of encouragement. Knowing she was nearly out the door and he was stuck here for another two months made him both angry and sad. He hid the anger, not so much the sadness.

If only he had gotten here sooner. *Sure, if only Angie had been courteous enough to die two months earlier your life would be so much the better.* The voice angered and embarrassed him. He ordered it silent.

"Can I look you up when I get out of here?" he heard himself ask. He was immediately self-conscious. He had just taken the biggest step forward of his life. The prospect of a real relationship with a real woman, not simply out of convenience but of genuine affection, frightened him. He winced, certain Sarah was about to smack him down.

"I hope so," she replied.

Nick's head snapped up. He scanned her eyes for any sign of bullshit, came up empty. She smiled. He returned the gesture. If not for Buckley's presence in the building, and Carol's imminent return from her "secret" trip outside, he would have hugged her. Maybe more than hugged.

Nick almost chanced it, but he heard the front door open. He leaned back, a child who was almost caught in the act of stealing a candy bar. He looked sideways at Sarah and shared a knowing smile.

The lights in the foyer winked out. Nick craned his neck, but could see nothing. He got to his feet and looked around the corner.

"Pete will take care of it," Sarah said with little interest.

Nick called, "Carol?"

The lights leading from the foyer into the hallway flickered and went dim. They joined their brethren in the foyer a moment later.

Nick looked back at Sarah. She read the look on his face and stood. She joined him at the corner.

Someone stood within the darkness. Nick could see only a vague shape surrounded by shadow. "Carol, is that you?" The figure made no reply, simply stood beside the door to the receptionist's office.

"Nick, who is that?" There was an undercurrent of fear in her voice. Her hands found their way to Nick's arm.

Nick shook his head. "Can't tell." He turned his head slightly to the right and raised his voice. "Dr. Buckley?" The door to her office was at the edge of the dark zone. He waited for the door to open.

The figure in the darkness took two or three lurching steps forward. He had yet to enter the light, but Nick could see a little more detail. He thought the man might be naked. Nick could see his skin, wet with rain, glisten in the dim light.

"It's Richie!" Sarah said. "He came back." She stepped out from around the corner and looked at the man standing in the shadows. "Richie!"

Nick grabbed her arm. "Wait a minute."

Buckley's door opened. She got one foot into the hall before she stopped. At first Nick thought she was looking at Richie, but the doctor's eyes travelled up. They blossomed into the size of saucers. Her mouth worked, but Nick could hear nothing.

Something flashed out of the shadows. It was big and fast. To Nick it seemed part of the darkness extended itself in Buckley's direction in a swift, powerful arc. The doctor's head separated from her shoulders with an explosion of gore. It sailed through the air in their direction and bounced off the wall next to Nick before it ricocheted across the hallway. It ended its pinball course on the floor outside the cafeteria. Sarah screamed. Buckley's body staggered in the doorway, her hands gripping feebly for the wall. Her legs bent and skewed in different directions, making Nick think of old time comedians playing at being drunk. At last the dead woman's knees buckled and the body collapsed to the floor. The legs and arms twitched and bounced as if the body were being hit with an electrical charge.

"Oh shit, oh shit," Sarah whispered. Then, "*Oh my God*!"

"Wade," said the thing behind Richie.

Richie stepped forward. The darkness at his back moved with him. Nick could see a man within the darkness. He was tall, with broad shoulders and thin arms. He wore what looked to be a black trench coat and a top hat. The lights between Nick and Buckley's body winked out. Nick backed up slowly. Sarah was still at his back, still holding onto his arm with both hands. But now her fingers dug into his flesh hard enough to make him jerk his arm out of her grip.

"Back up, Sarah," Nick told her.

"Richie, how could you?" Sarah wailed. "You killed her!"

Nick continued to retreat, pushing Sarah behind him. "Sarah, *move*!"

He felt more than heard Sarah back up toward the stairs. Nick took his eyes off the man and the darkness now no more than fifteen feet away and glanced at the open doorway to the rec room. He could hear vague laughter from within. Movie night. He had no idea who was inside the room, but he liked his chances better in there. Nick reached back and grabbed hold of Sarah and changed course for the rec room.

The lights in the den went dark and took the TV with them. Nick could still hear the television pitchman raving about whichever product they gave him that week, but the screen was black. Just like the TV at Santos's apartment in his dream. Nick continued his retreat in the direction of the rec room. He gauged the distance until he was sure they were close enough. Then he turned and shoved Sarah at the opening and followed her inside.

Pedro, Ricky and Jenna sat grouped around the television. Meg Ryan has just found a child's backpack on the observation deck of the Empire State Building. Jenna looked heartbroken; the men in the room mostly looked bored, although Ricky was at least paying attention to the movie.

"Help us!" Sarah screamed.

Everyone started and turned in their direction. Pedro and Ricky were on their feet in an instant.

"What is it?" Pedro asked. "What's the matter?"

The television screen went black. The room was plunged into darkness.

Nick shoved Sarah away from the door. His right leg buckled and he nearly went down. He threw himself at Pedro, hoping the big man could see enough to catch him. Nick collided with Pedro, but both men kept their feet. Pedro helped steady Nick.

Someone stood in the doorway. It was almost total darkness in the rec room but Nick could tell it was Richie. Behind the mostly-naked methead stood the tall thin man with the impossibly broad shoulders.

The thing's arm shot to the side like a coiled snake. It caught Richie on his left side and launched him into the air. The only sound from Richie was a *humph* as the air was driven from his lungs. He smashed into the wall to the right of the doorway. Nick could hear the distinct sound of bones pulverizing under the impact.

"Wade," it said again.

Nick backed up. He felt Pedro next to him, but he had lost track of Sarah. He heard a woman moan in fear somewhere behind him and to his left. Sarah or Jenna. "We have to get out of here," Nick said.

"What the hell is going on?" Ricky shouted. He did not sound scared, not exactly, but he was almost there.

"Buckley's dead," Sarah shouted from the darkness. "This fucker killed her!"

Pedro surged in the direction of the door. Nick grabbed for him. His fingertips brushed Pedro's shirt sleeve but that was all. Nick could see very little but he thought the mass of shadows in front of him were Pedro and the tall man, who seemed so keen on introducing himself to Nick.

He could hear the struggle taking place in the doorway. Pedro grunted and then screamed, a short, ear-piercing wail. "No!" Nick limped forward, ignoring the pain in his right leg. "Ricky, help us!"

Nick ran straight into Pedro's back. His hands flew about, trying to find where the big man ended and the thing of darkness began. Nick felt something wet and hot around Pedro's head. His fellow patient continued to struggle, but weakly.

"Ricky!"

Nick heard footsteps coming in his direction. His eyes adjusted enough that he could see the thin man's fingers clamped around Pedro's throat. Pedro gurgled. Nick seized on those fingers and tried to pry them loose. At first he thought he succeeded in pulling one set away from Pedro's throat. He realized his mistake when the tall man grabbed at his wrist. Nick felt as if his skin was on fire.

He felt and heard the bones in his wrist snap and he cried at the unexpected pain. The fire worked its way into his hand and up his forearm. Nick's right knee buckled and he sagged to the floor.

Ricky was there as well. He seemed blind; he swiped at empty air. What the hell was wrong with him? How could he not see Pedro and the man holding him? Ricky landed a blow on the back of Pedro's head. The bigger man sunk to his knees, more to do with his lack of oxygen than the feeble blow struck by his roommate.

The tall man twisted his hand and Nick heard Pedro's neck snap. It was followed by the loud, dull thud of the body crumpling to the floor. The man in the top hat turned his attention to Nick.

That was when Ricky got lucky. He threw a half-assed roundhouse and caught the intruder a square blow in the middle of his back. Nick felt the pressure on his wrist disappear. He backed away slowly, pushed himself along the floor, and cradled his broken wrist. The sensation of his arm being on fire lessened and then dissipated.

He could hear Ricky struggling. He could also hear the two girls, perhaps ten feet away. He peered into the darkness of the room and thought he could make out Sarah and Jenna. They stood near the opposite wall, clutching each other.

Ricky landed another shot, this one right across the tall man's jaw. His target responded by whipping his arm in a tight arc in front of him. Ricky stopped his attack. He stumbled back, both hands clutching his throat. Something that sounded like water pattered on the floor. Ricky tripped on an overturned chair and went down in a heap, his hands still wrapped around his own throat and gasping.

Nick limped across the room until he was next to Sarah and Jenna. Sarah caught him and steadied him. Nick's legs felt like rubber, but he seemed to draw strength from the two women.

"Nick, what happened?" Sarah asked. Her voice was high-pitched, panicked.

"Where's Pedro?" Jenna asked.

There was enough light from the area around the stairs that now Nick could see the tall man framed in the doorway. He flexed his long fingers; something wet dripped from them. "Wade," he repeated.

Nick felt about until his fingers found one of the plastic chairs. He lifted it, braced himself.

The tall man took a step forward.

That was when Curran leaped on his back, wrapping his arms around the tall man's chest. "Motherfucker!" he shouted. He took turns with each fist, raining blows on his target. Curran reared back, threw all his weight behind him. The tall man staggered back, hands trying to grasp Curran. Their momentum carried them out of the room.

Nick grabbed Sarah's hand and limped forward as quickly as he was able. "C'mon, I have to help him."

Nick rushed at the doorway. He did his best to guide the women around the spot where he thought Pedro fell. He was relieved when no one tripped over the body. The lights by the stairs had now gone out, but those nearest the foyer had returned to life. The illumination was weak but it was enough for Nick to see his roommate struggling against the tall man. Nick turned and placed Sarah and Jenna against the wall. "I think you two should get outta here. Find a phone and call the cops."

Sarah nodded; Jenna simply stood and stared with mute horror at the scene before her. "Go!" Nick shouted.

He did not wait to see if they followed his advice. He turned toward the stairs.

Curran was still on the tall man's back, but his grip seemed weaker than before. The dark thing succeeded in landing several blows against him, but they were mostly ineffective. He was off-balance and seemed unable to connect with anything other than a glancing blow. The effects were still dramatic; Curran bled from his nose and mouth. Nick did not know why, but he received the distinct impression the tall man was toying with Curran.

Nick limped toward them. He glanced up and saw Phil standing on the first floor landing, Jessica and Patty behind him. All three looked terrified. "Get out of here!" Nick shouted at them. They remained in place, as if their feet had grown roots into the floor. The girls cried and held their hands to their mouths. Phil looked stunned.

The tall man finally succeeded in flipping Curran off his back. Nick's roommate landed hard on the floor, flat on his back, the air exploding from his lungs. Nick was nearly there when the tall man lifted Curran by his arm and swung him through the air. Curran's legs caught Nick and sent him stumbling back. Nick's bad leg gave and he crumpled to the floor. Curran's trajectory carried him into the wall. The impact produced a dull thud and Curran's body went limp. The tall man tossed him down the side hallway that led to the backyard.

Jessica shrieked. She was followed a moment later by Patty. The sound echoed off the walls of Springbrook and pierced Nick's skull and made him wince.

The tall man seemed to collapse into darkness. One moment he was standing outside the rec room and the next he was no longer there. A flat, undulating mass of pure darkness slithered up the stairs quickly. It pooled around the feet of the three people on the landing. They seemed not to notice, although Nick could not see how that was possible. Even at a distance he could see it quite clearly.

The puddle of darkness that had just murdered four people in front of Nick began to roil. In less than a heartbeat it had become the tall man once again. It stood among Phil and the girls. Nick began to shout a warning.

A thin but long tendril of darkness shoved Phil to the side with so much force Nick heard the old man's bones crack on impact with the wall. Phil's hands pushed weakly against the wall, trying to free himself from the depression his body had made in the drywall. He succeeded, took a single drunken step back. A tendril of darkness shot toward the stunned man too quickly for Nick to follow. It struck Phil in the back and this time the old man crumpled to the floor. The Shadow Man picked up the corpse with one hand and tossed it over the side. Phil landed in the hallway next to Curran.

Patty screamed again. Her feet shuffled back but she bumped into Jessica who was still frozen in place. The shadow that was the tall man reacted. Another tendril that Nick realized was an arm shot forward. It impaled Patty through her abdomen. The young blonde girl gasped. The tendril of darkness continued unimpeded through Patty's body and caught Jessica in the same spot. Jessica managed a scream, but it ended abruptly. The tall man withdrew the tendril amid a fountain of blood that erupted from one or both of the girls. Patty and Jessica folded to the floor, puppets of a master who had grown bored with them.

When Nick glanced up again the tall man stood plainly on the first floor landing and stared at him. Nick kept his eyes on him as he backed up. If he pulled that collapsing-into-a-shadow trick again Nick would be defenseless. He wondered what the tall man was waiting for. And then it hit him. *He's savoring the moment.* Nick did not know how he knew it, but he was certainly correct.

Nick retreated another step. He took his eyes from the top of the stairs and looked at the two crumpled bodies in the hallway. Neither had moved but Nick had to know. He limped as quickly as his wounded leg would allow.

"Nick, what are you doing?" Sarah shouted.

Nick turned and saw her and Jenna standing in the well-lit den. They looked to be a thousand miles away. "Get out of here," Nick waved at them. "Get out now!"

To his horror Sarah started toward him. Jenna reached for her, but missed. Sarah ran the length of the building quickly. She reached Nick and grabbed his hand and pulled him toward the foyer. Nick pulled away and limped toward Curran and Phil.

He stopped when he reached the two bodies on the floor. Neither moved. Phil lay on this stomach, his arms and legs splayed at odd angles to his body. Curran was on his back, groaning and writhing weakly.

"C'mon, John, get up. We have to leave right now."

Curran grimaced and rolled onto his stomach. "What the hell was that?" he mumbled. He got his hands beneath him and pushed himself to his knees. Blood spilled from his mouth and pooled on the floor. "He fucked me up pretty good," Curran slurred.

"We'll get you to a hospital but we have to go *right now*." Nick helped his roommate to his feet as much as his broken wrist and bum leg would allow.

Curran swayed and leaned against the wall. "Hospital sounds pretty good about now." More blood spilled from his mouth.

The ceiling lights dimmed and went out when they were perhaps ten feet from the door. Nick stopped and turned. The Shadow Man stood just on the other side of Phil's corpse. He leered at Nick.

Nick's first thought was to run, but that was ridiculous. His injured leg would never allow him to outrun whatever the hell this thing was. The best he could hope for was to get Sarah and Curran out of the line of fire. It was after him, God knew why, so perhaps it would let them go if they weren't in his way. Nick braced himself to shove them toward the door.

Someone shouted something from somewhere far away. Nick could not make it out. A moment later several shots rang out and echoed off the walls. The tall man's body stiffened under what looked to be several impacts. Slowly, as if reluctant to take his eyes from Nick, the Shadow Man turned.

Nick could see little beyond the dark shape of the tall man. There was someone in the foyer, someone familiar, and he held a gun and snapped off several shots at the thing in the shadows. Nick thought he saw Jenna cringing behind the newcomer.

"Come on," Sarah whispered to him. "We have to go. Let the cops deal with this fucker."

The cops won't stop him. They won't even come close. Yet he allowed Sarah to lead him away. They were outside and making for the wall and Nick could still hear shots coming from within Springbrook.

They skirted the swimming pool and were close to the wall when Curran collapsed. "Jesus," he muttered.

Nick staggered to him. "C'mon, John, let's go."

Blood saturated Curran's shirt and the front of his sweatpants. He tried to sit up, failed.

Nick turned to Sarah. "Help me."

Sarah ran to him. Together they lifted Curran into a sitting position. Nick cast glances over his shoulder, but the tall man had yet to emerge into the backyard. His knee and his wrist screamed for him to stop but Nick ignored their pleas. With Sarah's help he got Curran to his feet. "That's it, brother, we're almost there."

Nick and Sarah half-carried Curran to the wall. His feet dragged on the concrete walkway that surrounded the pool. He coughed blood into the air. When they reached the wall Nick looked at its seven foot height. He made a weak attempt to grab the top of the wall and surprised himself when he succeeded. He dropped back down, careful to land on his left foot. His right leg barked at him anyway.

He stepped back and laced his hands together. "Let's go, Sarah."

She placed her hands on the wall and her foot in the stirrup he created. Nick grimaced against the pain in his right wrist. Sarah pushed against his hands and mounted the wall with some effort. When Nick was sure she had made it he turned his attention to Curran.

His roommate sat slumped against the stucco wall. He drooled blood onto his shirt.

"C'mon, man, we gotta go." Nick bent forward to lift him.

"Ain't happening," Curran said weakly. Bubbles of blood coated his lips. "Just go."

"We ain't leaving you," Nick replied. He got his hands under Curran's arms.

Curran's hand landed on Nick's shoulder with surprising strength. He pulled Nick down until they were nearly eye-to-eye. "Just go, Wade. Get Sarah and go. I'll be fine. The cavalry's here, right?"

Nick scanned Curran's eyes. There was much pain there but the man had clearly made up his mind. And Nick was in no condition to force him to do anything. "Fuck."

"Got that right," Curran replied. He smiled, then, and blood trickled from the corners of his lips. "Go on. Get outta here."

Nick closed his eyes and squeezed Curran's hands. "We'll come back for you."

"I'll be here chillin'."

Nick straightened and looked atop the wall, where Sarah's eyes whipped from the door to Nick. He jumped and grabbed for the top. Sarah caught his hand and helped.

Chapter 15

A Sitting Duck

Connelly pulled up to Springbrook Healing and Recover Center and turned off the car. He still did not know why he was here. Nicholas Wade was not a suspect, nor was he likely to have any knowledge of the copycat Shadow Man. But something clawed at the back of Connelly's mind, an itch he could not scratch. He hoped a talk with Wade would accomplish something, even if it was only to get rid of that goddamned itch.

He stepped out of the car and walked around to the sidewalk. He regarded the façade of the building and it reminded him of school. Light spilled from the front doors and from one of the windows on the second floor. He hoped that window was Wade's room and he was awake. It was only 9:45 by his watch, but addicts were not known for keeping a regular schedule. If he was not awake and Connelly was forced to return in the morning, when he was on duty, it would be a little more difficult to explain this visit to Captain Calabrese.

Connelly started for the stairs. He slipped in something on the sidewalk. It was dark and wet and Connelly's stomach did a backflip. He pulled his small penlight from his pocket and knelt beside the small puddle. The blood was still wet, still fresh. A streak of gore led away from the puddle onto the grass in the direction of the bushes that lined the front of the building. Instinctively Connelly reached for his walkie. He cursed himself when he remembered it was in his locker at the precinct house.

He followed the trail up the front lawn. Behind the bushes, in the small space between them and the building, lay a dead woman. She wore the baby blue scrubs of a nurse. Her dark hair of loose curls was matted with blood. It ran from the corners of her mouth and coated her chin. The top of her head was crushed as if by a giant vice. Her sightless, blood-filled eyes stared at him.

Connelly pulled his weapon. Thank God he had not left that in his locker as well. Now he no longer had an option about going inside. Even if things turned out to be normal and everyone accounted for, except the poor, dead nurse, he would still need to call in the CSI team. He left the body and made for the front door.

It was unlocked and he went inside. There was some commotion from around the corner where the reception area was located. Connelly poked his head out and looked. There was a young woman standing no more than five feet in front of him. She hugged herself and wept. He could see little beyond her because the rest of the main floor was in darkness.

Connelly placed his hand on the girl's shoulder. She screamed and spun and her fists beat a meager rhythm on his chest. "Whoa, whoa," he said, and grabbed her wrists. Her eyes were wide, wild. She tried to say something, but she was terrified beyond words. Instead she took a step back and pointed.

Connelly followed her directions. Just in front of the girl was a woman's body minus her head. The corpse wore the white coat of a doctor. Blood had poured from the top of her neck and saturated the carpet around the corpse. Beyond the dead doctor, down the hallway past an open area and near what looked to be stairs,

Connelly saw something else. It was dark, black, even, but there was someone moving about within the darkness. It had the vague shape of a man, albeit one drawn by a child. Its shoulders were broad, but its arms appeared to be too long and too thin. The one detail of the figure that Connelly could recognize was the top hat on its head.

"Jesus," Connelly said.

"Help them," the girl whispered through her tears.

Connelly got a better grip on his gun and aimed it into the mass of darkness roughly sixty feet away. "Police!" he shouted. He saw no reaction to his challenge. Connelly fired wide, the one and only warning this pretender was going to receive. The Shadow Man ignored both him and the shot that missed him by no more than five or six feet. He was focused on someone Connelly could not see, someone in the far corridor.

Connelly aimed as best he could, still without a good bead on his target, and pulled the trigger. He had no idea if the shot hit home or not. He fired again, and a third time. Connelly saw no indication that any of his shots hit the perp. It was difficult to tell, but he thought the man turned his way.

The darkness surged in his direction, suddenly and more quickly than his eye could follow. He had a vague sense of the ceiling lights above him going dark. Then something very big and very heavy crashed into him. The breath was driven from his lungs and he was knocked off his feet. He landed in the corner of the lobby. He heard the girl scream and then a thud.

Dazed, not even sure of where he was, Connelly crawled along the floor, fingers searching for his gun. He coughed, felt the pain in his chest and side. He gave himself a quick pat down and his hands were still dry. "Miss, where are you?" he called into the darkness. He still could not find his gun. He wondered if it would do any good even if he came across it. The way that thing moved…

The lights flickered and came on. Connelly winced at the sudden brightness and shielded his eyes. He never felt more vulnerable in his life. He was all but blind, unarmed, and in the room with a murderer. Connelly ticked off the seconds, wondering when he would feel the killer's touch. After several moments his eyes adjusted to the light and he looked about.

He and the young girl were alone in the foyer. She was huddled in the corner, curled up into a ball with her hands wrapped around her head. There was no sign of the Shadow Man. Connelly crawled quickly to her side and put his arms around her. She trembled and whimpered but she did not scream. "It's okay, it's okay," he said and stroked her hair. "He's gone. We're okay." He spotted his gun on the floor next to the girl. He picked it up and held it and rocked her back and forth until her tremors subsided.

With the lights back on he looked about. In addition to the headless woman in the foyer he spotted another body in the far hallway. There also appeared to be a pool of blood seeping from an open doorway farther down on the left.

"Jesus," he said again.

****

"I need to stop," Nick said breathlessly.

"No, we have to keep going."

Nick leaned back against a rotted wooden fence in a garbage-strewn alley two blocks from Springbrook. His chest felt as if it was on fire, and his right leg throbbed worse than at any time since the cast came off. The edges of the brace had rubbed the skin raw around it. He could see Rorschach blots of blood on his sweatpants. His shirt was soaked through with sweat and it dripped endlessly from his hair into his eyes. He blinked it away and felt the heat radiating from his body. He could not remember a time when he felt more exhausted.

Sarah must have realized he was not going anywhere because she returned to his side and joined him in leaning on the fence. She was breathing hard, too, and she sported dark stains under her arms and around her collar. The sweat on her skin reacted in the moonlight and created the illusion that she was aglow. Nick might have found it erotic if not for the scene from which they had just fled.

"Christ, did you see that thing?" Sarah asked. "What the hell was it?"

Nick shook his head. Sweat flew from his hair. "I don't know," he said between gasps of air. "But it was familiar. Something about it was. Don't ask me how, though."

"What?" Sarah sounded incredulous as well as out of breath.

Nick tapped his temple. "I don't know." He licked his lips. "It's just a feeling."

He became aware Sarah was staring at him. He gave her a sideways glance. She looked upon him with a mix of horror and disbelief. She stuttered.

Nick held up a hand that shook. "All I'm saying is there was something very familiar about it. I just don't know what." He took another deep breath. "I'm pretty sure he's the one who killed all those people in Manayunk and those drug dealers in West Philly."

Sarah wiped wet hair from her forehead. "Why was he after you? He said your name, Nick. Why was he after you? Is this some kind of leg breaker? You owe a dealer somewhere?"

"You know any leg breakers who can do what that thing did to Pedro and Ricky? Or John?" He wanted to say more but he was stopped by a coughing fit. He doubled over and waited for the sledgehammer in his chest to stop pounding.

When Sarah spoke again, her voice held none of the accusatory tone from a moment before. Her voice was soft, so soft Nick had to strain to hear it. "What kind of man can do that?"

Nick wiped sweat from his forehead. "That isn't a man. I don't know what it is but it's not a man." He looked at her. "And if it's after me, then you should leave right now before it finds us."

Sarah raised her head and looked about. Nick could see her deciding whether or not to take his advice. She straitened and took a single step away from the fence. She paused. Finally she turned in his direction and shook her head. "No."

"Sarah—"

"No. En. Oh." She stood in front of him. "Look at you. You won't last three seconds if it comes back, not in the shape you're in."

Nick laughed. It ended with a cough. "I won't last three seconds, anyway. You saw it."

"Yeah, but you can't even run. Look at your leg." She pointed to the slowly-blossoming crimson flowers on his sweatpants. "You're a sitting duck."

"Quack quack."

She reached for him and got her hands beneath his arm. She pulled him away from the fence. "C'mon, we have to keep moving."

"I still say you should split now, while you can."

"Shut the fuck up." But her tone was friendly, even playful.

Nick allowed her to lead him down the alley.

They made it three more blocks before he had to stop again. The pain from his leg brace was unbearable. "Hang on," he whispered. "I have to ditch this fucking thing before it cuts my leg off."

They were in someone's backyard. A storage shed that had seen better days stood before them. Sarah pulled him toward it. The doors were closed, but there was no lock. Sarah looked over her shoulder at the house. It was dark and silent. She eased the doors open and cringed when the hinges squealed. She shot another look at the house. It remained dark. After a moment she looked inside the shed. There was very little to see, a few stray gardening implements hung from the walls, but the rest of the space was empty.

"You can take it off in there."

"Sure." Nick limped inside the shed. He leaned against the wall as Sarah closed the door. "Leave it open a crack, will ya? Hot as hell in here." She frowned, but did as he asked. She kept her eyes on the house.

Nick brought his leg up as much as the brace would allow and began loosening its straps. A moment later he dropped it to the dirt floor. It clanged softly. He gently massaged the swollen skin, taking care not to touch the bloody areas where the brace had rubbed the skin raw. "Ouch," he whispered through gritted teeth.

Sarah looked over her shoulder at him. "Back in a minute." She crept outside.

Nick continued to massage his throbbing leg. The adrenaline left him all at once and he felt tired. Despite the temperature inside the shed gooseflesh rose on his arms. He leaned against the wall and breathed deeply.

Sarah returned a moment later. "House is empty. I thought as much after no one came out to chase us away. I think I can get us inside." She looked over several of the abandoned gardening tools before she selected a rake.

"Well-versed in breaking and entering?" He smiled weakly.

"Well, I'm not an expert, but I've done it a time or two." She broke a tine from the rake and shoved it into her pocket. Then she went to him and boosted him up and wedged herself beneath his right shoulder. "C'mon." She led him from the shed to the darkened back porch. Nick leaned on the rotted railing while Sarah went to work on the lock. It took several moments but the door swung open slowly. She turned a triumphant smile in Nick's direction. "It'll be better than in there with the dirt floor."

"I'm not arguing."

She boosted him again and helped him inside.

They were in the kitchen. The house was clearly deserted; dust coated the countertops and the cabinet doors were open, exposing bare shelves. There was no telltale hum from the refrigerator. Sarah tried the light switch anyway. The kitchen remained dark. "No power. Guess that makes sense."

Nick followed her into the living room. An ancient sofa took up nearly an entire wall. A large and dead fireplace stood against the wall closest to the front door. A ceiling fan hung low in the center of the room like an Old West outlaw hanged for his crimes. The carpet was threadbare and the plywood beneath peeked through in several places.

"Have a seat. I'm gonna check out the rest of the place. Make sure we have it to ourselves."

"Be careful," Nick replied.

Sarah smirked. "Little late for that now." She went upstairs.

Nick eased himself onto the sofa. Dust plumed up and formed a small cloud that dissipated quickly. He closed his eyes and leaned back and listened for any sound coming from the house. If Sarah encountered anyone upstairs he hoped they would be accommodating enough to share the house, at least for one night. Then again, anyone staying here would most likely not want someone else under their roof, not without paying a fee, anyway. Nick had neither cash nor H to pay for their shelter. If a confrontation became unavoidable, Nick did not like their chances. He was next to useless at the moment and Sarah would likely be an easy target. He hoped she would find no one upstairs.

She did not. Sarah came back to him after a few moments. She plopped down on the sofa next to him, releasing another plume of dust. "Place is empty. Looks like our fellow addicts haven't found it yet."

Nick relaxed his shoulders. "Give it time."

They sat in silence, in darkness, for some time without speaking. The house was cooler than the shed although the odor of decay was somewhat strong. The air was still thick from the day's heat but Nick could live with it. He glanced out the picture window at the neighborhood street outside. A few houses were illuminated from within but many others were dark. A couple of kids walked by, obviously up to no good. That was all. He felt himself starting to drift.

"Did you see Jenna? Did she make it?"

Sarah's question brought him back to full wakefulness. He rubbed his eyes before he answered. "I don't know. I didn't see that thing go after her, if that's any help. Last I saw she was standing next to that guy with the gun. Probably a cop."

Sarah seemed to relax a little. "I hope she's okay. We've been sharing that room for two months. She's a good friend."

Nick did not reply.

Sarah leaned over and placed her head on his chest. The move surprised Nick, if only for a moment. He gently draped his arm around her shoulders.

"I don't think anyone else made it," she said after a while. "Jess and Patty, Pedro, Ricky. He killed them all." Her voice was soft, almost a whisper, but there was no fear in it. She simply stated a fact.

"I didn't see Carol or Pete. They might be okay."

She looked up without taking her head from his chest. "Think so?"

Nick thought about it, shrugged. "I don't know."

Sarah began to trace little circles on his chest. The feel of her fingers relaxed him despite their surroundings and what they had just witnessed. The circles slowly got bigger and wider. She raised her head and looked at him. Nick leaned down and his lips brushed hers. The hint of contact aroused him and the gesture became a kiss. Her lips parted and suddenly her tongue was inside his mouth. Nick reciprocated.

His hands moved on their own to her breasts. Her shirt was still damp with sweat. His hands found their way beneath the fabric and inside her bra. He thought she might hesitate, even pull back. Instead she reached behind her and unhooked the clasp of her bra. The cups fell away and Nick felt her hard nipples between his fingers. She inhaled a short, quick breath when he pinched them gently.

Then her hand was travelling south. It grasped his penis and he felt a jolt of electricity. He kissed her harder and was rewarded when she returned the gesture. She was breathing heavily now; he felt her breath in his mouth and around his lips.

Sarah continued kissing him as her hands worked at his sweatpants. He removed his hands from her breasts long enough to slide his sweatpants down to his ankles. He kicked them off awkwardly, the pain in his leg momentarily forgotten. She stripped her own pants from her legs.

Still kissing him, her tongue still working the inside of his mouth, Sarah straddled him. Nick felt sudden pressure and warmth as he entered her. She began to raise and lower herself slowly. Her breathing became heavier, but still she would not pull back from the kiss.

Nick cupped her buttocks and assisted her in the slow, rhythmic up-and-down motion. At last she pulled back. Her eyes were shut, her lips parted. She was at that moment the most beautiful woman in the world. Her breath was coming in short, forceful gasps. She moaned and kissed him again, cupping his face in her hands as she did so. Nick felt the pressure inside himself beginning to build.

Here, on this shitty old couch in this shitty old house he and Sarah were making love for the first time. It was not how he would have imagined it if given a choice but all of that fell away, inconsequential nonsense. All that mattered was the two of them and this moment.

Nick's breathing matched hers. She moaned and her pace quickened until she began to piston up and down, forcing him deeper inside her. Sarah moaned again and this time it became a scream. Her fingers dug themselves into his shoulders as she climaxed.

Her reaction triggered Nick's own orgasm a moment later. He felt himself explode inside her, filling her. She continued to piston up and down for several more moments, her fingers welded to his shoulders. Nick smelled the sweat in her hair and on her neck. The scent filled his world and Nick allowed himself to drown in it.

At last they were both spent. Her movements slowed and then stopped. Sarah collapsed on top of him, her heart slamming the inside of her chest so powerfully Nick could feel it against his skin. He wrapped his arms around her and held her close. She remained in that position, straddling him with his penis still inside her, her breath still coming in rapid gulps of air. It took her several moments to recover. When she did she eased herself off him. She plopped herself next to him and lay her head on his chest once again.

"Thank you, Nick," she whispered.

Nick was genuinely surprised. "For what?" he asked breathlessly.

She raised her head and looked at him. She leaned in and planted another kiss on his lips. "Just for being here."

Nick held her once again. He brushed at some stray strands of her hair and kissed her forehead. They sat in silence and held each other for some time.

****

Connelly watched the ambulance depart with Springbrook's lone survivor in the back. She was physically unhurt but certainly in shock. He could not blame her. He was nearly in shock himself, and he was a homicide detective with twenty years of dealing with things like this. How could this innocent little girl expect to come out of that slaughter inside with her mind one-hundred-percent? He followed the course of the ambulance and its shattered cargo until it turned the corner and was lost from view. Then he returned his attention on the chaos around him.

There were numerous patrol cars, two detective's cars, another ambulance and the captain's car all taking up space in front of Springbrook. People stood in their front yards and watched the proceedings. One of the ambulance jockeys was still working on him, applying a compress against his right side. It hurt like a son of a bitch, but he was told there were no broken bones or lacerations. Just a contusion, a giant fucking contusion that would probably be there for at least a couple weeks. Connelly could live with that, gladly. After that mass of darkness crashed past him and out of the building, after Connelly had calmed the girl enough to leave her side, he had called for backup on the facility's landline. And after that he had surveyed the building up to the two female victims on the landing between the first and second floors. He saw what this bastard was capable of doing. If he could walk away with a bruise, well, he would take that any day.

Calabrese exited the building and made a bee line for him. The ambulance jockey finished his handiwork in time to vacate the area, leaving the two men alone by the ambulance's rear bumper.

"Nine dead, in all," Calabrese said with a backward glance at the building. "Seven inside, one out back by the wall, plus the nurse over there." He indicated the bushes, now cordoned off with yellow tape.

Connelly swallowed. "Any other survivors?"

"Yeah, one."

Connelly raised an eyebrow.

"Night janitor. Found him hiding in a closet on the top floor. Said he didn't see anything, but he heard enough to decide discretion was the better part of valor."

Connelly nodded. "He's right. He wouldn't have been able to do shit and we'd have another victim."

Calabrese chewed his lower lip. "What the hell happened in there, Mike?"

"I told you."

"Well, tell me again because I need to hear it at least three more times."

Connelly related his report again. When he finished Calabrese was shaking his head slowly and looking at the front of the building. "I'm gonna assume it was too dark in there for you to see clearly. Because if I go ahead with your report the chief will be up my ass in a minute, to say nothing of the press."

Connelly shrugged. "So be it. But I know what I saw."

"One other thing, Mike. According to the patient registry, we're two short. Nicholas Wade, aged thirty-one, and Sarah McCallister, aged twenty-six. They're nowhere inside. We're trying to contact their families and putting out an APB, see if we can pick them up. Maybe they can shed some light on what the hell happened in there."

Connelly started. Until that moment he had forgotten about Wade, the sole reason he had come to Springbrook in the first place. "I know what he looks like, Cap. I'll keep an eye out."

Calabrese and Connelly surveyed the emergency responders who continued to enter and exit the building. The first stretcher with its dead occupant was carried from the front entrance and down the steps. Connelly put his shirt back on gingerly and limped to his car.

Chapter 16

The Land of the Wealthy

Nick sat on the sofa with Sarah's head in his lap and listened to the soft rhythm of her breathing. She had fallen asleep not long after they made love. Nick, not so much. He was exhausted physically and mentally, to be sure. What energy he had left after their escape from Springbrook Sarah drained from him in that one orgasmic moment. He should have nodded off almost right away and yet here he was, wide awake and looking out the filthy picture window on a dark, deserted street.

Not long after Sarah closed her eyes Nick did the same. He felt himself just starting to drift when he was startled back to full consciousness. He blinked his eyes, seeing not the squalid living room but a wooded area. The night air felt cold on his skin. A small fire burned in a shallow pit off a walking path. He approached and found three men huddled around it, warming their hands. They were scraggly, with unkempt beards and holes in their clothes. They laughed among themselves. The laughter stopped when they noticed Nick standing nearby. One of them lifted a half-empty bottle in his direction. The other two got slowly to their feet and backed away a step. Nick felt himself advance quickly on them. He awoke at that moment.

Whatever fatigue had allowed him to nearly fall asleep was gone now. Nick was wide awake and shaking. He knew what the image meant, of course he did. The appearance of the thing at Springbrook had driven home exactly what was happening. The knowledge did him little good now, sitting on a decrepit couch in a decrepit living room with a beautiful woman dozing on his lap. But since sleep seemed no longer an option he simply sat and looked out the window.

Since then he had seen no cars and only one person outside. A drunk or junkie, stumbling aimlessly from sidewalk to blacktop, arms swaying to keep his balance, had wandered by perhaps twenty minutes before. Nick watched him with little interest. It was nearly impossible to see the poor bastard and not remember the many times Nick himself had made that directionless walk down a nameless side street. *Christ, is that what* I *looked like?* He knew the answer, of course. Yes. Precisely like that. For the first time in a long time, Nick felt shame.

The sky was still black but Nick could detect a slight brightening in the distance. He had lost all track of time since their climb over the backyard wall at Springbrook. He did not keep track of how far they ran or for how long. They were still in West Philly, that much he knew. He even recognized the area, if only vaguely. But it must have been much later than he thought. The last thing he wanted was to be inside the abandoned home when the sun came up. He thought about easing Sarah's head off his lap and having a look around but he did not want to risk waking her. She slept soundly; her dreams, if any, were peaceful. Nick could not bring himself to wake her. Not yet, anyway. He could afford to give her a bit longer.

He surprised himself by nodding off a short while later. He did not sleep long, perhaps as little as fifteen minutes, and he awoke with a start. He caught himself in time to avoid any big movements that would wake Sarah. He looked down and saw she was still asleep. He brushed a stray lock of her hair that had fallen across her eyes. In the near-dark of the decrepit living room, he thought he saw the ghost of a smile tug on the corner of her mouth.

If he dreamed during his nap he remembered no details. Maybe that was for the best. After what he had seen at Springbrook he needed no more nightmares of the man (*thing*) in the top hat. He glanced quickly out the window, almost expecting to see it just on the other side of the glass, staring in at him and grinning. There was no one there, of course. The street remained deserted, as did the outside of the window. Nick settled back and placed his hand on Sarah's shoulder. She reacted by snuggling closer to him. He spent the next hour alternating his gaze from the sleeping woman next to him and the street outside.

He still had no idea of the time but the sky to the east was beginning to lighten considerably. It was still dark, but the streetlights seemed less distinct than they had just a short time before. 5:30, maybe 6 in the AM. He could already see a few illuminated windows in the houses near them. As much as he disliked the idea of waking Sarah he no longer had a choice.

He prodded her and she stirred. He did it again. "Sarah, you have to wake up now." His voice was a whisper but in the silence of the empty living room it nearly echoed.

Slowly she lifted her head off his lap and looked up at him. "Hi." Her voice was a croak. She cleared her throat and tried again, then rubbed her eyes and stretched her arms and legs.

"Good morning." He was still whispering. "I think it's time we hit the road."

"Mmm. Just another couple minutes." She put her head back on his lap and closed her eyes.

"I'm afraid not. We have to get moving. C'mon, wake up."
He nudged her again.

She started. She drew a sharp breath and pushed herself off his lap. Her eyes were wide as they darted about the room. "Where is—" She stopped, looked at Nick. "Jesus, it wasn't a dream."

Nick could practically see the memories of the previous night flood back into her. Her lips trembled, her shoulders shook. He expected the tears to start any moment. She surprised him by blinking them back. She sniffled and looked at him. He placed his arms around her and pulled her close. "It's okay, hon. We're okay."

They kept the embrace for another few moments before she straitened on the couch. She composed herself quickly, dabbing at her eyes before looking at him again. "I'm okay."

Nick stood and stretched. Pins and needles poked into his arm where Sarah's head had rested. His leg and his wrist hurt like hell but he tried to push the pain away. He was partially successful; the fire was replaced by a dull throb. He looked out the window. More houses around them were illuminated from within. There were no people out there yet. Nick took that as a good sign. "I think it's time to go."

"Where to?"

Nick turned and smiled. "How about the Bahamas?"

Sarah returned a much weaker version of his smile. "That'll do just fine."

"Well, until then, I'd suggest getting the hell out of West Philly. Maybe the city altogether."

"I wanna go home, Nick. My brother is probably worried sick about this. I'm sure what happened last night is all over the news by now. I have to let him know I'm okay." She paused. "My mom, too, I suppose."

Nick nodded. "And you will. I'm thinking of going to my cousin's house. It's a hike from here, but it's safe. You can call them from there."

Sarah mulled it over, nodded after a moment. "Deal."

****

Sarah's mother did indeed know of the events from the night before. Connelly sat with her in the living room of her one-story ranch and took a few notes. The woman sat calmly in an old recliner and regarded Connelly and the news he brought with what he could only label as pained indifference.

He assured her there was no evidence her daughter was dead, and was, in fact, one of the two patients missing. No, Sarah was not a suspect. He stressed that she needed to call him right away should Sarah show up at her door. Mrs. McCallister did not think Sarah would have the nerve to show up here. She calmly related to Connelly numerous stories of her daughter's struggles with drugs and the law and how she had thrown the girl out of the house three years earlier. They had not spoken since and she saw no reason for that to change. Her tone was neutral but Connelly caught her twice darting a look at a framed photograph on the fireplace mantle, a photo of a young girl of perhaps three or four years-old and smiling broadly from atop a plastic slide. Mrs. McCallister thanked him abruptly for the visit and walked him to the door.

Connelly sat in his car in front of the woman's house and looked over his notes. Nothing helpful. Mrs. McCallister turned out to be a dead end. He leaned back and closed his eyes, replaying the events of the night before for the thousandth time. He got as far as the Shadow Man turning in his direction when he heard the radio come to life. A number of bodies found in the South Garden section of Fairmount Park.

He was nowhere near it, but he started the car anyway and headed for the call.

****

Nick and Sarah had put a good two miles between them and their overnight shelter. The sun was up now and a late-summer breeze rippled their clothes. It was a beautiful morning, neither hot nor muggy, but Nick was already bathed in sweat. His leg throbbed and he had developed a noticeable limp. He tried to hide it from Sarah but he caught her looking a few times. She said nothing, simply walked beside him and held his hand. They must have looked like hell to anyone driving past, leftovers from some wild party the night before who were only now getting around to the Walk of Shame. That was okay with Nick. The more people offended by their appearance meant the fewer people taking too close a look at them. He was used to this reaction from civilians. So was Sarah, if her downturned eyes and slumped shoulders were any indication. Heroin addiction, it seemed, had its uses after all.

He glanced longingly at most of the parked cars they passed. He could imagine himself crawling under the dash and pulling ignition wires and starting the thing. The trip to Rebecca's would take no time at all if they had four wheels to take them there. But it was too late to try it now. It was mid-morning and there was enough traffic to provide a witness or two to the police. To say nothing of his broken wrist making it almost impossible for his fingers to make the delicate moves hotwiring would require. They would not make it to Rebecca's before they and their stolen vehicle were spotted, let alone out of Philadelphia.

So they walked, mostly in silence. Once or twice a cop drove past. Nick and Sarah did not rate much of a look, a new experience for him, and, he was willing to bet, for her, as well. It was Nick's experience that anytime a cop saw him he wound up checking Nick for drugs or paraphernalia, usually finding both. Maybe the cops' newfound ambivalence was the product of Nick and Sarah's time at Springbrook. Perhaps, for the first time, their body language did not scream, *Search me! I have drugs!* Maybe Springbrook had done something for them, after all.

Nick was forced to stop a few times. His leg was getting worse. New pinpricks of red were showing through the old rust-colored spots on his sweatpants. Sarah wanted to help but they had nothing to serve as a bandage, no medication. Each time Nick allowed himself only a few minutes to rest. The need to reach Rebecca grew inside him each moment he spent sitting on a curb or bus stop bench.

They were on another side street, walking as quickly as Nick's leg would allow them, when Sarah stopped suddenly. Nick turned and saw she was staring at a house across the street. There was nothing remarkable about the structure; it looked like every other house in the neighborhood. Nick knew instantly why she stopped.

"You used to score there."

Sarah nodded without taking her eyes from the house. "Yeah. All the time."

She was considering crossing the street and knocking on the door. Nick could see it in her eyes, her body language. It was subtle, probably recognizable only to a fellow addict. She may as well have been panting with excitement, so clearly did she want to knock on that door.

"Why don't you?" he asked, his voice neutral.

Sarah continued to look at the house for another few moments. Then she turned away and took Nick's hand again and pulled him down the sidewalk. "Nah. Not today. Maybe another time."

Nick smiled.

Sarah stopped and regarded him. "Were you testing me?"

"No," he answered immediately. "No, I'm in no position to test anyone. But I'm glad you didn't do it." He smiled again.

Sarah squeezed his hand and started to walk again. They were a block past the house when she looked at Nick and said, "God, I need a hit."

Nick continued walking. "I know. Me, too." He thought about the many houses he knew of where they could find what they needed. He wondered if he would have had the strength to walk away, especially after the events of last night. He continued wondering for the next two hours, until they reached Rebecca's house.

****

Connelly stood on the periphery of the three corpses lying around a makeshift fire pit. The CSI guys were already present when he arrived and were doing their thing. He walked a slow circle around the scene and looked at each corpse in turn. They were homeless, that much was obvious. Just as obvious to anyone who had been at Springbrook was they were killed by the same lunatic. One of the men was decapitated. His head lay a good ten or twelve feet from the rest of the body. Another's throat was slashed almost to the bone. The front of his ancient shirt was dark crimson. The third poor bastard sported a very large hole in his chest, as if a tank shell had been fired through him. Connelly found he could picture quite easily how each man had died. He also knew the CSI guys would find the word "Wade" written in blood somewhere among the carnage. He did not bother to point it out to anyone. They were thorough, if nothing else, and they would find it on their own. Besides, he did not need the murderer's signature to know who was responsible.

Connelly squinted at the mid-morning sun and rubbed his eyes. He was exhausted, even if he would admit it to no one but himself. He had been awake now for almost twenty-eight hours. He was also officially off-shift. There was no reason for him to be in the park. With one more orbit around the crime scene he walked back to his car and headed home.

He was asleep thirty seconds after his head hit the pillow.

****

Sarah felt out of place immediately upon entering the neighborhood where Nick's cousin lived. The houses were large with well-manicured lawns and three-car garages. In one of the driveways a man wearing an outfit Sarah associated with golfers washed his black Mercedes and treated them to a long, disgusted stare. Nick ignored him; Sarah resisted the urge to flip him off.

They saw no one else during their foray into the land of the wealthy. Sarah was thankful for that. If any of the rich bastards who lived around here took too close a look at her and Nick's appearance they might feel inclined to call the cops. So she kept her eyes down for the most part and followed Nick.

They stopped in front of a very large home with a long driveway and a Spanish tile roof. The façade was of brick and gray vinyl siding. Sarah counted no fewer than three chimneys and she could picture them spewing smoke into the air on cold winter nights, warming the inhabitants while they sat around and sipped brandy and talked about their country club. It was certainly a far cry from her experiences of staying in a crack house and burning a pile of discarded clothes for warmth.

She did not like the neighborhood. And she did not like being here. But Nick was too weak and wounded to go back now.

"She's home," Nick said, pointing to the dark green Hyundai in the driveway. "About time something went our way."

Sarah did not reply. She clasped his hand tighter when they turned up the walkway.

****

Rebecca's jaw dropped when she opened the door and saw who was standing on her front porch. She shouted Nick's name and threw her arms around him and hugged him so tightly he could not breathe. She began to cry and he felt her tears on his neck.

"It's okay, Becks, it's okay. I'm all right." He hugged her back and then tried to pull away. She pulled him closer and tighter. Nick half-turned to Sarah who stood on the walk behind him. Sarah suppressed a laugh, but not a smile. She shrugged her shoulders. *You're on your own.*

Nick allowed Rebecca to continue the embrace for another moment before he successfully pulled back. He placed his hands on her arms and smiled. "It's okay, Becks. We're all right."

"Nicky, I was so worried about you." She spoke so quickly her words blended together. "The news said everybody was dead at the rehab. They're calling it the worst mass murder in recent memory, but they wouldn't give the names of anyone. I thought you were dead!" She threw herself at him again.

Nick's leg buckled and he would have gone down if Sarah had not been there to grab him. She braced him and kept him on his feet. They must have presented quite a sight to any neighbors who happened to be looking in their direction.

"We're okay," Nick said again. "Really. Becks?"

Rebecca held the embrace for another moment before she separated herself from him. "I'm so happy you're alive, Nicky. I really thought you were dead." She wiped at some tears.

"Well, I'm not. And I'm happy to see you, too. Can we come in?"

Rebecca sniffled and opened the door. "Of course. Mom's at work so I have the place to myself for a while. Come on in." She stepped inside and held the door for them.

The furniture was not new but it was in nice shape and looked both expensive and comfortable. They stood in the living room and Nick introduced Rebecca to Sarah.

"I think I remember you from that family day at the rehab," Rebecca said as she shook Sarah's hand.

Nick asked if he could sit down and Rebecca showed him to the recliner. It was soft and Nick felt himself sink right into it. He grimaced at the pain in his leg, by now a steady ache, and asked Rebecca if she had any painkillers.

Rebecca blanched. "Are you supposed to take anything? I thought that was part of your program." She looked and sounded concerned.

"We can take medicine," Sarah said, "so long as it's on the approved list. He needs something like Aspirin or Tylenol. Nothing with 'oxy' in the name." As Rebecca went upstairs Sarah called after her, "And some kind of bandage. And peroxide or the next best thing. His leg is a mess."

Rebecca turned, nodded, and continued up the stairs.

Nick leaned back in the chair and closed his eyes. He felt Sarah roll up his pant leg and tried to ignore her gasp of surprise. He did not want to look at it. He did not want to look at anything. By the time Rebecca returned with the medicine and the bandages, Nick was out cold.

****

Rebecca placed a steaming cup of coffee on the table in front of Sarah. Sarah took it gratefully and sipped it and it was the best coffee she ever tasted. They sat at the kitchen table while Nick snored loudly from the living room recliner. Rebecca took the chair opposite her and sipped from her own cup. They drank in silence for several moments.

After they bandaged Nick's leg Sarah had asked to use the facilities. Rebecca had regarded her with suspicion, probably assuming Sarah was going to ingest something illegal behind the closed door. As much as the thought appealed to her she assured Rebecca that was not part of the plan. After she relieved herself she splashed cold water on her face and spent a moment looking at her haggard appearance in the mirror. Then she opened the medicine cabinet and popped two Advil and sat on the toilet seat and cried.

She would have remained like that for much longer but she could imagine Rebecca downstairs growing more suspicious the longer she stayed inside the bathroom. She washed her face again and headed downstairs.

She called her brother and got the answering machine. Sarah left a message that she was all right but stopped short of saying where she was. She also left out any mention of Nick and told the machine she would call back later. Scott's cell was a possibility but she was surprised to find her desire to speak with him was greatly diminished. It was enough for now that he would know she was all right and still among the living.

Now she sat at the table and drank coffee and caught Nick's cousin looking at her several times over the rim of her cup. Sarah was used to this reaction from civilians and she allowed the girl her curiosity. She had taken them in, after all.

"So what were you there for?" Rebecca asked. Her tone was guarded but still conversational.

"Heroin, same as Nick," Sarah replied.

Rebecca shrugged but Sarah knew what she was thinking. *Birds of a feather. You'd better not fuck up his sobriety. If he relapses because of you there'll be hell to pay.* Sarah could not begrudge Rebecca her feelings. Her own brother disliked the idea of Sarah sharing a room at Springbrook with a fellow addict. Non-addicts always seemed to assume the addict was just biding their time until they could make another score. And they would share the wealth with whoever was around. It was what her brother expected of Jenna even though heroin and meth were two entirely different substances. And it was what Rebecca expected of her and Nick. The girl was no more capable of hiding her suspicions than was Sarah's brother

"I have no plans to get high, you know. And neither does Nick. Believe me, if we were gonna do that we wouldn't be here. I know plenty of places around West Philly where I could score. I'm sure he does, too. We're here, not there. I hope you believe me."

"Of course," Rebecca replied too quickly. She returned her attention to her cup. ·

They sat in uncomfortable silence for several more moments. Sarah resisted the urge to glance around the kitchen. It was another fact of her lifestyle that civilians always expected addicts, especially those they did not know well, to case the house for items to steal, said items eventually finding their way into pawn shops. She had no such intentions but Rebecca did not know that, nor was she likely to believe much of what Sarah told her. So Sarah kept her eyes on her cup and said little.

"Oh! I should call my mom, tell her Nicky's okay and that you're here." Rebecca pushed her chair from the table.

Rebecca acted as if the thought had not occurred to her until just now but Sarah could see through that easily. Addicts had a wonderful bullshit detector, a byproduct of the lies they themselves employed on a regular basis. Even if she were stoned to the hilt Sarah still would have seen through Rebecca's pretense. "Um."

Rebecca paused, her hand inches from the phone. "What?"

Sarah squirmed. *How do I go about this?* She cleared her throat. "I don't know if that's a good idea," she began. "Nick wants us to keep a low profile."

"She's my mom," Rebecca replied. "And Nicky's aunt. I have to tell her he's okay."

Sarah frowned. What could she say? The girl was right. She sat back and rubbed her eyes as Rebecca picked up the phone.

A moment later she said, "Mom! Nicky is okay." A pause. "No, he's here. He got here a little while ago with a girl from the rehab." She looked at Sarah before she turned her back. "His leg and his wrist are a little messed up but he's okay." Another pause. "No, how can you say that?" She sounded unsure as she cast a glance into the living room. "Mom, mom, calm down. He's okay. Isn't that the important—" Another pause.

Sarah could just make out the woman's voice on the other end of the phone. She could not make out any words, merely the insect buzz of an adult in a Charlie Brown cartoon. Even the buzz sounded angry.

"I will *not*. What's wrong with you? I don't— Hello? Mom?" Rebecca held the phone away from her ear and regarded it. She pressed the button to end the call and replaced the phone on its wall-mounted cradle. She turned back to Sarah. "She hung up."

"I assume she's not crazy about me being here."

Rebecca looked again into the living room from whence the sound of snoring continued. "She said she saw the news report this morning. She assumed Nicky was dead. How could she say that? It's like she was disappointed he's alive." She took a deep breath. "She wants you both out right now."

Sarah pushed her chair back from the table and stood.

Rebecca held up both hands. "You're not going anywhere. I'm not throwing my cousin out on the streets. I don't know what's up her ass, but it's not happening."

"Rebecca, we don't want to cause any trouble."

Rebecca turned from the living room and regarded Sarah. "This isn't trouble. Trouble will be when she gets home. Until then, you're free to stay."

Sarah did not argue.

****

Nick awoke to the sound of raised voices. The commotion catapulted him out of the dream and erased it from his memory. He forgot himself at first, thinking he was in a drug den somewhere and people were arguing over a shot of heroin. Having woken up in just such a place more than once he could be forgiven his momentary confusion. The cloud lifted from his memory and he found himself back in his cousin's living room. He looked about groggily. The light outside was the cold electric illumination of a nearby streetlight. Nick shook his head and homed in on the angry voices coming from the kitchen. He lifted himself from the old recliner and grimaced at the dull throb in his knee. He placed his hand over the wounded area and limped into the kitchen.

Aunt Noreen was there, standing in front of the counter with her arms folded imperiously across her chest. She was dressed in a beige power suit and her small purse still hung from one forearm. She glowered at the two girls on the other side of the table. Rebecca and Sarah stood nearly side by side, as if seeking strength from one another against the onslaught that had surely targeted them since the older woman's arrival. They looked equally uncomfortable, although Nick was willing to bet Rebecca had borne the brunt of her mother's anger. Rebecca appeared to have something to say but she stopped herself when she saw Nick standing weakly in the doorway. Noreen noticed her daughter's hesitation and her gaze moved to Nick.

"Get out of my house, Nicholas," Noreen hissed. "Get out and take your fucking junkie girlfriend with you. I won't have you bring your bullshit under this roof." She threw her arm in Rebecca's direction. "I worked too hard to make sure Rebecca doesn't go down the same road you did. You're not gonna fuck up everything now. Understand me?"

"Mom, he's not—"

"*Stop interrupting me.*" Noreen's eyes drilled into Rebecca's.

The last of the girl's resistance crumbled beneath the weight of that glare. Her shoulders slumped. She shuffled her feet. Her lips trembled but she said nothing.

Sarah looked at Nick. "We'd better go." She started for the living room.

Nick held up his hand. "We're not leaving yet."

Noreen's cheeks turned an even brighter shade of red. Her shoulders shook with fury. It took her several moments to regain the ability to speak. When she did, her voice was perfectly level, nearly monotone. "I said leave."

Nick took a single step into the kitchen. "No."

Noreen flung her purse across the room, causing Sarah and Rebecca to duck. Rebecca emitted a surprised squeal. Noreen's eyes narrowed and her lips pulled back from her teeth. "Leave now or I call the police." She took a step toward the phone mounted on the wall beside the fridge.

Nick folded his arms across his chest. "Knock yourself out. When they get here you can explain to them why you slipped me some heroin that day at Springbrook. I'm sure they'd love to hear that story."

Noreen's hand froze inches from the phone.

"What?" Sarah sounded incredulous.

"That's impossible," Rebecca stuttered.

Noreen picked up the phone. "A lie. All junkies lie, isn't that right? Let's see who the police believe."

Nick did not release her eyes. "Yeah, let's."

For several moments no one moved. Noreen seemed to study him. Her eyes penetrated his in a way that made him want to run from the house. But he did not. Nick stood his ground and endured the hate in those eyes. The older woman's body shook with rage and, Nick guessed, the pure indignation of being called out in front of her daughter. He expected her to dial 911 and call his bluff. She was right, of course; the cops would take her at her word. He resisted the urge to look away.

Noreen placed the phone back on its cradle slowly, as if it were the last thing in the world she wanted to do. Her hands dropped to her side and her shoulders slumped. She walked slowly to the table and sat down. Rebecca and Sarah both backed up a step.

Nick approached the table. He pulled out a chair and motioned for the girls to join them. They both hesitated but Nick's attention was no longer on them. He sat gingerly and stared at his aunt. "Tell me everything."

Chapter 17

An Urban Legend

Noreen lit a cigarette and exhaled loudly. The smoke swirled around the small, elaborate light fixture dangling above the table. The small but expanding cloud hung in the air and silence. Noreen took another puff before she said, "Rebecca, put a pot of coffee on, will you?"

Rebecca stood rooted to the spot for a moment. She had not moved since her mother sat down. Her eyes went from Noreen to Nick and back before she mumbled, "Okay," and made for the stove.

Nick took his eyes off his aunt long enough to nod at Sarah. "Go ahead, she won't bite. I think."

Sarah walked around the table and pulled a chair next to Nick and sat. She placed her hands on the table and laced her fingers together. Nick placed his hand on hers and squeezed. Sarah offered him a weak smile. Nick mirrored her smile before he returned his eyes to the older woman across the table.

Noreen pushed her pack of cigarettes and lighter toward Nick. Nick sat back in the chair and folded his arms. Sarah looked hesitantly at the offering before she scooped them up and lit a cigarette for herself.

"Aunt Noreen, I think time is a factor, here. I don't know how I know that, but I'm pretty sure I'm right. So please, tell me what the hell is happening."

Noreen puffed on her cigarette, put it out in the ashtray, and lit another. "I'm not sure I know where to begin."

"Maybe you can start with why you smuggled heroin into the rehab. That might be a good place."

"Jesus," Sarah whispered.

"Mom, tell me you didn't." Rebecca stood by the counter, tending to the plug-in coffee maker. Her eyes were wide, her mouth agape.

Noreen remained motionless and silent. She kept her eyes on the table, inclining her head slightly only to puff on her cigarette. After a few moments she rubbed her eyes and regarded Nick. She looked much older than her fifty-three years, as if she had aged significantly in the past few moments. Most of her customary Aunt Noreen Hostility seemed, not quite absent, but dormant. Her lips parted as if she were about to speak before she closed them again.

Nick almost reached across the table to take her free hand in his. He stopped himself when he thought about the small baggie she slipped into his hands and the conspiratorial *I'm-on-your-side* look she threw him. "Aunt Noreen."

"I did it for your own good," she blurted out. She sat back as if surprised by what she said. Her eyes darted about nervously, a woman looking for the person who had just sucker-punched her. After a moment during which she seemed to steady herself, she repeated, "For your own good, Nicholas."

"How could that have been for his own good?" Sarah asked. She sounded both horrified and angry. "You have no idea what that was like for him."

Nick held up his hand. "It's okay, Sarah. Let her talk."

Noreen seemed unfazed by Sarah's outburst or her accusatory tone. That alone made Nick nervous. He doubted many people had gotten away with speaking like that to Noreen Wade-Davies, and certainly no one in her own home, least of all a stranger. Nick wiped his sweaty palms on his pants.

"It was for your own good," Noreen repeated. "Yours and everyone else's."

"Okay, that you're gonna have to explain," Nick replied. "You went from not wanting me around Rebecca—and I'm not saying you were wrong about that, by the way—to scoring some H for me. How does that happen?"

Rebecca placed a cup in front of each person and filled them with coffee. She took the last empty chair and watched her mother with a mixture of hope and dread. "Mom, how could you do that? After everything you drilled into my head about drugs…" She stopped and looked at Nick.

"She said she had a reason, Becks." He returned his gaze to his aunt. "And I'm dying to hear it."

Noreen took one more puff on her cigarette before she snubbed it out. She reached for the pack again but stopped herself. Instead she laced her fingers together and looked at Nick. "You won't believe me, but like I said, it was for your own good. And my daughter's, and everyone else's, too."

"Yeah, you keep saying that. I need an explanation, Aunt Noreen. And I need it now."

Noreen took a deep, shuddering breath. "I don't think you want to know, Nicholas. I really don't."

"Oh, for fuck's sake, *just tell us*," Sarah shouted. She slammed her palm on the tabletop for emphasis. "Christ, lady, do you have any fucking idea what happened last night?"

Noreen did not react to Sarah's outburst. Instead, she said, "Nothing would have happened last night if Nicholas had used what I gave him. That was the whole point."

"What the hell are you talking about?"

Nick was about to say the same thing before Sarah beat him to it. He only nodded in the girl's direction. "That's a pretty valid question, Aunt Noreen."

"I agree," Rebecca added. The hope was gone from her eyes. She regarded her mother with sadness and anger.

Noreen continued as if no one had spoken. "The man who showed up at the junkie hospital last night. You saw him?"

Nick held up his injured wrist. "Up close and personal."

Noreen leaned forward a bit. "Did he seem familiar to you?"

Nick rubbed his eyes. "Yes. I mean, kinda. I'm not completely sure. But he definitely knew me. How?"

"Oh, he's known you for a long time, Nicholas. From your dreams, mostly."

Nick felt something cold wrap itself around his heart and for a moment he could not breathe. He tried to speak but he was no longer capable of producing a coherent sound. He stuttered and blinked. Sarah put her arm around him and pulled him a bit closer.

"Nick? Are you okay?"

Nick's throat constricted. The gooseflesh rose on his arms and legs. He ceased to see his aunt's kitchen and instead found himself in the MacKennedy backyard. The scene shifted to Santos's living room before he found himself in a parking garage. Sweat coated his forehead and dripped into his eyes. The rapid change of location caused his stomach to rumble. Quickly and without conscious thought, Nick bolted for the sink. Somehow he made it in time. His stomach was empty but he managed to void a small amount of bile. It burned his throat and brought him back to his aunt's kitchen. Nick wiped at the tears in his eyes and concentrated on keeping his legs under him.

Someone patted him on the back and brushed his sweaty hair from his eyes. "It's okay, Nick," Sarah soothed. "It's okay. You're okay."

Nick coughed and spat into the sink. He turned on the tap and stuck his mouth under it, slurping water as quickly as he could. He spat again before he turned off the tap and looked back at his aunt. "How…how do you know about that?" He wiped weakly at the remaining moisture around his eyes.

Sarah helped him back to the table. His leg gave at the last moment and Nick collapsed into his chair. He landed with a thud, grimaced at the fresh pain in his knee.

Noreen sipped her coffee. It seemed to return some of her emotional stability. She sat a little straighter, there was a renewed confidence in her eyes. She lit another cigarette and regarded her nephew through the smoke. "You're not the first Wade to go through this."

****

Connelly sat at his kitchen table and absently munched on an English muffin. The wound to his side had turned an ugly shade of dark purple while he slept. There was little pain but it was certainly uncomfortable. He shifted continuously in the chair as he scrolled through the preliminary report from both Springbrook and the park on his laptop. The CSI tech in charge of the investigation, Rizzo, was probably the best the city had and Connelly was confident she would find and file all the evidence. He was just as confident she would not believe her own findings.

The female survivor from Springbrook, Jenna Davino, was released from the hospital with a clean bill of health. Connelly was happy to read that; it was the one bit of good news so far. Wade and McCallister remained among the missing but an APB had been sent out. Connelly was less confident that would produce any results. They were both addicts, and addicts had a way of avoiding attention. He knew—*knew*—Wade was the key to the whole thing, but he had no evidence to back up that assertion. And until the man surfaced, willingly, the question mark would continue to hang over the investigation.

There was no new information from McCallister's mother, at least not at the time the report was filed. Connelly could not go back to her; if the woman's daughter was still incommunicado his presence would do nothing but irritate her again. That left Wade's family.

Connelly scrolled to the section that detailed Nicholas Wade. Both parents deceased, no siblings. So much for that. It would have been an obvious avenue for the investigating officers, anyway. Connelly continued to scroll through the report.

Buried at the back of the report was the sign-in roster for the rehab's most recent family day. Connelly saw McCallister's brother attended the event. A few spaces below was Wade's name. His two visitors were Noreen and Rebecca Davies.

"Slim," Connelly said. "In fact, probably nothing." He minimized the report and brought up the search engine. A few moments later he was moving for the door as quickly as his wounded side would allow.

****

Noreen polished off her coffee and slid the empty cup toward Rebecca. "Get me another one, please, honey."

"Yes, mom." Rebecca stood and picked up the cup. "Anyone else?"

Sarah said, "No, thanks," and Nick waved her off. He never felt less like coffee in his life.

"Aunt Noreen, please, I wasn't kidding about time being a factor."

"Oh, I believe you. In fact, I'm gonna wrap this up right now so the two of you can hit the road as quickly as possible."

"Whatever you say."

"My brother had those same dreams," Noreen began. "So did our father. And our grandfather. I don't know all the details or even how far back this goes. At least 150 years, if my grandmother was to be believed, maybe even longer than that." She accepted the fresh cup from Rebecca and took a thoughtful sip. "He's been called by a bunch of names. The one that stuck was put on him when our family still lived in North Jersey. Some small town rag dubbed him the Shadow Man. Have you ever heard of him?"

Nick shook his head. "No, I don't think so."

Sarah said, "I remember something about that. He's an urban legend, isn't he? Some psycho serial killer or something like that."

"*Something* like that, yes," Noreen replied. "His appearances are so infrequent and spread out that no one's ever put two and two together." She leaned forward and folded her hands on the table. "He only shows up when a male Wade dies."

Nick blinked at her. "What?"

"That doesn't make any sense," Sarah added. "Who died last night? Was there someone in the family who passed away?"

"It wasn't just last night," Nick said. "This has been going on for a couple weeks now. Who died, Aunt Noreen?"

The older woman shook her head. "No one, as far as I know. That's not why he's here this time."

"But you just said—"

Noreen slammed her open palm on the tabletop and Nick yelped; the vibration from the impact sent a jolt into his broken wrist. The coffee cups and the ashtray jumped a bit. Sarah instinctively backed away as far as her chair would allow. Rebecca jumped, too, and emitted a startled yelp.

"Don't interrupt me, young lady. I believe my nephew when he says we're running short of time and I want you two out of here ASAP. So let me finish, okay?"

Sarah's lips pressed into a thin line. She sat back in the chair and folded her arms across her chest. Nick massaged his wrist gently.

Noreen held Sarah's gaze for another moment before she returned her attention to Nick. "I was saying?"

Nick placed his uninjured hand on Sarah's knee without taking his eyes from his aunt. "He only shows up when someone dies."

"Right." Noreen took another sip of her coffee. "He showed up sixteen years ago when your father died. Before that he popped up again when my father died, and on and on and on."

"And he disappears again after we all die? Is that it?"

Noreen shook her head. "No, not exactly. The deaths have something to do with it but that's not what makes him appear and disappear. You know your father OD'd, correct? What you might not realize is he did it on purpose."

"Come again?"

Noreen nodded. "He had his reasons. Before he killed himself, my brother had been trying to beat his addiction. He actually went a couple weeks without heroin. That was when the Shadow Man showed up."

"And Nick's been off the stuff for a while now," Rebecca said. She turned to her mother. "Is that why?"

Noreen inclined her head in her daughter's direction. Her lips pulled back from her teeth in a bad imitation of a proud smile. "Yes, dear, that's why."

Sarah started to speak, but Nick held up his hand. "You're saying this is my fault."

Noreen waved him off. "That's one way to look at it, I suppose." Nick thought she tried to sound sympathetic but she failed miserably. "Like I said, I don't have all the details. What I know is, a very long time ago this...*thing* became--I'm not sure of the right word. Connected, maybe?--to our family. My guess is it doesn't like this any more than you do. It wants out, and my grandmother thought that if it kills the last male Wade it'll get its wish. If that happens it'll never go away. It'll just go on killing until it gets bored."

"Jesus," Sarah whispered.

"He won't help you," Noreen said. "No one will. Because no one can."

"And my father knew all this?"

Noreen nodded. "Our grandmother told us when dad died. That's why she introduced my brother to heroin."

Nick stuttered.

Noreen picked up her lighter and began to tap it on the tabletop. "Sometime in the 1800s, probably right after this thing became attached to our family, one of the Wade men discovered that taking opiates blocks the connection to this creature. At some point along the way opium gave way to heroin. They both work on the brain in the same way. Since then every male in the family has eventually become hooked on that shit."

"Bullshit," Sarah remarked.

"Oh, I'm afraid it's quite true," Noreen replied.

Sarah looked at Nick. "It's not possible, Nick. Okay? Not fucking possible."

Noreen continued as if the girl had not spoken. "This thing, this Shadow Man, it remains linked, if that's the right word, to the same male until that male dies. Then it latches onto the next in line. When your father died, it was free to do whatever it wanted to do."

"So my mother got me on heroin to stop it."

Noreen nodded. "Yes."

Nick lowered his head. "Fuck me."

"She got herself hooked on it, too, Nicholas. She must have felt that you would do it more easily if she did it with you. Your mother was what we used to call a goody-goody. She didn't drink, smoke, swear, nothing. Until your father died."

Nick looked at Sarah. Her eyes were wide and red-rimmed. She blinked back tears until she lost the battle. She hugged him tightly and he felt her tears on his shirt sleeve. He placed his hand on the back of her head.

"You knew all this and you never said anything?" Rebecca asked. She sounded horrified, from the story or her mother's secrecy, or a combination of both, Nick did not know.

"It never should have reached this point," Noreen replied. "Nicholas should have stayed hooked on that shit. Even when he went into that place I didn't think he'd actually make it. When I started hearing about those killings on the news, I knew what was behind it. I also knew Nicholas had to get back on the drug so the killings would stop." She returned her attention to Nick. "That's why I gave you that baggie at the rehab."

"All those people would still be alive if I hadn't gone to Springbrook," Nick whispered.

Sarah pulled away from him and placed her hands on his cheeks. "Even if all this is true, you couldn't have known, Nick. There's no way you could have known."

"You two need to leave now," Noreen said. "I've told you everything. I need you out the door before that thing finds you here. I won't allow you to put my daughter in harm's way any longer than you already have."

"Right." Nick stood a bit too suddenly. His knee gave and he just managed to brace himself against the table before he fell.

Sarah stood up to help him. "Hang on, hang on a minute." She had a good grip on his arm and Nick steadied himself. "I'm still not clear on something. What are all these men in your family supposed to do? Stay on heroin for their whole lives? What happens when they accidentally overdose and die? Because it sounds to me that's what you're hoping for."

Noreen swallowed. For the first time she looked genuinely saddened. "If you die of an overdose and there are no more male Wades around, that might trap this thing forever. That's what my brother and I thought. But toward the end he was so fucked up his mind was gone. When he drove out to the airport he planned to shoot himself in the head. The Shadow Man went after him. If he can kill you while you're free of the drug, he'll be free. I don't think your father knew anything by then, except he wanted the pain to stop." She lowered her eyes. "I think it caught up to him and maybe they fought. The gun got knocked away and he did the only thing he could think to do."

"He overdosed."

"I think it was his last resort, the only way he could stop the thing from killing him and freeing itself."

"You *bitch*!" Sarah let go of Nick suddenly. She reached across the table so quickly Nick had no time to react. Neither did

Noreen. Sarah's open hand connected solidly with Noreen's cheek. The older woman took a surprised step back. Rebecca jumped to her feet and steadied her mother. Nick got his hands on Sarah's shoulders and pulled her back. Fortunately she did not resist; Nick was in no shape to restrain her for more than a moment or two. Noreen took another step back from the table, her hand holding her cheek and her eyes wide with shock.

"That's enough," Rebecca shouted. Her hands remained on her mother's arms. When she was convinced Sarah would not launch another attack Rebecca gave her mother her full attention.

"We need to go," Nick said. He limped in the direction of the back door.

Sarah glared at Noreen, but the older woman apparently thought better of challenging her. She kept her eyes either on the floor or focused on Rebecca. Sarah caught up to Nick and placed her arm around his waist.

Nick stopped when he reached the back door. He half-turned. "Thanks, Becks. For everything."

Rebecca wiped at some tears. "You're not leaving?"

"Oh, yes we are."

"Nicky…"

"We'll be okay, Becks." He smiled his most reassuring smile. "Promise."

The girl stuttered. At last, she managed, "Please, be careful."

"You, too." He flashed his confident smile again. He glanced at Noreen, who rubbed her cheek gently and spoke too softly for Nick to hear what she said. He redirected his attention to Sarah. "Let's go."

Sarah opened the back door. "Any idea where to?"

Nick shrugged. "No idea. We'll come up with something."

Rebecca crossed the kitchen and threw her arms around Nick. The sudden move threw him off-balance, but the doorway caught him and kept him on his feet. Sarah moved out of the way. Rebecca kissed his cheek and held him tightly and whispered, "I love you," in his ear. Nick held her close and stroked her hair. "Be careful, Nicky. Please be careful."

"Of course, Becks. Don't worry about me. I'll be fine. Take care of your mom, okay?" He pulled away and was relieved when she did not try to hold onto him. "We gotta go now, Becks."

Rebecca grasped his hand again before she took a step back.

Nick looked at his hand, at the ring of keys she had left there. "I can't take your car, Becks."

"You can and you will." She glanced briefly at Sarah before her eyes settled again on her cousin. "Love you, Nicky."

"Rebecca…"

"Go."

He hugged her again. "Thanks. And I love you, too."

She toggled the light switch next to the door and the expansive backyard was illuminated weakly. Rebecca sniffled and smiled. "Anytime." She looked past him into the backyard. She frowned and flicked the light switch several times. "Looks like we lost a couple lights at the other end."

The hair on Nick's arms rose to attention quite suddenly. He turned back toward Rebecca.

That was when something large and covered in darkness crashed through the window to Nick's left.

****

Connelly had never been to this neighborhood in his professional career although he had cruised past it once or twice. He was starting to regret his decision to call on Wade's visitors at Springbrook. The people who lived in this neighborhood were unused to dealing with the police and were certainly unused to being questioned. He could already envision the woman calling her attorney to report his appearance on her doorstep. It would not deter him, of course; he had a legitimate reason for being here, after all. But he was still uneasy.

"Just a quick conversation," he said to the dashboard. "A quick in-and-out, five minutes at most. Who knows, they might even be able to point me in the right direction."

Connelly shrugged and followed the directions of his GPS.

****

Shards of glass flew in all directions. Nick and Sarah, to the side of the window, were not hit. Rebecca screamed and shielded her eyes. Bits of glass pelted her arms and left small beads of blood in their wake. Noreen caught the brunt of it. She shrieked and backed away until she bumped into the refrigerator.

The momentum of the alien object carried it across the kitchen. It crashed into the table and splintered it. Three of the legs snapped and the table split and collapsed. Bits of window glass skittered across the linoleum. The light hanging above the table swung wildly but Nick could barely make out its shape; the kitchen had gone dark.

For a moment there was no sound in the kitchen, no sound in the house. Nick stood by the door and held his breath. He peered into the sudden darkness but could make out little. The bright light from the outside floods seemed powerless to penetrate the shadows that enveloped the kitchen. Nick closed his eyes and concentrated. It took a moment but he could just barely hear the sound of short, quick breaths coming from Rebecca's direction. He reached into the darkness. Rebecca shrieked and pulled her arm back when Nick brushed it.

"Becks, it's me, it's me." He reached farther into the darkness until he felt her arm again. Nick grasped it and pulled her closer. "It's okay, Becks. It's me. I'm right in front on you."

"Nicky?" Rebecca stepped forward. Nick could see the outline of her body against the meager light spilling through the open kitchen door. There was a sharp intake of breath when he pulled her closer and embraced her. "Where's mom?"

Nick shoved Rebecca and Sarah through the open door. "Run."

Three steps descended from the kitchen door to the very large deck. Rebecca stopped at the bottom of the stairs and turned. "Nick, my mom!"

Nick could hear and see nothing from within the kitchen. "I'll get her. You two need to go, *now*."

"We're not leaving you," Sarah told him.

"Yes, you are." Nick closed the kitchen door forcefully. He could hear the two women on the other side, banging on the door and shouting his name. Nick turned back to the kitchen.

Something rustled in the darkness, something that sounded like dead leaves blowing gently but quickly across the linoleum. He could see little but he knew the thing was getting to its feet. He could not see his aunt but he could now hear her breathing from across the room.

"Aunt Noreen? Are you okay?"

"I can't see." Her voice was weak. It came from somewhere ahead and to his left.

"Get out of the house. Get out now."

Nick saw something rise in front of him perhaps ten feet away. It was tall. The oblong shape atop the thing's head brushed the light fixture dangling from the ceiling and sent it swinging on its thin cable.

On the other side of the thing, a step or two in front of the refrigerator, Noreen held both her arms in front of her. Her hands probed into the darkness blindly. Nick could barely see her but it seemed his eyes were becoming accustomed to the darkness.

"Wade," said the Shadow Man.

Noreen shrieked.

He chanced a quick glance at the door behind him. Rebecca and Sarah stood on the other side of the glass. They implored him to open the door.

Noreen screamed again. She had shrunk back against the refrigerator with her hands outstretched before her. The scream bounced off the walls and hurt Nick's ears.

The Shadow Man swung its emaciated arm in a wide, rapid arc. The back of its fist connected solidly with Noreen's head. Her skull exploded in a black haze of blood and bone. Her arms, still outstretched, began a series of intricate gestures in the air, as if she were a sorceress casting a complicated magic spell. Her body staggered across the kitchen floor until her feet became entangled on the ruins of the table. The corpse tripped and landed hard on the linoleum. One of her arms reached out as if to stop the fall before it folded at the elbow. Her legs and arms twitched a few times before the cadaver lay still.

"Wade," the thing repeated. The Shadow Man squared its shoulders and faced Nick. It stepped toward him.

Nick heard glass shatter behind him and the kitchen door flew open. Two pairs of hands grabbed him and pulled him back violently. Nick, all semblance of balance lost, tumbled backward and down the steps that led to the backyard. He landed atop both Sarah and Rebecca, heard them gasp for air.

Nick rolled off them quickly and got to his knees. He eyed the darkened doorway in front of him.

"Run!" Rebecca screamed.

Nick was on his feet, standing between his cousin and Sarah. Both girls ran for the side of the house, each with a hand on his arms. His leg hurt but the adrenaline pumping through his veins pushed away the pain and he was able to match the speed of his two companions.

"Nicky, my mom?" Rebecca asked breathlessly.

Nick did not reply.

They rounded the side of the house and Nick zeroed in on Rebecca's Hyundai. He fumbled with the key ring until he found the fob. He pointed it at the car as they ran.

An unremarkable sedan pulled in front of the house and rocked a bit on its suspension when the driver slammed on the brakes. The driver's door flew open and a man stepped out. His hand was already reaching inside his jacket. "Nicholas Wade? Philly PD."

The front door of Noreen Wade-Davies's home vanished in an explosion of expensive wood. There was nothing but darkness there, as if the pulverized door had been replaced by one made of obsidian. Nick thought he could see movement somewhere within that darkness.

Rebecca stopped dead in her tracks. The sudden move threw Nick and Sarah off-balance and they tumbled onto the grass. "Shoot it!" Rebecca shouted and pointed at the doorway.

The cop glanced briefly at the empty doorway before he returned his attention to Nick.

Nick regained his feet and helped Sarah to hers. They made for the Hyundai.

The Shadow Man emerged from the house. The area directly in front of it darkened but Nick could see its hulking shape well enough. The cop must have seen it, too.

The sound of the gunshot echoed off the homes and picket fences in the immediate area. The Shadow Man's body shuddered with the impact. It stopped its advance on Nick and turned toward the police officer. It did not appear hurt. If anything the impact of the bullet seemed to irritate the creature.

The cop from the rehab stood in front of his car and leveled his weapon at the mass of darkness.

"It's directly in front of you," Nick shouted. "Run!"

The Shadow Man turned from Nick. The cop seemed unsure of its exact position. He pointed his gun in the general direction of the creature's last location.

The zone of darkness moved toward the cop.

He fired several rounds. The muzzle flash of the gun was muted in the shadows, appearing like the tiny spark of a cigarette lighter that refused to light.

"No!" Nick broke from Sarah and ran as fast as his wounded leg would allow at the Shadow Man. He landed on the thing's back and dug his fingers into its arms. The Shadow Man spun quickly. Nick's legs shot out almost vertically from the creature's body. His feet smashed into the cop and sent the man tumbling backward, off-balance. The gun discharged and buried a slug in the Hyundai's door.

Nick's broken wrist finally gave out. He lost his grip and for a moment he was weightless. Sarah and Rebecca scrambled to avoid the missile he had become. Only one of them was successful. Nick collided with Rebecca and the two of them went down hard on the grass. The breath was driven from his lungs and pain lanced from his leg up his spine.

"Nick!" Sarah shouted. She was at his side instantly.

He groaned and rolled off his cousin. "Becks, you okay?"

Rebecca echoed his moan and rolled onto her side, clutching her abdomen.

"Nick?" Sarah asked. She placed her arm around his shoulders as he struggled to lift himself from the cold ground.

"How's Rebecca?" Nick got to his knees and looked at his cousin. She lay on her side, coughing weakly and protecting her middle with both hands. "Becks."

"She'll be okay," Sarah replied. She yanked Nick to his feet so quickly he lost his balance. He would have gone down again had Sarah not braced herself. She threw her arm around him and moved as quickly as she was able for the driveway. "C'mon!" she screamed.

Nick felt slow and clumsy and it took him several tries to get his feet under him. He saw the cop rise to one knee and aim his weapon into the approaching mass of darkness. "Get outta here!" Nick shouted.

The Shadow Man turned in their direction.

Sarah did not pause. She all but dragged him in the direction of Rebecca's car. She threw open the passenger's door and tossed Nick inside.

"We have to go back for Rebecca," Nick said weakly. "Sarah, we have to go back."

Sarah got in behind the wheel. "It doesn't want her, it wants us." She slammed the door closed and threw a glance over her shoulder. The mass of darkness had changed course and was closing on the Hyundai. Sarah jammed the key into the ignition and turned it. The engine roared to life. She slapped the shifter into D and mashed the gas pedal. The car surged down the driveway and she did not look back.

****

Connelly saw the Shadow Man turn away from him and focus on Wade and McCallister. The thing appeared to deflate and became an amorphous black stain on the lawn. It flowed swiftly across the grass in the direction of the Hyundai. McCallister was behind the wheel and she nearly smoked the tires on the way out of the driveway. The mass of darkness pursued, but it was not fast enough. The car fishtailed a bit when McCallister spun the wheel, then she and Wade vanished down the tree-lined street. Connelly quickly lost sight of the Shadow Man but he was able to track its progress by the streetlights winking out in succession. He lowered his weapon.

He heard someone gasping for air nearby. The young girl left behind by Wade and McCallister lay on the ground, struggling to push herself into a sitting position. Connelly rushed to her.

"They're gone," the girl gasped. She winced and covered her abdomen. "They're all gone."

Connelly knelt beside her. "Are you injured, miss?" It was a stupid question, cop 101 stuff. It was all he could think to say. He glanced about the yard but he knew the girl spoke the truth. Wade was gone, as was Sarah McCallister. And the Shadow Man. Connelly swallowed and turned his attention back to the young girl.

"Lay down, miss. I'll call for an ambulance. Just stay still."

The girl did as he directed

Chapter 18

The Familiar Itch

Nick jounced around the front seat as Sarah struggled to control the unfamiliar vehicle. She took the first corner much too quickly. The tires squealed and Nick was thrown against the door. He pulled himself into a sitting position and fumbled for the seatbelt. "Sarah, slow down. Slow down or we're gonna die." He kept his voice as level as he could, which was not very. His heart hammered inside his chest and it had little to do with her driving skills.

"No way, no way," she said, and Nick did not know if she was speaking to him or to herself.

"Sarah, slow down." He did a much better job of keeping his voice level and calm the second time. He looked out the window and concluded he had no idea where they were. His aunt's house was three blocks away, maybe four. He did not know how quickly the Shadow Man could move but he doubted the thing could outpace the six cylinder Hyundai, and certainly not with Sarah's foot mashing the gas pedal into the floorboards. He looked out the back window and saw nothing but empty street. "He's not behind us, we're clear. C'mon, slow down."

She took another corner at full speed. Nick was once again acquainted with the passenger door. The armrest dug into his side and caused him to yelp. He looked at the frightened girl behind the wheel. Sarah took one hand from the wheel long enough to wipe at her eyes. Her breath was coming short and fast and when the street gave her a straightaway she pounded one hand on the wheel.

"Babe, slow down or you're gonna kill us. We're safe, okay?"

She shot him a quick glance as if noticing for the first time he was seated next to her, albeit plastered against the passenger door with one hand braced against the dashboard. Her foot came off the gas pedal and the furious roar of the engine became a low, relieved growl. She pulled to the curb between a red pickup and someone's driveway. She licked her lips nervously and put the car in park. Then she leaned back in the seat and closed her eyes and did not bother trying to stop the tears.

Nick sat up and wrapped both his arms around her. The sobs came more freely now and he held her tight and patted her head gently. "We're okay, we're okay," he repeated. "Take a deep breath, calm down. It's okay."

She pulled away from him and regarded him with wet eyes. "How can you say that, Nick? Didn't you just watch that thing murder your aunt? If that cop didn't show up you'd be dead, too."

Nick started to argue but stopped himself. She was right, of course. For the second time in less than twenty-four hours the unknown cop had saved his life. And he had, indeed, watched Aunt Noreen killed in front of him. He tried not to think of what may have happened to the cop. Or to Rebecca.

"We'll be okay," he said after a moment. "Switch places with me. I'll drive."

Sarah said nothing but she stepped out of the car and walked around to the other side. Nick worked his way into the seat and behind the wheel and opened the passenger door for her. She sat down and closed the door and said nothing. She looked out the back window every few moments.

Nick glanced at the dashboard clock. 9:18 PM it flashed at him. He turned to Sarah. "What day is it?"

She looked confused for a moment before she said, "Wednesday. No, Thursday. I think it's Thursday. Why?"

"Nothing." He put the car in drive and pulled away from the curb. "Where do you live? I'll take you home."

"I'm not leaving you," she said matter-of-factly.

"Sarah, you've done enough for me. I'm taking you home. Where do you live?"

She wiped at her eyes and sniffled but said nothing, just stared out the windshield.

Nick grimaced. "Fine. I have a stop to make, a quick one. Then we're going our separate ways. Even if ten percent of what Aunt Noreen told us is true, that's enough to know this thing won't stop as long as I'm alive and clean. And I don't want it coming after you. So after that stop I'm taking you home and that's all there is to it. Got me?"

Sarah continued to stare out the window silently.

Nick shook his head.

It took almost twenty minutes to get to O'Toole's, mostly because Nick had never been there while sober and it took him a few tries to remember where it was. The bar was obviously a dive; even from the outside he felt like he needed an STD shot just from looking at it. He parked the Hyundai across from the front entrance and put it in park.

Sarah looked out her window and then at Nick. "Do I even want to know?"

"Probably not." He killed the engine and opened the door and stepped into the cool night air. A few people wandered the streets around O'Toole's, mostly the type of people Nick would expect to frequent such a place. A few of the night people stumbled as they walked. He spotted a few telltale orange glows from cigarettes, joints as they walked. At the edge of the alley between the bar and the Chinese place next door a pair of junkies shot up beneath the streetlight. Nick's mouth was suddenly dry.

Sarah got out of the car and regarded O'Toole's. Nick detested the idea of her being anywhere near the place, let alone venturing inside. But he also knew he could not leave her in the car, either. Not alone. Not around here. He closed his door and walked around to her side and took her hand. "You really wanna do this? I'm sure you can guess what goes on around here."

"I can smell it," she replied. Her voice was equal parts longing and disgust. She inclined her head in the direction of the two junkies in the alley. "And it's not like I'm blind, either."

Nick watched her. Sarah did not lick her lips or fidget with her hands but he knew what she was thinking. *Just one hit. Just one to take the edge off. Really, that's all I'll take. I'll stay clean after that.* He thought the exact the same thing. He hoped when they walked out of O'Toole's she would still be sober.

"Let's go." He led the way across the street.

He did not recognize any of the junkies hanging around the entrance. That was not odd in and of itself. He rarely associated with the street people, preferring to do his business inside and then vacate the area as quickly as possible. Lingering was a good way to get robbed and nothing would ruin a night more than exiting the club with a brick of H only to have it taken by some lowlife scumbag after he delivered a few surprise kicks to the balls. One of them nodded to Nick and Nick nodded back and pulled Sarah a bit closer.

The inside of the place seemed both familiar and alien. On the rare occasions Nick had come here sober he was usually too sick to pay much attention to his surroundings. It was typical of any smoke-choked dive in the country. The lighting was subdued, the air thick with the stench of old smoke and alcohol. Several framed photographs of Peter O'Toole decorated the walls as well as movie posters of *Lawrence of Arabia*, *The Lion in Winter* and *Caligula*, among others. Behind the bar, the centerpiece of the whole place, was an autographed 8X10 of the actor. Nick could not remember noticing that before but it had certainly been present every time he had come here; the photograph was almost obscured completely by a film of grime on the glass that doubtless took years to build up.

Several people sat on stools at the bar, drinking their Das Saftiges and Bud Lights. Not one of them so much as looked in their direction. Nick shot a nod to the bartender, whose name was either Eric or Derek, and made for the door opposite the pool table. Two bikers stood at the pool table and eyed Sarah, and Nick grasped her hand a bit more tightly.

He knocked twice on the door and waited. After a moment it opened a crack. A rather large and bloodshot eye peered at him from the other side. Nick looked back but said nothing. The eye studied him before moving over to Sarah. A moment later the door swung open.

The large man attached to the eye stepped back. Nick crossed the threshold with a confidence he did not possess. Sarah stayed at his side and shrunk away from the large man's attention. The door closed behind them.

The back room at O'Toole's, where the club's real business took place, was dark and smelled of stale smoke and vomit. There were two ancient sofas opposite each other on either side of the room. Straight ahead from the door was a large, ornate desk that seemed wildly out of place amid the squalor of the rest of the room. Seated in the high-backed chair behind the desk was the man himself.

Bryan McMillan was perhaps fifty although he looked older. What was left of the hair on his head was white with wisps of light brown. He was overweight but not grossly so. A thick gold chain hung from his ample neck and his fingers were adorned with rings of every shape. Nick had forgotten about the man's tattoo. It was on his right forearm and looked to be Peter O'Toole sporting ancient Greek robes. Nick had never been close enough to it to verify precisely what it was. McMillan nodded once. "Wade."

Nick returned the nod. "Bryan. Been a while."

McMillan spread his arms and smiled. "You used to come see me all the time. Then you disappeared. I thought you didn't love me no more. But now here you stand."

"Here I stand," Nick agreed. He could feel his bile rise. Being in this room again made his skin crawl and his palms sweat. He shifted his grip on Sarah's hand.

McMillan pushed his chair back and stood. He was head and shoulders taller than Nick and doubled his weight, easily. His smile widened as he walked around his desk. "Come say hello to your old friend."

Nick swallowed and let go of Sarah's hand. He approached the big man and stopped a few feet in front of him. McMillan spread his arms and wrapped them around Nick in a bear hug. The breath was driven from Nick's lungs but he managed not to squawk. He could smell the sweat and smoke emanating like radiation from the man. Nick turned his head and grimaced. McMillan ended the hug with a few pats on the back that Nick knew would leave bruises by morning.

McMillan laughed. "You look good, you son of a bitch. Been a long time." He grasped Nick's arms. "A long time. What brings you to my door this fine evening?"

"I'd like to reopen my account," Nick replied. "If that's okay with you."

Sarah was suddenly behind him. She grasped his hand and whispered into his ear, "Nick, what are you doing?"

Nick squeezed her hand but otherwise ignored her. He knew from experience McMillan expected to be the center of attention when conducting business. Anything that distracted from that business was a liability, and liabilities tended to disappear rapidly and permanently where Bryan McMillan was concerned.

The saloon owner regarded Nick with open suspicion. He stroked his chin and appeared to look Nick up and down. It was an act and Nick knew it. He also knew he would have to play along to get what he came here to get.

"Oh, I'm sure we can arrive at a mutually-satisfying arrangement," McMillan said after a moment. "How much are we talking about?"

Nick swallowed again. "How much do you have?"

McMillan laughed. Spittle flew from his thick lips. He looked past Nick and Sarah at the large man behind them. He laughed, too. "Oh, Wade, you always did manage to put a smile on my face." He wagged a finger at him. "That's why I always liked you. You shoulda gone into standup with that shit. You'd be making more than Lewis Black and Chris Rock combined!" He retreated a few steps and leaned back against his desk. The laughter subsided after a moment although the smile remained. "Seriously, how much do you need?"

Nick returned the smile. "Seriously, how much do you have?"

McMillan guffawed one last time before his smile vanished. "I guess you don't remember how you left it the last time you were here." He looked past Nick and Sarah again and nodded.

Nick heard the big man move quickly. He turned and shoved Sarah toward one of the sofas just as the bouncer reached him. Nick threw everything he had into a haymaker aimed at the man's jaw. His fist instead crashed into the man's thick neck. The bouncer's momentum carried him forward, but he was no longer in fighting mode. Both hands were on his throat and his face shaded to dark crimson. He tripped himself and sprawled loudly onto the floor, his arms and legs splayed.

"You motherfucker!" McMillan roared. He grabbed Nick from behind, wrapped his arms around Nick's waist and pinned his arms to his side.

Nick cursed himself for underestimating McMillan's speed. He squirmed in the big man's grip but he had no chance of breaking free. He watched Sarah recover her balance. She launched herself off the sofa at McMillan. Nick tried to shout a warning but he did not have enough breath in his lungs.

McMillan spun quickly and threw his back at Sarah. The girl crashed into him and rebounded violently. She nearly landed on the couch again but fell a foot or two short. She squealed when she hit the floor.

Nick managed to get one foot on the edge of the desk. He pushed off with everything he had. He felt McMillan backpedal, slightly off-balance because of Nick's weight. McMillan roared and spun again. Nick saw the wall approaching rapidly. He could do nothing but brace himself. The impact drove out what little air he had left in his lungs.

"You rip me off and then you got the balls to come back here?" McMillan sounded both astonished and insane with rage. "It's motherfucking Christmas in August!" He spun and released his grip.

Nick sailed through the air and landed hard on the sofa across from Sarah. He bounced off and wound up on the floor. Nick gasped and rubbed his chest.

McMillan advanced on him. He paused and glanced at his bouncer. The big man had risen to one knee and looked stupidly at his boss. "What the fuck are you lookin at? Get the bitch. We'll have fun with her later. Leave this fucker here to me."

The bouncer turned his attention to Sarah. She pulled herself to her feet and retreated until she backed into the wall. Her eyes were wide and focused entirely on the bouncer. He grinned and licked his lips.

Sarah brought her foot up with what must have been all her strength. It collided perfectly with the bouncer's genitals. The man harrumphed and crumpled to the floor, clutching his wounded manhood with both hands.

McMillan paused a few feet from Nick. He looked from his employee to the young girl. "That was dumb, sweetheart. When Matt gets up he's gonna ass rape you into a coma."

Nick scrambled to his feet as quickly as his wounded leg would allow. He was still gasping for breath but he believed McMillan's threat. McMillan turned in time to see Nick throw a haymaker in his direction.

Nick felt the broken bones in his wrist grind under the impact and he screamed. McMillan reeled, off-balance and holding his nose. Blood fountained into the air from between his fingers. He stumbled about blindly, one hand covering his broken nose and the other taking powerful but off-target swings through the air.

Nick charged him. He tackled the larger man around his knees and they both crashed to the floor. Nick managed to remain on top. He brought his uninjured left hand down hard on the side of McMillan's head. He landed three such blows before McMillan had the sense to roll over. Nick tumbled away to avoid being squashed.

Sarah was at his back in an instant and lifted him onto his feet. Nick stumbled but steadied himself against McMillan's desk. "Nick, Jesus," Sarah muttered.

McMillan rolled slowly back and forth holding his nose. There was an astonishing amount of blood, much more than Nick thought possible. He glanced at the bouncer, Matt, who was no closer to regaining his feet. Nick rushed behind the desk and rifled through the drawers. He found what he was looking for in the bottom drawer. Stamp bags of heroin tied together with elastic bands. He grabbed as many as he could with his one good hand and stuffed them into his pocket. The rest he handed off to Sarah.

She froze and looked at them. She turned them over slowly, as if studying something she had never before seen. "God, no," she whispered.

Nick had started for the rear door. He stopped and turned back to her. "Sarah."

She did not move, simply looked at the stamp bags in her hand.

He knew what she was thinking, what she was feeling. Under different circumstances he would take the time to talk with her. But not here. McMillan and his buddy would recover any moment now and they would not underestimate Nick and Sarah a second time. He grabbed her arm and dragged her toward the rear door. She did not pull her eyes from the objects in her hand until they reached it.

Nick opened the door and peeked outside. The alley between O'Toole's and the Chinese restaurant was empty. Odd but he could not take the time to figure out where everyone had gone. He stepped outside and pulled Sarah after him.

They reached the street and Nick knew why the junkies had cleared out. Two police cruisers were parked across the street. Three officers stood by Rebecca's car and shined flashlights through the windows. Nick pulled Sarah closer and emerged from the alley. The cops looked in their direction but quickly returned to their find. One was talking into the radio.

Nick placed his arm around Sarah and guided her gently but firmly down the street. He did not pull his arm back until they were out of sight of the police.

****

Connelly stood by the rear of the ambulance and looked at the young woman seated inside. She was wrapped in a blanket and stared straight ahead as the paramedic worked on her. She seemed undamaged, at least physically. Her blank eyes told a different story. Connelly looked away. He simply waited for the ambulance jockeys to do their thing with the girl before taking them both to the hospital.

He stared at the darkened swath on the lawn. He could not banish the image of the Shadow Man collapsing into an oil slick of darkness and surging after the car. The adrenaline surge at the time had insulated him somewhat from the shock but it was gone now. Connelly felt his heart pick up the pace as the scene replayed in his head. He willed himself to look at something else, anything else.

A CSI crew moved about the exterior and interior of the house. Several neighbors stood on their porches and their lawns and watched the proceedings. Several gestured toward the house and the ambulances and the police units. A news van was parked as close as the cordon would allow and a woman in a smart business suit spoke into the camera.

Connelly looked at the house again and the CSI crew going about their business. They would find nothing, of course. The Shadow Man left no fingerprints or DNA. They would reconstruct what occurred—or try their damnedest—but in the end they would come up with nothing. Just the headless corpse of a woman and the testimony of a shattered girl and a police detective.

Connelly had put out an APB on Wade and McCallister and a description of the car they had taken from the driveway but Connelly knew it would do little good. Addicts were simply too good at laying low when the situation called for it, and this one certainly met the requirements. But could they hide from the Shadow Man? No. That fucker had Wade Radar. Connelly hoped the man would stay one step ahead of the thing chasing him, but he suspected Wade's run was close to the end. And he believed Wade believed it, too.

****

"What are you gonna do with that?"

Nick sat on the bus stop bench and looked at the stamp bags of heroin in his hand. He turned them over, seeing through the thin wax paper envelopes at the small white powder inside. He could actually see very little; the streetlights were too dim to make out much of the envelopes' contents. But he could imagine what it looked like, and just as he had when Aunt Noreen slipped him the contraband at Springbrook, he thought he could taste the white smoke.

His heart was still racing from the fight with McMillan. It was a conscious effort for him to keep his hands from shaking. Nick could count on the fingers of one hand the number of fights in which he participated, going back to grade school. Now he looked at his bruised and bloodied knuckles and concentrated on slowing his breathing. The throbbing in his broken wrist had yet to subside and sent jolts of electricity up his arm.

"Nick?" Sarah leaned over him. Her feet shifted nervously. It was probably to do with the fight, but it also might have had something to do with what he held in his hand.

"What?"

"I said, what are you gonna do with that?"

Nick swallowed. "You heard what Aunt Noreen said. If this is the only way to stop that thing…" He stuffed the stamp bags into his pocket. "I need a delivery system. Snorting this shit always gives me a fucking headache." He stood, wobbled a bit on his bad leg. The weight of the bags in his pocket seemed much heavier than it should have been and it seemed to throw off his balance. *It's all in your head, asshole. Get your shit together.*

Sarah moved to support him, but she stopped herself. She drew back her hands as if Nick's body would burn her. "After everything you went through at Springbrook? All those nights you couldn't sleep and the throwing up and being too sick to even lift your head. You're gonna throw all that away now?"

Nick steadied himself against the bench. "I don't think I have a choice, Sarah. This fucker isn't gonna stop on his own. And it's not just me he's after. He's killing everyone he comes across. This has to stop, and according to my aunt I'm the only one who can make that happen."

Sarah lowered her head. Her breath hitched in her throat.

Nick wrapped his arms around her. Sarah returned the gesture, even if she seemed reluctant to be so close to him. He held her close, tried to concentrate on her and not the contents of his pocket. The stamp bags seemed, not just too heavy, now, but to radiate heat, as well. He felt the familiar itch return, the one that scratched at the inside of his head. His mouth was dry and Nick licked his lips.

"Your part in this is over, Sarah. It's not after you. It wants me. Go home, baby."

Sarah did not move although she did stop breathing for a moment. At last she shook her head. "I'm not gonna let you face this alone. Not after everything you went through."

Nick pulled back, looked at her. "Sarah. You need to go. Now."

She shook her head.

Nick swore. "I can't protect you if you stay."

Sarah actually laughed. "You can't even protect yourself, the shape you're in. So I'm sticking around. That's the end of it."

Nick frowned, swore again. "Fine." He started away from the bus stop.

"Where are we going?" Sarah asked.

"Anywhere I can use this. And the sooner the better." Nick licked his lips again. The dry mouth was getting worse by the moment. "I know a place."

Chapter 19

The White Powder

Nearly an hour after they left the bus stop Nick and Sarah stood in front of a single-family house in West Philly. It was a far cry from Noreen Wade-Davies's Colonial, as was the neighborhood around it. Several of the houses on the street were clearly abandoned. Their windows were boarded or broken, their lawns overgrown. Piles of garbage dotted the yards and the gutters. Even the trees appeared sickly, their branches hanging low and sparse with leaves.

The house in front of them matched its environment. The windows were intact but filthy, even in the dim illumination of the sputtering streetlights. The lawn was mostly dirt with patches of crabgrass here and there that somehow clung to life. The house was dark but for a single window on the second floor.

Nick scooped up a small stone and tossed it at the window. He waited, standing next to Sarah and holding her hand. The contents of his pocket were uncomfortably heavy and warm. Nick shifted his feet every few moments.

Someone appeared at the second floor window. "Who the fuck?" called a female voice.

"Stacie, it's Nick. Nick Wade."

"Nick? What the fuck, man? What time is it?"

"No idea. Gonna let us in?"

It was too dark to see her face but Nick was sure Staci was weighing her options. It was not simply the time of night that made her pause. She did not know Sarah, and she most likely did not trust Nick in the first place. Nick hoped their shared past would be enough for her to open the door.

After a few uncomfortable moments, Stacie said, "Hang on. Lemme get some clothes on." She disappeared from the window.

"Cool." She was not putting on clothes, he knew. Likely she was hiding her stash just in case they were here to rob her. Not that her caution was completely unwarranted. Nick had indeed left her house a few times with some undeclared cargo in his pockets. He would do the same thing in her position. He guided Sarah to the front door and waited.

A few moments later Stacie opened the door. She was clearly high. Nick's hands began to sweat.

"Christ, Nick, it's almost midnight."

"Yeah. Sorry about that. This is Sarah, by the way. Sarah, Stacie."

Stacie looked her up and down before she stepped aside. Sarah gave a short wave and followed Nick into the house.

The cape was in much better shape on the inside. Stacie might not have been one for yard work, but the interior of her house was close to immaculate. The furniture looked comfortable. The walls were adorned with framed photos and paintings likely purchased at Target or Wal-Mart. Aside from the ashtrays piled high with cigarette butts on the coffee table and end tables, and the empty bags of heroin and various paraphernalia scattered about, this might have been the residence of an upper-middle-class family.

Nick and Sarah stood in the center of the room while Stacie closed the door behind them. She joined them, looked over Sarah again. "This your girlfriend?"

Nick looked at Sarah, back to Stacie. "We met in rehab."

"How'd that work out for ya?" Staci plopped herself on the sofa and took a cigarette from one of the packs on the coffee table. She exhaled slowly and loudly.

Nick shrugged. "Stace, I need a favor."

Stacie guffawed. "I figured that much. Y'know, I don't mind hooking you up from time to time, but you really pushed it last time. You probably don't even know how much shit we burned through before you went to your country club. I can tell you, it was a lot."

"Sorry." It was ridiculous, of course. Stacie had participated one-hundred-percent in those last blurry days before he left for Springbrook. And he had paid for the heroin, if not with cash. Stacie's anger had less to do with the amount of H consumed than with his entering rehab in the first place. It was the same with most addicts and alcoholics. When one of their own tried to free themselves of their demons, the others resented them. It was almost always out of fear that they themselves would never be able to stop, but whatever the reason, the resentment always managed to show itself.

"How much do you need?" Stacie asked. She leaned forward and placed her elbows on her knees. She glanced at Sarah. "And how are you going to pay for it?"

Sarah shifted her feet. She must have been in this type of situation herself at some point, but her time away from this environment had made her uncomfortable. She squeezed Nick's hand with a bit more strength.

"I don't need any H," Nick replied. "I just need some foil and a toilet paper tube or something." She would know what he meant. So would Sarah.

Stacie regarded him coldly. When she spoke, her voice had dropped an octave. "So now you don't even want my shit, you just want some place to do it. You're seriously fucked up, Wade. I think you should leave now."

Nick held up his free hand. "It ain't like that, Stace. Well, it kind of is, but not really. It's hard to explain and you wouldn't believe me, anyway."

"No shit."

"But I need to do some H and I need to do it now." Nick winced as Sarah squeezed his injured hand more tightly. "Then we're gone. And believe me, that's for the best."

Stacie regarded him through a haze of cigarette smoke. She no longer glanced at Sarah; her attention was focused solely on Nick. He could feel her eyes drilling into him, looking for the reason that brought him to her door in the middle of the night. She would not find it because she would be unable to believe. At last, she said, "I'm out of foil. But I have a syringe you can use."

Nick winced. She was lying, and she was quite obvious about it. No heroin addict was ever without foil. This was his punishment for rehab, and for showing up with Sarah. He swallowed and forced a smile. "Sure."

Stacie mashed her cigarette in one of the overflowing ashtrays. She reached for the nearest end table and pulled the drawer open. Her hand emerged with two syringes. She made sure they were capped and tossed them to Nick. "One for each of you. Don't say I never gave you nothing."

Nick caught them. "Thanks," he said as he shoved them into his pocket. "I'll need a lighter if you can spare one. And a spoon if you're out of foil."

"Want me to fucking shoot it for you, too?"

"I think I can manage that part."

Stacie stood and walked into the kitchen. Nick resisted the urge to follow her and rush her along. The hair on his arms was at attention. The Shadow Man was close and getting closer.

"Nick, are you sure about this? It's not too late to stop." Sarah's voice was a whisper.

Nick did not reply. He listened to Stacie rummaging around the kitchen and wished she would speed things up. As much as he disliked her he had no wish to put her in harm's way any more than he had already.

At last she emerged from the kitchen with a spoon and one of her many spare lighters. She tossed them both to Nick. "Here ya go. That all you need or can I get you your slippers and the paper? Maybe your new friend can feed you grapes while I fan you with a giant fucking palm frond."

Nick made for the door wordlessly, pulling Sarah behind him.

"This is it for us, Wade. You used me one time too many. In fact, I hope you OD on that shit. You hear me? I hope you fucking OD!"

Nick made it past the front door with Sarah in tow. They were down the walk before Stacie slammed the door closed behind them.

Nick stood on the sidewalk and closed his eyes. His heart pounded the inside of his chest and sweat covered his face and arms. He took his hand back from Sarah and wiped it on his sweatpants. Before he realized it Nick had dropped to one knee.

"Nick? Nick!" Sarah knelt beside him, one hand on his back and the other holding his arm. "What is it? Are you okay?"

Nick said nothing, simply knelt on the sidewalk and willed his heart to slow. He brought up his wounded hand and tried not to notice it shook and placed it on Sarah's arm. It took a few moments but at last his heart slowed its pace. Nick took in great gulps of air. He patted Sarah's hand. "I'm okay, I'm okay."

"Like hell you are."

Nick staggered to his feet, leaned on Sarah. "No, I'm okay. Or as okay as I'm likely to get, anyway." He looked at her, smiled weakly. His eyes were drawn to movement above and well behind Sarah. Stacie looked out from her bedroom window. She smoked a cigarette and watched him quite neutrally. Nick managed a wave. Stacie ducked back inside before Sarah could follow the gesture. *Yeah, burned the shit outta that bridge.* It might have concerned him if he thought he had any chance of seeing Stacie again.

Nick refocused on Sarah. "I have to do this, babe. Believe me, I wish I didn't. Come on."

He took two or three steps when he noticed the streetlights farther down the road were winking out one after the other

****

"He's here."

At first Sarah had no idea what Nick meant. She followed his gaze down the street. The streetlights on the next block were going dark in sequence, as if someone had their hand on a row of switches and was flipping them one at a time. She squinted. Something moved within the darkness, something big. Its pace was both casual and with purpose. Sarah could just make out the outline of the top hat on its head.

"Jesus."

****

Nick could see the Shadow Man, as well. In fact, he found he could see the thing quite clearly. It was as if he were blind up to this point in his life and suddenly been granted the gift of sight. Despite the distance—Nick estimated it was still a good hundred, hundred-twenty yards away—he could see the thing clenching and unclenching its fists, a bare-knuckle fighter anticipating the start of the first round…or the last.

"We need to leave right now." Sarah pulled at him.

Nick did not have the strength to resist. He stumbled after her. The sidewalk felt uneven beneath his feet, although Sarah seemed to have no trouble navigating it. His knee started to protest and a low-level throbbing had taken up residence behind his eyes. "He'll kill you, babe. You need to go."

Sarah did not reply. She continued along as quickly as Nick's nearly-dead weight would allow. He watched her chance a look over her shoulder every few moments. Her reaction to what she saw grew more pronounced each time. Nick glanced back. Only four streetlights remained lit behind them. Within the darkness strode the Shadow Man, now no more than sixty or seventy yards behind.

They had made it one block from Stacie's house when Nick's right knee gave completely. He nearly collapsed and brought Sarah with him. At the last moment she heaved him back up, grunting with the effort.

"Pick it up, Nick, pick it up."

"Trying," he replied through clenched teeth. And he was. But it would not be enough. Nick saw there was only a single illuminated streetlight behind them. He glanced about frantically. An abandoned house stood in the center of an overgrown yard twenty feet ahead. "There." He pointed to it.

"No choice, anyway." Sarah was breathing heavily. "Hope no one's in there."

"It's empty." It *appeared* empty, but in this part of town all bets were off. The house could just as easily be home to a dozen addicts. Nick prayed it was empty as Sarah helped him up the front walkway.

They stopped on the small porch. To their right was a rather large bay window boarded up completely. On their left a smaller window was also boarded. Sarah tried the door, found it locked. "Fuck!" She tried it again before she turned away in disgust. "Stand back, Nick." Before Nick could begin to move Sarah kicked at the door with everything she had. Nick heard the wood crack but the door held. Sarah tried again. This time the door splintered and flew open. Sarah did not even look inside. She grabbed Nick and guided him across the threshold. Nick stumbled and went down on a dusty, mildewed carpet.

Sarah shouted something and slammed the door closed. Something large, possibly a chest-of-drawers, stood beside the door. She grabbed it and rocked it back and forth until it fell across the door. The sound reverberated around the room and made Nick wince.

"It's too close, Nick. We're outta time."

"Sarah, I need you," Nick told her. She went to him and helped him up. "Upstairs. We need to go upstairs. We have to hide until I can get this shit going."

"You're still going through with this? Nick, I'm sorry but your aunt was a crazy old bitch. This won't do anything except kill you."

"Then I'm dead either way," he replied with more edge than he intended. "Come on."

Sarah swore again and headed for the stairs.

They were not as difficult to negotiate as Nick expected. His right leg was useless and bumped up each step painfully but they still reached the top quickly. There were several rooms upstairs and Nick indicated the closest one on their left. Sarah obediently moved in that direction. She tried the door and found it unlocked. A moment later they were inside the small room and Sarah slammed the door closed behind them.

"There's a lock but I doubt it'll hold for long."

"We don't need it to," Nick replied. The single window was boarded from the outside but several gaps between the boards allowed slivers of light from outside to paint thin and uneven lines on the floor. He plopped down on a sagging couch as Sarah locked the door. Nick dropped the syringes next to him and placed the spoon and the lighter beside them. He pulled the stamp bags from his pocket. The elastic snapped and the bags flew in all directions. Nick grabbed for them and managed to catch one. Not enough. "Sarah, help me." He felt about the floor for more of the bags.

"I can't believe we're doing this," Sarah spat. She dropped to her knees and searched for more bags. After a moment she passed two to Nick. "Here. Last chance, Nick. Don't do this."

He ripped open the bags gingerly and upended their contents onto the spoon. He substituted spittle for tap water and then held the lighter beneath the spoon. It took several tries before the flame sputtered to life. It was weak, maybe too weak to do the job. Nick swore and prayed.

They heard the chest-of-drawers skid across the decayed carpet on the ground floor. It was followed by what Nick took to be the sound of the front door being torn from its hinges. Heavy footsteps reverberated throughout the house.

"Quiet, Sarah. Get behind the couch and stay there, no matter what happens." His voice was so soft he barely heard it himself.

"I'm not leaving you," she whispered back.

"Get the fuck behind the couch *now*," he hissed.

Sarah looked at the door, then at the couch. "Fuck." She scrambled across the floor for the small, dark area between the couch and the wall.

Nick could make out the outline of the spoon from the dim light provided by the flame. He could not tell if the heroin was cooking or not. He glanced at the door before returning his attention to the spoon. "C'mon, c'mon."

Footsteps on the stairs.

Nick willed the flame to burn hotter. For all he knew the crumbs of heroin were swimming about in his own spit, completely intact. "Cook, goddammit," he whispered.

The heavy footsteps stopped in the small hallway outside. Nick could imagine the Shadow Man looking at each of the closed doors, weighing its options. A moment later he heard the sound of one of the other doors splintering.

He was out of time. Nick dropped the lighter and picked up one of the syringes. He removed the cap with his teeth and held the point to the spoon. He could not tell if the syringe sucked up anything when he drew back the plunger.

More sounds of splintering wood from the hallway.

Nick glanced nervously at the door.

More footsteps outside. They stopped outside the door. "Wade," the Shadow Man said.

The door vanished, torn from its hinges and cast back inside the hallway. The Shadow Man stood framed in the doorway. It smiled at him.

Nick froze.

The Shadow Man stepped inside the room.

Sarah screamed something and threw herself at the creature. The Shadow Man swung its arm in a wide arc. Its fist caught Sarah cleanly on the side of her head. The impact knocked her back and off her feet. She bounced once on the hardwood and skidded into the corner of the room, limp as a rag doll.

"No!" Nick shouted. He was on his feet, the needle in his hand temporarily forgotten. He charged the Shadow Man. Its other hand shot from the darkness of its body. Cold, steel fingers closed around Nick's throat. Nick gasped. Intense heat radiated from its palm and scorched his skin. Both hands went reflexively to the thing's fingers. The needle dropped and clattered on the floor.

The Shadow Man pulled him closer. Nick tilted his head back and to the side, anything to avoid being any closer to the darkness that enveloped the thing's head. "Wade." The malevolence in its tone had changed. If Nick put any thought into it he might have concluded the creature sounded pleased, triumphant.

Nick could feel the cold of its breath on his face. Against his will he turned and squinted into the darkness in front of him. He could make out very little, even this close. Its eyes shined a shade of black Nick had never before seen. It possessed no nose he could see beyond a slightly raised bump where it should have been. Two long slits that might have been nostrils puffed out rancid air. Its teeth were gray and sharp and inches away from Nick's face.

The darkness that was the Shadow Man spread to the corners of Nick's vision. His head swam. "Get it—Get it…" *Get it over with.* He did not know if the thing could read his mind. He hoped so.

Nick caught a flash of movement from behind the Shadow Man. He heard the sound of an impact and felt it travel up the thing's arm and into its fingers around his throat. The creature turned and Nick saw the syringe sticking out from its shoulder. Sarah stood by the door, glaring at it. Blood trickled from her nose and the side of her mouth. Her eyes were defiant and blazed anger and fear. "Die, you fucker!" she shouted.

The Shadow Man dropped Nick, who landed in a heap on the floor. Nick had the presence of mind to lift his head and reach an arm toward Sarah.

She backed away slowly.

The Shadow Man turned toward her.

Nick rolled away, gasping and rubbing his throat. The skin on his neck felt cold and scabrous, as if he had just come inside after spending hours in a January wind. He blinked the darkness clear from his vision and rose to his knees.

The syringe was gone, its contents emptied into the Shadow Man. If Sarah had expected the liquefied powder to have any effect on the creature she would be disappointed; the Shadow Man showed no reaction to the syringe's contents beyond anger at Sarah.

Nick scrambled on hands and knees to where he thought the remainder of his stash had landed. His fingers felt numb as they scraped along the floor. He found and grasped four stray stamp bags. "Sarah, run," he gasped. He tried for a shout but his bruised throat allowed little sound to escape.

The Shadow Man grabbed for her and Sarah made for the doorway. Its fingers caught in her hair and Sarah screamed. The Shadow Man pulled her back violently. In one fluid motion it hurled her through the window. The glass exploded and the boards on the other side splintered and flew apart. Sarah disappeared into the darkness outside.

Nick tried to shout again but could manage only a croak. Wind rippled the curtains but did little to dissipate the smell of decay and death within the room.

The Shadow Man returned its attention to Nick. Its eyes drilling their way into his, it casually reached back and pulled the syringe from its shoulder. It dropped the device on the floor and stepped on it. Even from across the room Nick could hear the plastic cylinder crack within the darkness.

"Just you and me," Nick croaked. He pushed himself backward toward the couch. His left hand found five more stamp bags and he scooped them up. He grasped the tops and tore them free. One of the bags flew out of his hand and was lost in the darkness. Nick closed his fist more tightly around the rest.

The Shadow Man approached him.

"This is hardcore, motherfucker. Here's to us." Nick brought up the stamp bags and held them in front of his eyes. Without another look at the creature now standing just a few feet from him, Nick held the bags to his nose and breathed in deeply and with as much force as he could muster.

Some of the bags were probably pinched closed but he still received a full blast. The familiar smell and taste of the white powder filled his world. Nick nearly choked. He swayed and then fell upon his back.

He felt suddenly lightheaded. Nick lay flat on his back and looked dumbly at the hulking figure who stood only a few feet from him. "Oh, yeah," Nick warbled. "That's the shit." He forgot how good it felt, the white powder circumnavigating his bloodstream. It was more than worth the brief burning sensation in his nostrils. Not as enjoyable as smoking it but the result was always the same. And this time he would not even have to worry about the headache he always got when he snorted the stuff.

Nick felt himself being lifted from the floor. The sensation of weightlessness was something he had forgotten about until that moment. Christ, he missed this. Fuck Buckley and Springbrook and the judge who sent him there. Nothing mattered but this. Nick felt himself drifting, his consciousness seeming to float free of his body. By chance he looked down on himself.

Someone was holding him a few inches off the floor. He was big and dressed all in black and he wore a top hat, of all things. He could not see the man's face clearly from this angle but Nick got the impression he was disfigured. His arms were too long for his body and appeared to end in talons. There was something familiar about this man. Nick felt a twinge of frustration at not being able to remember who he was or why he was lifting Nick from the floor. And there was someone else here, as well, or there should have been. A woman, he was sure of that much. Angie? No, not Angie. Angie was gone. He searched through the fog that enveloped his head.

Sarah.

The man holding him reacted as if Nick had spoken the name aloud. Nick watched his other body reach an arm in the direction of the shattered window. Then the fog closed in again.

****

Sarah shook her head to clear it, winced at the pain that lanced through her right side. She had landed in an overgrown shrub. One of the thicker branches refused to bend and instead punctured the side of her torso. Her shirt was soaked with blood but a cursory self-examination revealed what looked to be a minor flesh wound.

274

She crawled away from the shrub and looked up at the shattered window. She could see nothing but darkness within the house. Worse was the silence that reached her. She expected to hear Nick fighting for his life but she heard nothing. Was it over already?

Sarah struggled to her feet, moaned as the pain in her side upped the wattage. She staggered toward the front door.

****

It was the most wonderful hit of heroin Nick had ever taken. Like a man dying of thirst suddenly being presented with a two-gallon jug of water, Nick welcomed the long-absent sensation of the powder circulating throughout his body. It filled him in a way no words could explain, no non-addict could possibly understand. For the first time since he walked through the front door of Springbrook, Nick felt complete.

He continued to observe himself and the dark, malformed man who held him in his arms. Nick had a much better idea of the man's deformities now that he was fully in the zone. It could not be human. Its movements were wrong, unnatural, but graceful if such a term could be applied to such a creature. Its body rippled as if waves of fluid moved just beneath its black skin. There was something behind the man, beyond the mask it presented to the world, but whatever it was Nick decided he did not want to see it. He tried to look away but his head would not turn and his eyes refused to close. It was the one unpleasant aspect of his otherwise-euphoric state.

The thing holding his physical body paused. It smiled, revealing teeth that were too numerous and far too long. Its black eyes sparkled with anticipation.

Nick felt himself, quite against his will, descending rapidly down toward his body. A moment later he was back in his familiar shell. This, too, he had forgotten about. It was not the end of his high, just a lessening of the initial effect of the powder. There was no pain from his leg or wrist, no pain at all, in fact, and that was a plus. But there was the unpleasant sensation of the dark man holding him and grinning and savoring the moment.

"Nick," Sarah whimpered from somewhere close.

Nick lifted his head and looked about the room. The dark man turned slowly in that direction and Nick saw Sarah standing in the doorway. She leaned to her right and held one hand tightly against her side. Most of her shirt had turned crimson.

The fog parted, at least a little, and Nick remembered everything. He yelped and rolled his body away from the Shadow Man. Perhaps unprepared for such a move, the thing released its grip and Nick tumbled to the floor. He landed hard on his side, directly on his wounded knee. There was little pain, more an unpleasant throbbing. Nick caught sight of the remaining stamp bags lying on the floor just out of arm's reach.

He squirmed forward as quickly as his drug-slowed muscles would allow. His hand closed around the stamp bags and Nick tore off the tops. He turned over on his back and looked up.

The Shadow Man loomed above him. Its grin was even wider. Something like saliva but much more syrupy dripped from its teeth and the corners of its mouth. It reached for him.

Nick brought the bags up to his nose and inhaled for all he was worth. The powder burned his nostrils, his sinuses. His head snapped back involuntarily and he smacked it on the floor. He closed his eyes against the onslaught of stars that filled his vision. The powder burned its way down his throat and he felt his heart, already hammering away, pick up the pace.

He felt the burning grip of the Shadow Man's hand on his arm, lifting him from the floor. Nick managed to look at it, into the void of the thing's eyes.

"First. You. Then. Her." The Shadow Man's voice was rough, like truck tires rolling slowly over broken glass. Its enunciation was all too clear.

"Fuck you." Nick spat at it.

That was when he felt his chest explode.

****

Sarah watched Nick's body go rigid, his arms and legs splayed out, as if he had just received a monstrous electric shock. At the same moment the Shadow Man staggered back and released its grip on Nick's arm.   Nick fell the rest of the way to the floor and continued to convulse. Sarah shot forward but stopped short when the creature stumbled in her direction. She shrieked and backed away, holding her hands out in front of her.

The Shadow Man seemed to lose its balance. It sashayed past Sarah and crashed into the wall next to the door. The drywall gave and the studs behind them creaked. The Shadow Man slid down the wall, its talons fighting for purchase on the pulverized drywall. It sank to one knee and its great bulk heaved as if it were a marathon runner who just crossed the finish line.

Sarah saw a gap of perhaps five feet between the Shadow Man and the wall to her left. She shot through it, angling her body to stay out of its reach. It did indeed swipe at her as she passed but the effort was weak and she was able to dodge it easily.

She reached Nick's side. He lay where he fell, back arched and head thrown back. The muscles in his neck and arms were corded, his veins bulging. White foam coated his lips and dripped down his cheeks. He produced gurgled moans.

"Nick, no!" She reached for him and stopped. She had no idea what to do. She began to pat his back but gave up after a few moments. She looked at him helplessly. "Nick, tell me what to do."

Nick gurgled again and this time the sound kept going until it reached a scream. One of his hands went to his chest. His fingers drove themselves into his skin with enough force they produces tiny beads of blood on his shirt. The scream stopped—interrupted was a better word—and it occurred to Sarah he was trying to speak. Before he could enunciate anything he screamed again.

His hand came away from his chest and just missed her head on its path to the floor. He slammed his fist into the floorboards hard enough to put a small crack in the wood. His body convulsed again. His feet kicked out and he produced a scream that sent white foam and spittle into the air.

"Jesus, no." Sarah placed her hands on his chest. "Nick, please."

All at once his body went limp. Whatever electrical current had kept him rigid departed abruptly. His head lolled to one side.

Tears streaked down Sarah's cheeks. She continued to rub his chest. "Nick. Nick, please. Nick, don't do this. Come back, *please*."

His lips parted and he said something. Sarah leaned down and placed her ear directly in front of his mouth. "Safe now," he repeated weakly. His lips upturned at the corners, the ghost of the smile he had flashed at her back at Springbrook.

"Yes," Sarah replied, although her voice broke and she could not be sure Nick understood her.

She turned and looked at the Shadow Man. It sat against the wall and looked at him, at her. Tendrils of black undulated on the floor and the wall around it, but weakly, a nest of pythons dying a slow death. One of its arms was suspended in the air, reaching for the two people in front of it. It might have been the darkness around the thing but it seemed the arm trembled with the effort.

The darkness that was the Shadow Man retreated back into its body. The area around the door began to brighten in the weak illumination from the nearest streetlight outside. Without its shield of darkness the creature looked small, weak, pathetic. She still could not see much of its features, the darkness was still absolute closest to its body, but it already looked much smaller than before.

"Wade," it croaked. Its arm dropped to the floor.

The darkness around the creature simply dissipated all at once. The Shadow Man grew small—even its top hat seemed to melt away—until it resembled a blackened skeleton slouched in the corner. It grew smaller and thinner still, seeming to melt into the floorboards until the spot it had occupied was vacant.

Sarah watched the area for another few moments, convinced the thing would reappear, crashing through the doorway and flinging her aside to get to its prey. Nothing happened. After another moment Sarah returned her attention to Nick.

He lay perfectly still, his eyes half-lidded and seeing nothing. Sarah lowered her head and laid it on his chest and wept in the dark room.

****

Sarah opened the front door to her apartment and saw Jenna Davino smiling at her, a bottle of wine clutched in each hand. Sarah smiled back and stepped aside. "C'mon in, hon."

"Thanks." Jenna crossed the threshold and looked about the small apartment. "Nice place."

"It'll do for now." Sarah moved to close the door, but stopped short when she saw the unmarked police unit parked across the street. The detective who investigated the Shadow Man case, and Nick's death, sat behind the wheel and looked at her, as he had nearly every day since her brother helped her get the apartment. She knew why he was there, and why he would continue to show up for as long as he could keep it up. She swallowed hard and closed the door.

Sarah led Jenna into the kitchen. She took the tea kettle off the stove and poured the water into two cups. She placed them on the table and indicated one of the chairs. "Have a seat."

"Coffee doesn't really go well with this," Jenna said, indicating the two bottles now sitting on the table between them.

"I'm allowed one cup of coffee a day. The doc didn't say anything about wine but I'm gonna err on the side of caution and say I can only have one of those, too." She got up and rummaged around one of the drawers and came back to the table with a corkscrew. "You can do the honors." Sarah returned to the cupboard and snatched up two wineglasses.

She watched her old roommate open the first bottle. Fresh scabs decorated Jenna's cheeks and neck. When she smiled Sarah noticed one of her molars had gone AWOL. She recognized the gleam in Jenna's eyes as the girl poured the wine. It was the look only a fellow addict could recognize. Alcohol was a poor substitute for meth, but Jenna would make do until she left Sarah's apartment. And so would Sarah.

They drank their wine and chatted and gossiped. Jenna was living with her new boyfriend on the other side of town. She was thus far unemployed but her boyfriend made good money— dealing, no doubt, although Jenna did not say—and he was willing to support her until she found something. Sarah had managed to find a job. It was only part time waitressing at the White Castle but her brother helped with bills. Jenna finished her first glass of wine quickly and topped it off again. Sarah nursed hers.

"So when are you due?" Jenna asked after another sip.

"I'm only eighteen weeks," Sarah replied, "so it'll be a while yet." She rubbed her belly. "But I'm looking forward to it."

Jenna reached across the table and squeezed Sarah's hand. "You'll make a great mom, babe."

Sarah smiled. "Thanks. I hope so."

"Still clean?"

Sarah nodded. "Yep. Haven't had anything since Springbrook. You?"

Jenna smiled a wide smile. "Clean and sober," she lied. "One-hundred-percent."

Sarah expected the answer, as Jenna no doubt expected hers. Addicts, after all, lied to everyone, especially fellow addicts. They were both full of shit and they both knew it. "Glad to hear it."

The rest of the visit consisted mostly of reminiscing about Springbrook and their time there. Jenna finished off the first bottle by herself, Sarah having stuck to her guns about having one glass. Jenna offered to leave the second bottle behind but Sarah convinced her to take it with her. In her present condition it would take her weeks to polish off that bottle, whereas Jenna and her boyfriend could probably do so within thirty minutes ("Fifteen," Jenna corrected her with a laugh.). When her old roommate left Sarah rinsed the glasses and tossed the empty wine bottle into the recycling bin. Then she went into the bedroom.

In the top middle drawer of her dresser she found the small bundle of stamp bags. She counted them for the hundredth time and calculated how long they would last, as she always did. She took the one bag that was already open and sprinkled a little of its contents onto her fingertip.

She held the tiny crystals to her eyes. In the old days, pre-Springbrook and pre-pregnancy, this miniscule amount would not have been enough to even register with her. In truth, it did little for her now. It made her nostrils tingle and gave her a slight sensation of lightheadedness, but little more. That was okay. She could not afford to get really wasted, anyway. Her brother was coming over in a little while and Sarah could not be comatose when he arrived.

She snorted the powder and felt its familiar burn. The lightheadedness came a moment later, for a split-second making the world around her gray and indistinct. She tried to hold on to that euphoria, to go even deeper into the warm darkness. She had plenty of H right in front of her. One hit, one *real* hit, and she would be on her way. She felt this temptation each and every time she used these days. But the result today would be the same as it had been since she discovered she was pregnant. She sat and looked at the tiny bags in her hand, turned them over, felt their weight. Then she returned them to their hiding place as she always did, licking her lips as she closed the drawer.

The baby kicked, then, as it was starting to do now every time she used. Nicky Jr., getting his first taste of what will be a lifelong relationship. She rubbed her belly again and smiled sadly.

Then she stood and walked into the bathroom and stepped into the shower. The hot water always felt good after a hit and the steam helped to clear her mind. Sarah stood under the showerhead and breathed deeply and felt good. She had another hour or so before her brother arrived. By then she would be in tiptop shape, clearheaded and ready to chat.

And if the conversation turned accusatory, as they sometimes did, well, Sarah always had the contents of her dresser drawer to help her after her brother left. The thought made her smile. Sarah rubbed her belly again.

Acknowledgments
The Author wishes to thank:

Monica Talarino
Marie Bohrer
Nancy Christiano, R.N.
Rachel Christiano, R.N.
Elizabeth Fortin-Hinds
Taria A Reed
Shelia Powers

About the Author

Author photograph by Taria A Reed

Joseph J. Christiano's published works include the novels *The Last Battleship*, *Moon Dust*, *Dark Annie* and *Old Ghosts*.

He resides in Connecticut.

Tell-Tale Publishing Group would like to thank you for your purchase. If you enjoyed this work and would like to read more by Joseph or some of our other fine authors, please visit our website:

www.tell-talepublishing.com